Five Nights at Freddy's™

TALES FROM THE PIZZAPLEX

#5 THE BOBBIEDOTS CONCLUSION

Five Nights at Freddy's™

TALES FROM THE PIZZAPLEX

#5 THE BOBBIEDOTS CONCLUSION

BY

SCOTT CAWTHON
ANDREA WAGGENER

Scholastic Inc.

Copyright © 2023 by Scott Cawthon. All rights reserved.

Photo of TV static: © Klikk/Dreamstime

All rights reserved. Published by Scholastic Inc., *Publishers since 1920.* SCHOLASTIC and associated logos are trademarks and/or registered trademarks of Scholastic Inc.

The publisher does not have any control over and does not assume any responsibility for author or third-party websites or their content.

No part of this publication may be reproduced, stored in a retrieval system, or transmitted in any form or by any means, electronic, mechanical, photocopying, recording, or otherwise, without written permission of the publisher. For information regarding permission, write to Scholastic Inc., Attention: Permissions Department, 557 Broadway, New York, NY 10012.

This book is a work of fiction. Names, characters, places, and incidents are either the product of the author's imagination or are used fictitiously, and any resemblance to actual persons, living or dead, business establishments, events, or locales is entirely coincidental.

Library of Congress Cataloging-in-Publication Data available

ISBN 978-1-338-85143-4

10 9 8 7 6 5 4 3 2 1   23 24 25 26 27

Printed in the U.S.A.   131

First printing 2023 • Book design by Jeff Shake

TABLE OF CONTENTS

GGY

A BARRAGE OF THUNDER RATTLED THE SCHOOL'S OLD, MURKY WINDOWS JUST AS MRS. SOTO WROTE ON THE BLACKBOARD, "FICTION STRETCHES THE BOUNDARIES OF REALITY." TONY GLANCED FROM MRS. SOTO'S PRECISE BLOCK LETTERS TO THE PLUMP RAINDROPS THAT WERE NOW PELTING THE WINDOW NEAREST TO TONY'S DESK IN THE BACK ROW OF THE MUSTY, HIGH-CEILINGED CLASSROOM.

Tony blinked. No longer interested in anything Mrs. Soto was doing, he put all his attention on the storm.

For just an instant, Tony could have sworn he'd seen something moving in the downpour. An elongated, human-size shape seemed to have slithered through the torrents of water just as the thunder's rumble had faded away.

But that, of course, wasn't possible because Mrs. Soto's creative writing class was on the third floor of the 120-year-old limestone school building. The only thing Tony could have seen out in the rain, forty-five feet above the ground, was something falling or flying.

Tony wished he could get up and go look out the window to see if anything had hit the ground. But getting out of his seat would have earned him one of Mrs. Soto's dirty looks. He hated those.

Letting Mrs. Soto's voice merge with the rain's thrumming rhythm, Tony resigned himself to simply wondering about what he'd seen. And that was okay. Tony liked life's little mysteries. Poking around to find answers to why things happened fascinated him.

Tony continued to watch the rain as he pondered what he might have seen. It hadn't been a person, obviously. If a person had fallen through the rain, Tony would have heard the splat even over the sound of the storm. And surely someone would have screamed. Or maybe not. Sometimes bad things happened right under people's noses. Danger lurked everywhere, even in the places you thought were safe. Many of Tony's investigations had taught him that.

Thunder boomed again. The whole building shook this time. Two seconds later, Tony saw piercing white tendrils of light streak down in front of the hills beyond the school's grounds. *That was close*, he thought.

On the heels of the lightning, a tree branch speared through the rain. It shot downward, then disappeared out of view. That must have been what he'd seen, Tony realized. Some of the trees on the school grounds had pale gray bark. He wasn't sure what kind of trees they were.

The sudden squall had come out of nowhere. One minute, the hundred-foot trees that guarded the school grounds like a stolid line of stern principals had been still, their branches limp and relaxed. The next minute, the trees' branches had begun to whip around, tossed by wind gusts that arrived with no warning.

Life was like that, Tony thought. He'd learned that from his investigations, too. One second, all was well. The next second could bring surprises of the worst kind.

Something prodded Tony's shoulder. He gasped as he spun to his right.

"Space out much?" Tony's best friend asked as he leaned across the space between his desk and Tony's. He handed Tony a stack of pale blue papers.

Tony grinned nonchalantly, as if he hadn't nearly just jumped out of his skin. He took one of the pieces of paper. They were assignment sheets, he realized; Mrs. Soto color-coded her handouts. Blue was for writing homework.

Tony leaned across the aisle and handed the rest of the assignment sheets to Zoey, the pretty blonde girl who sat in the desk next to his. Zoey didn't even look at him as she took the stack. She was one of the popular girls in the seventh-grade class, several rungs above Tony and his friends on the social ladder.

Tony glanced down and read the assignment. He sighed. Another fiction story.

In preparation for his goal of becoming an investigative reporter someday (he was only twelve, but he believed in planning ahead), Tony had been eager to hone his writing skills in Mrs. Soto's class . . . his *nonfiction* writing skills. The class syllabus had said that it would be about all aspects of good composition, but so far, Mrs. Soto was focusing only on fiction.

Outside, the rain stopped as suddenly as it had started. A shaft of sunlight shot through the wet window, throwing prisms of refracted light across Tony's desk. He put his finger in the pink-and-yellow streaks that played across the scarred, dark-stained oak. *See*, he thought. Reality was much more interesting than fiction.

Now that the rain had stopped, Tony could hear the assignment sheets rustling as everyone in the class read over what they were supposed to do. Several kids started murmuring to one another. Tony could hear his friends whispering next to him.

The creative writing classroom was, surprisingly, not particularly creative in its appearance. Although nearly all the other classrooms in the building were decorated with posters or charts—whatever was related to the subject matter being taught in the room—this one was oddly bare. The yellowish plaster walls held nothing but the blackboard at the front of the room, a whiteboard on the inner wall, and a shelf of novels at the back. The fifteen desks that were lined up neatly in the middle of the room weren't enough to fill out the vast space, so sound tended to bounce between the bank of windows and the other barren walls. Even the quiet noises seemed amplified.

"Okay, hush, please," Mrs. Soto called out.

Tony looked up from the blue paper he held. Mrs. Soto's gaze met his. He smiled at her. She didn't smile back.

Although she was one of the younger teachers in the school, Mrs. Soto wasn't one of the friendlier ones. Tall and thin, Mrs. Soto dressed solely in dark brown and tan, and she wore her brown hair in a blunt, chin-length style. The bottom edge of her hair was so straight that it looked sharp, like it could cut her jaw if she moved wrong. Mrs. Soto was a good teacher; Tony had learned a lot from her, even though she didn't assign enough nonfiction. He often wondered, though, why she was so unhappy. He'd like to write a story about that.

"The goal of this story," Mrs. Soto said when the paper rustling and murmuring died down, "is to focus on a mystery while also wrapping it in subplots that seem to have nothing to do with the plot but actually are essential to it. You'll work in teams of three. You can pick who you work with. If anyone needs help partnering up, let me know. Any questions?" She looked out at the class.

Tony raised his hand. "What if we can find a non-fiction mystery that fits that description?" he asked.

Mrs. Soto shook her head. "You can let reality spark your imagination," she said, "but I want you to look past the real world."

Just as Mrs. Soto finished speaking, the bell rang. It was Friday, and this was the last class of the day. Half the kids in the class were out of their seats before the bell's insistent buzz ended. Tony didn't move. He frowned at the assignment sheet, his mind already starting to toy with ideas for the story. He was going to be the one who would take the lead on it; he always was.

"As usual, the three amigos, oh great and wondrous Great American Writer?" Tony's best friend asked, pulling Tony's attention from his thoughts.

Tony glanced at his friends.

"We've already picked our numb de plumbs." The curly-black-haired kid—who Tony had been friends with ever since their moms, across-the-street neighbors, had brought them together for a playdate when they were four years old—flashed his signature lopsided grin. "I'm going to be Boots," he said.

Tony shook his head. When his friends had learned the

term *nom de plume* at the start of the school year, they'd twisted it into "numb de plumb." Since then, they'd insisted on choosing different pen names every time they got a new writing assignment. For the duration of the assignment, they demanded that they had to call one another by the crazy names they picked out.

Tony stood and stuffed his assignment sheet into his backpack. "Why Boots?" he asked.

"For Puss in Boots. Clever cat. That's me."

"Okay. Got it, Boots," Tony said.

"He's going to be Dr. Rabbit," "Boots" said, pointing at the last of "the three amigos."

Tony looked at "Dr. Rabbit" and lifted an eyebrow. "Why Dr. Rabbit?"

"You can call me Rab for short," "Rab" said. He shrugged. "The name just came to me." He grinned as he ran a hand through his unruly brown hair. He'd admitted the week before that he cut it himself; it looked it.

"Rab" was a relatively new friend. Spotting the unfamiliar kid who'd looked a little lost at the start of the school year a couple months before, Tony had introduced himself just to be friendly. He and "the new guy" had hit it off, and Tony had invited him to work with him—and Boots—when they'd gotten their first creative writing assignment.

Rab pointed a finger gun at Tony. "What about you?"

Tony thought for a second. "I'll be Tarbell."

Boots grabbed his backpack and started toward the classroom door. "Don't tell me," Boots said, looking back over his shoulder. "A reporter, right?"

Tony nodded. He didn't bother to explain that Ida Tarbell was a famous muckraker in the late nineteenth to early twentieth centuries. Neither Boots nor Rab would have cared. Their interest in history was even more nonexistent than their interest in current events.

As Tony followed Boots and Rab from the classroom and the three of them started pushing through the throng of kids filling the hallway, Tony wondered, not for the first time, how much longer he and Boots and Rab would be friends. Over the summer, Tony had started feeling a little impatient with his best friend, Boots. It felt like Tony was starting to grow up, but his longtime friend was content to stay a little boy.

Adding a new friend to the mix had helped a little because it shook things up a bit. Rab was kind of halfway between Boots and Tony; he liked to cut up and goof off, but he also had moments when he said interesting, even deep, things. More than once, Tony had caught Rab with a rigid expression on his face, as if he was contemplating something intense. Tony had a feeling that Rab had layers that Boots would probably never have. Tony had a terrible feeling that he was outgrowing Boots and might soon just want to hang with Rab. That would be awkward in the extreme.

Tony realized he was lagging behind his friends, and he hurried to catch up. "Hey, you guys want to get together and start brainstorming ideas for our story?" he called out.

Boots and Rab turned and looked at Tony. Boots rolled his eyes, and Rab shook his head.

"The story can wait," Boots said. "We were just talking about hitting the arcades at the Pizzaplex."

Tony twisted his lips in frustration. "But—"

"The best creative ideas can't be pushed out," Rab said. "They need to sprout from the fertile soil of distraction."

Case in point, Tony thought. Rab could definitely be deep.

They'd reached the end of the hall and started to make the turn down the side hall that led to their lockers. Boots sidestepped a couple of eighth graders, one of whom deliberately bumped Rab as he passed. Rab's eyes narrowed as he gave the jerk a hard stare. Of course the guy—a popular kid the girls fawned over—didn't even notice.

Tony and his friends tended to be invisible to most of the kids in their school. Tony acted like he didn't care . . . but he was lying to himself.

Tony, who loved trying to get to the bottom of life's mysteries, had spent hours attempting to figure out what made a kid popular or not. He'd reached some obvious conclusions. Being a nerd, for example, was not the way to popularity. Neither was being funny looking or having strange habits. Speaking up too much in class was a surefire way not to be popular. So was dressing wrong. But there was something intangible, too. There had to be, because Tony and his friends weren't nerds. They had no strange habits. They didn't talk too much in class, and they dressed like everyone else. They also weren't bad looking . . . or at least Tony didn't think they were.

Tony and Boots and Rab were all dark haired (Tony's hair color was somewhere between Boots's jet black and Rab's chocolate brown), and all had pretty regular features. Boots was probably the best looking of "the three amigos." The tallest boy in their class, Boots was wiry, had deep green eyes, a normal-looking nose, a mouth that was usually quirked into a grin, and a square jaw.

In contrast to Boots, Rab was one of the smallest boys in their class. He, too, was skinny, and because his skin was paler than Boots's dusky skin, Rab could appear a little weak and frail. He had really big brown eyes, and those made him look like a wide-eyed little kid sometimes. But the rest of his features were fine. Tony had overheard a couple girls say that Rab was cute.

Tony's height was somewhere between Boots's tallness and Rab's shortness. Tony figured he was average for his age. Maybe he'd always be average. Tony had dark blue eyes that might have been a little too small and a little too close together, but they weren't weird looking. His nose didn't have anything odd about it, and his mouth, though a touch small, wasn't goofy looking. Maybe his cheeks were a little pudgier than was ideal (and if they were less so, his aunt Melva might not pinch them every time she saw him), but he didn't think any of his features were cause for social exclusion.

"Earth to Tinkerbell!"

Tony was jerked to the side. He blinked and realized Boots was dragging him toward their lockers.

"It's Tarbell," Tony said automatically. "Not Tinkerbell."

"Says you," Boots said. "It's going to be Space Cadet if you don't stop standing in the middle of the hall looking like your brain took a vacation."

"Sorry," Tony said. "I was just thinking."

"That's your problem," Rab said as they reached their lockers. He began spinning the numbers on his lock. "You think too much. That's bad for your health."

"He's right," Boots agreed, flinging his locker door open with a resounding bang. The door bounced back and almost hit him in the face. He didn't seem to notice.

Tony stepped over to his locker, whipped through his lock combo, and opened the dented metal door. Unzipping his backpack, Tony swapped out some notebooks for what he needed to take home for the weekend.

"C'mon, c'mon," Boots said, bouncing on his heels like he always did when he was impatient . . . which was nearly all the time. "The Fazcade is waiting!"

"I still think we should start brainstorming," Tony said.

Boots snorted. "The story's not due for two weeks. We've got plenty of time."

"We'll be able to knock out the story in a few hours," Rab said. "Why do now what we can put off till later?"

"Besides, Tinkerbell," Boots said, bumping Tony's shoulder, "we know you'll get started without us. You always do."

Tony sighed and slammed his locker shut. Part of him resented his friends for just assuming he'd do most of the work on their story, but part of him was relieved. He always got excited about a new writing project. He planned to work on it every day, and he'd have fun doing it.

Freddy Fazbear's Mega Pizzaplex was exactly as its name advertised; it was *mega*. Even though Tony wasn't quite as into the place as his friends were, he had to admit the Pizzaplex was ginormous. And every square inch of the entertainment complex was stuffed full of dazzling—and fun—sights and sounds and experiences.

Tony and his buddies had tried every venue in the massive domed compound. They'd ridden the high-tech roller coaster a couple dozen times, explored the climbing tubes, played countless rounds on the course at Monty's Gator Golf, bowled a bunch of games at Bonnie Bowl, and raced frequently at Roxy Raceway. They'd also seen so many animatronic stage shows that Tony could pretty much sing the band's songs word for word.

The best part of the Pizzaplex, though—at least in Tony's opinion—was the largest of the dome's multiple arcades: the Fazcade, a three-story arcade connected with spiral staircases. Billed as a "disco arcade," the Fazcade was the home of DJ Music Man, an animatronic DJ that spun tunes for the arcade's game players and for weird people who used the karaoke rooms on the Fazcade's third floor (Tony thought anyone who wanted to stand up and sing in front of other people was totally bonkers).

Lit with the same amount of over-the-top multi-colored neon lights and LCDs that radiated throughout the

Pizzaplex, the Fazcade had eye-popping purple walls and plush light purple carpet that was patterned with stars and swirls and likenesses of Freddy Fazbear, the animatronic bear that was the linchpin of the Fazbear empire. This purple backdrop was stuffed full of shiny chrome and painted metal game machines in nearly every color imaginable. The Fazcade was so iridescent that Tony always felt like he was leaving the real world and entering some kaleidoscopic parallel universe when he stepped into the Fazcade.

It wasn't just the sights that transported you to another realm in the massive arcade; it was also the sounds. Overlaid with the pulsing bass beats of the tunes that DJ Music Man played, the arcade was an eruption of noise. It was like an auditory multiverse—layers and layers of sounds were packed together in the Fazcade. Sometimes, because he liked to try to describe things in his head (to help him be a better writer), Tony tried to pick out every sound he heard in the arcade, but he never felt like he could parse them out. The machine's pings, zings, zips, dings, buzzes, pops, trills, and gongs and the players' shouts, laughter, chatter, and whoops converged on one another and just became one compressed din that made Tony's head hurt sometimes.

Like today. Probably because he would have preferred to kick around ideas for their story assignment instead of playing arcade games, Tony was finding the arcade's racket and barrage of light and movement more annoying than fun.

After playing *Bon-Bon Funball*, *Chica's Feeding Frenzy*, and *Monty's Gator Golf* (an arcade game version of the real mini golf course), Tony was bored with the games. Leaving Rab and Boots firing up basketballs in a heated competition at the *Puppet's Basketball* game machine, Tony started wandering aimlessly through the arcade.

Actually, Tony's meandering wasn't exactly aimless. In fact, he had a purpose for strolling up and down every aisle in the Fazcade and watching players at the various games. Tony was in search of an idea for their story. From past experience, Tony knew that he might find what he was looking for if he engaged in a little people watching.

Although the games in the Fazcade were creative—all of them Fazbear-character themed—and fun to play, Tony thought watching the *people* who played the games was more interesting. Everyone, from the littlest kids to the oldest seniors (usually grandmas or grandpas who brought their grandkids to the Pizzaplex), tended to lose themselves when they played arcade games. Caught up in manipulating the game machines' controls, gazes fixed on the screens, mental focus completely captured by the desire to rack up points, people ceased caring about "real life" when they played. Kids stopped acting self-consciously, unworried about what others thought of them when they played, and adults visibly relaxed because they got to set aside their daily problems.

Tony was only twelve but was old enough to know that living could be a hard and heavy thing to do. Maybe other twelve-year-olds hadn't yet come face-to-face with how awful life could be, but Tony had.

Over the last two years, Tony's dad had gone from being a successful, well-paid accountant for a big corporation to a convicted felon. Accused of embezzling hundreds of thousands of dollars from the company he'd worked for, Tony's dad had denied the charge. A jury, however, hadn't believed him. A group of twelve people had decided that the prosecution's arguments were more convincing than Tony's dad's claims of innocence. Tony's dad was given a sentence of twenty years and a fine that he couldn't possibly pay.

Tony had spent the first eleven and a half years of his life living in a nice, big house with an even bigger backyard in one of the best neighborhoods in town. Now he and his mom shared a small, old house sitting on a not-much-bigger-than-the-house scruffy yard just outside town with his grandma (his mom's mom). Instead of looking out his window and seeing green lawns and fancy cars, Tony now looked out his window at his grandma's patch of yellowing grass and a run-down trailer park across the road. Instead of waking to the *spurt-spurt-spurt* of automatic sprinkler systems or the laughter of playing kids, Tony woke to the *clackety-clack* of the early morning train that ran on the tracks just a couple hundred feet behind the house.

Of course it could have been worse. If his grandma hadn't taken him and his mother in, who knows where they may have ended up? His mom hadn't worked since Tony had been born, and got a job as an administrative assistant after his dad went to prison. She made just enough for them to get by. The only reason Tony could afford to go to the Pizzaplex so often now was because he spent most of his afternoons and many of his evenings doing yardwork, painting, and minor repairs for retired people in the trailer park and a few others who lived in the older homes sprinkled along the road north and south of his grandma's house.

Kids like Boots and Rab, who came from well-off families, didn't understand yet what kind of worries and struggles most people had to carry around. Life came easy to kids like Tony's friends (and most of his classmates), but Tony knew many kids, and most adults, got beaten down by life.

Even before Tony's dad was arrested, Tony was fascinated by the stuff he heard on the news and saw in the paper that his dad had read from cover to cover every day. Tony had started pretending to be a reporter when he was in second grade. When his parents gave him a digital camera for his birthday in third grade, he had started wandering all over his neighborhood taking pictures. The pictures had led to stories about neighborhood events. Painstakingly typing the stories with two fingers (that was before he'd learned to type for real), Tony had used his dad's home-office printer to make copies, which he'd "delivered" to the front porch of everyone on their street. "Crows Make Off with Neighborhood Girl's Favorite Doll," "Solar Panels Ruin Neighbor's View," "Stray Dog Eats Prize Tomatoes"— these were just a few examples of his early work.

When Tony's obsession with investigative reporting began, his parents had encouraged him. They'd become a little less enthusiastic, though, when Tony had written a story titled "How Does Mr. Markham Get So Many Channels without Cable?" After Tony distributed that story around the neighborhood, a few official-looking men in suits visited the Markham house. The next day, someone slashed Tony's dad's tires.

After that happened, Tony's parents had told him he couldn't pass out his stories anymore. "Maybe you should write fiction, sweetie," his mom had suggested. "It's safer."

"What do you mean?" Tony had asked.

Tony's dad had sat down with Tony and explained, "Writing about real-life events can be tricky, son. It's hard to get all the facts, and if you don't get them right . . . or even if you do . . . you can cause problems for people. Investigative journalism is important to our society, but it can be . . . ," Tony's dad had frowned, ". . . dangerous."

Tony didn't get it then. He did now, but he didn't care.

Now, more than ever, after what had happened to Tony's dad, Tony wanted to find answers. He wanted to get to the bottom of things.

Tony had tried to do that with his dad's situation, but after he'd gone to jail, Tony's dad had told Tony that he had to promise not to look into who'd really embezzled the money. "Drop it," Tony's dad had said. "Promise me you'll drop it."

Tony hadn't had a choice. He had to promise.

And so far, he'd kept his promise.

But not being able to find out what had really happened to the money everyone said his dad had stolen had made Tony even more determined to unravel other mysteries when he encountered them. He hated unanswered questions.

And speaking of unanswered questions.

As his thoughts had wandered, Tony had reached a row of pinball machines. Two pretty teen girls, probably at least two or three years older than Tony, were tearing it up on two side-by-side machines. From their exchange of insults and constant razzing, Tony could tell they were trying to outdo each other's scores.

"Oh, don't you even," the taller of the two girls, who wore her black hair in a long braid, cried out when her friend's flipper lit up and her point values quadrupled.

The other girl, a petite redhead, let out a bell-like laugh. "Catch me if you can," she trilled.

Tony's gaze went to the machines' scoreboards, and when it did, something niggled at the back of his brain. He frowned and studied the machines' high scores listings.

"GGY," he said out loud when he read the initials next to the highest score. GGY, whoever that was, had outscored the other high scorers by millions of points. They had done it on both the machines the girls were playing.

Tony returned his attention to the girls' pinball competition. Their faces set in fierce concentration, both girls were masters at the game. Tony liked to think he was pretty good at pinball, but these girls were unbelievable. They were like pinball queens! They both had extraordinary ball control, and they both obviously were familiar with the tilt sensitivity of their game machines. Both girls nudged their machines frequently and got away with it.

The girl with the long braid stood soldier-at-attention straight in front of her machine. Her mouth was set in a grimace; she had huge teeth, and it looked like she was grinding them as her ring and middle fingers fluttered so quickly over the controls that they were almost a blur.

The redhead, who had several thousand more points on her machine than the black-haired girl did, stood in a more relaxed stance. She looked like she was leaning casually on the machine as her fingers patted the controls. Although her teeth weren't bared like her friend's were, the redhead's jaw was tight, and the veins of her neck were distended enough that Tony could actually see her quickened pulse.

While the silver balls zinged and pinged off the bumpers and shot from flipper to flipper as the girls executed perfect tip passes and bounce passes, the games' lights strobed, throwing up red-and-orange glows that lit up the girls' faces. Mesmerized, Tony continued to watch the girls, but his attention vacillated between their amazing pinball skills to the points racking up on the scoreboard at the back of the machines.

The scoring systems on the pinball machines in the Fazcade varied wildly. The same shot in one game might get you 100 points, so a 1,000,000-point score was impressive. In other games, you could score 100,000 in one shot. High scores in those games could push to a billion. The two machines the girls were playing had the same scoring systems—they had to, or the girls wouldn't have been able to compete one-on-one on separate machines. On these machines, most of the high scores were in the low millions. These girls had already topped 5,000,000, and their scores were higher than all the others on the high scorer list—all except for GGY. GGY held the top three high score spots on both of these machines, and their scores were all over 50,000,000, millions above the other players.

Tony turned and looked back along the aisle he'd just come down. Where had he seen the initials GGY before?

Leaving the girls to their competition, Tony retraced his steps, his gaze on the high scorers rosters on each game. He found GGY quickly on another pinball machine, a few down from where the girls were playing.

Continuing on, Tony scanned the high point rosters on all the game machines as he did a systematic survey of this level of the Fazcade. GGY hadn't played that many games here, but the ones they'd played, they'd dominated. Whenever GGY was on the high scorers roster, their scores blew all the other ones out of the water.

Who was this arcade phenom? And how did they get such high scores? Were they just that good . . . and if so, how did they do it . . . or were they cheating somehow?

Tony grinned as he felt a little tickle of excitement. These were the kind of questions that got his creative juices flowing. It was a real-life mystery, one Tony intended to solve. And it could be the basis of their story. It didn't matter that it wasn't fiction. All Tony would have to do was change a few details about whatever he discovered, and his investigation could be the meat of their story.

The first thing Tony had to do was find GGY, and to find GGY, he had to find out who they were. Surely, if GGY had achieved such amazing scores on several machines, someone had seen GGY play.

Turning, Tony started retracing his steps back toward the pinball queens. Clearly, they had played at least the two machines they were now using *a lot*. There was a good chance they'd seen GGY play.

A couple rowdy boys careened toward Tony as he turned a corner, and he shook his head as the boys each bounced off a nearby arcade machine in their attempt to avoid Tony.

Both boys wore gray shirts and baseball caps. *They looked like little human pinballs*, Tony thought, grinning.

The boys shouted to each other to hurry up, and they tore away. Tony continued on, tuning out the rest of the noise around him as he contemplated the mysterious GGY and their high scores.

Reaching the pinball queens, Tony wondered if he could talk to them while they played. Some arcade game players had no problem chatting while they played. Others were hard-core, and they'd lash out if you tried to interrupt them mid-game.

As Tony approached the girls, he figured he might as well try talking to them. The worst they could do was give him a dirty look or call him a name. He'd gone through worse than that. Being the son of a convicted embezzler had given Tony a pretty thick skin. His dad's case had gotten a lot of media attention; they'd had the press camping out on their front lawn for a while. Tony learned quickly that caring about what someone else thought was a surefire way to be miserable all the time.

The pinball queens were still at it. The redhead was no longer in the lead, and now that the black-haired girl had the advantage, her grimace had been replaced by a cocky smirk.

Tony decided that the redhead looked more approachable, so he sidled around to her. Making sure he didn't get too close (no gamer liked to be hovered over), he waited until she glanced his way. Then he lifted a hand in a casual wave and said, "You've got mad skills." To be sure the black-haired girl didn't feel left out, he added, "Both of you do. You're incredible."

The black-haired girl didn't acknowledge Tony, but he noticed that her smirk widened into a smile. The redhead pursed her lips as she manipulated her flipper to perform a picture-perfect drop catch, slowing the ball's momentum flawlessly to set up her next shot. And her next shot was a doozy. In a hypnotic series of missile-like streaks, the redhead's ball careened through the pinball machine, and her point total soared. Her score shot past the black-haired girl's total, and then the redhead was on fire.

For the next full minute, Tony stood silently while the redhead dominated her machine and the competition with her friend. When the girl slowed things down with a live catch every bit as good as her drop catch, she looked over at Tony.

"Are you a stalker?" she asked. "You look a little young to be a stalker."

Tony smiled. It wasn't the best conversation opener, but at least she hadn't told him to go away.

"Not a stalker," he said. "I'm trying to find out who GGY is, and I thought since you and your friend obviously play a lot, you might have seen them."

"GGY?" the black-haired girl said. She flipped her ball at just the right time, and it caromed into a ricochet that brought her point total almost even with her friend's.

Tony pointed at the high scorers roster. "GGY's scores are way higher than anyone else's," he said. "You two are the best scorers on these machines, besides GGY. But GGY's scores are, like, in another reality."

The redhead made a face. "I never look at the high scorers roster. I couldn't care less. All I want to do is beat her." She used her chin to indicate her friend.

"In your dreams," the black-haired girl said.

"Delusional, are we?" the redhead flung back.

Tony laughed. The redhead flicked another look at him. "You're kind of cute," she said. "How old are you?"

Tony flushed. "I'm in seventh grade. I'm twelve."

The redhead heaved a loud sigh. "Too young. We're sophomores."

Tony didn't know what to say to that. He decided to ignore it. "So, you don't know who GGY is?" he asked.

The redhead shrugged. "No idea. You should ask Axel."

"Who's Axel?" Tony asked.

The black-haired girl let out a guffaw. "ABC," she said.

Baffled by the introduction to the alphabet, Tony said, "Huh?"

The redhead used her head to indicate the high scorers roster. "Axel Brandon Campbell. He's probably up there."

Tony looked up at the high scorers roster. Sure enough. ABC was a couple lines below the two girls' initials, KXT and CRF. He idly wondered what their initials stood for, but he didn't ask.

The redhead concentrated on her play for a few seconds, then she said, "Axel's in our class, and he's always blathering about how he's on the high scorers rosters on a bunch of games here. He's the one who told us we're on the board on these machines. He'll probably know who GGY is."

"What does Axel look like?" Tony asked.

"Short," the redhead said, "about your height, but he's four years older than you are. Really long face, little mouth. Big ears."

"Wears a stupid hat," the black-haired girl said.

"Yeah," her friend agreed.

"What kind of hat?" Tony asked.

The redhead shrugged. "The kind of hat you wear to fish in, or at least my dad does."

"Bucket hat," the black-haired girl said.

"That's it," the redhead said. "Ugly green."

"Now go away," the black-haired girl said. "You're messing with my groove."

The redhead snorted. "Like you even have a groove," she flung at her friend.

The black-haired girl growled, and the two kept playing. Tony smiled.

"Thanks," he said.

Neither girl acknowledged him.

Tony turned and craned his neck to scan the players within his line of sight. He didn't spot any ugly green bucket hats.

Starting down the aisle, Tony's head swiveled right and left as he went. He had something to go on now. How hard would it be to find a frequent player who wore an ugly green hat?

"There you are!" Boots called out.

Tony turned. Boots and Rab were strolling toward him.

"Where've you been?" Rab asked.

Tony shrugged. "I was people watching."

Boots made a loud snorting sound. "Snore," he said. He punched Tony lightly in the bicep. "You really need a better hobby."

Tony shrugged again. He didn't want to tell Boots or Rab about his new investigation. They'd just rag on him about his curiosity and tell him his idea was dumb. They always thought his real-life investigations were lame.

"We're hungry," Rab said. "Pizza?"

Tony nodded. "Sure." He figured he could come back later to look for Axel. He didn't want his friends around while he was investigating anyway.

Tony had to concentrate to keep a grin off his face as he and his friends strolled out of the Fazcade. He couldn't wait to dive into the GGY mystery. He had a really strong feeling about it, like it was just the tip of an iceberg that was going to knock his socks off. He didn't know why he thought that, but he'd learned to trust his instincts. There was something here, something that he was going to unravel. And it was going to be epic.

★ ★ ★

Tony didn't get to come back to the Pizzaplex on his own until Sunday afternoon. Between Friday afternoon and Sunday, he'd either been with Rab and Boots or he'd been doing odd jobs for his grandma or her neighbors.

Boots's dad insisted Sundays were family time, so Tony and his friends never got together on Sundays. Tony usually spent Sunday afternoons with his mom—they played board games or went on long walks together. Today, though, his mom wasn't feeling good, and she wanted to take a nap. Tony was sorry she felt bad, but it was good for him. It gave him time to head back to the Pizzaplex while he knew his friends weren't there. Tony wasn't sure what Rab did on Sundays. Tony had never asked him, and Rab had never said.

Sunday afternoons were busy times at the Fazcade, and all the games were in use when Tony arrived. That was fine. He didn't want to play any games; he was on a mission. The big crowd drawn to the arcade on Sundays—because that was when the animatronics often strolled through the arcade, joking around and performing impromptu routines—raised the odds of finding either Axel or someone else who might have seen GGY play.

Tony eased himself into the throng of players. Backing out of the way when Montgomery Gator suddenly appeared and did a breakdance in the middle of the aisle, he thought about just picking someone at random to ask about GGY. That, however, was probably a total waste of time. It sounded like Axel was more of a sure thing. So, Tony decided to walk through the arcade in search of the ugly green hat . . . and long face, small mouth, and big ears.

For the first time, Tony wondered if the girls had been messing with him. Their description of Axel was a little out there. If the guy really fit that description, he was pretty funny looking.

And he was.

It only took Tony ten minutes to find Axel, who looked exactly as the pinball queens had described. The guy was truly unique looking.

Axel Brandon Campbell was leaning into the game machine's controls on *The Bunbarians.* His "ugly green" (army green) bucket hat was perched atop stringy brown hair that trailed down the back of a long neck red and bumpy with angry acne.

Hanging back behind Axel, Tony watched the game screen. Axel was doing a great job of controlling the game's "heroes," little axe-throwing Bon-Bons. The Bon-Bons drove their army tanks expertly through a dark, mottled landscape that looked like it was made of chocolate.

Lifting his gaze from the play, Tony checked out the high scorers roster on the game. ABC held the third-highest spot. Two other sets of initials unfamiliar to Tony were ahead of Axel. GGY obviously hadn't played this game.

Guessing that Axel was probably one of those intense players who would get angry if he was interrupted, Tony waited until Axel lost the game he was playing before stepping up beside the strange-looking teen. Then, before Axel could put another token in the machine, Tony said, "That was impressive. You're really good at this game."

Axel whipped his head toward Tony so quickly that the bucket hat nearly flew off. Axel reached up to tug the hat down more firmly on his head. He scowled at Tony.

Tony tried to look friendly. He gestured at the high scorers roster. "I've seen your initials on other games, too. Which game is your favorite?"

"What's your deal?" Axel asked

Tony frowned. "My deal? I don't have a deal."

"Sure you do," Axel said. "You wouldn't be talking to me if you didn't have a deal."

Since that was true, Tony shrugged and decided to just launch into it. "Okay," he said. "I'm trying to find out who GGY is, the person whose scores are so much higher than anyone else's on several games in the Fazcade, and I was told that you might know."

"Who told you?" Axel asked.

Tony shrugged again. "I don't know their names, but their initials are KXT and CRF. Two girls, one a redhead and one with a long black braid."

"Kenzie and Crystal," Axel said. "Couple of stuck-up snobs."

Tony decided to try to get on Axel's good side. "Yeah, I got that feeling. But are they right? Do you know who GGY is?"

A couple little girls started looking at *The Bunbarians*. "I'm not done playing," Axel growled at them. The little girls stuck their tongues out at him and scampered off.

Axel leaned back against the game console like he owned it. He crossed his arms and shook his head. "Nah, I don't know who GGY is." He rubbed a pointy chin and narrowed his eyes. "But the guy's scores are too high. Way too high."

"That's what I thought," Tony said.

"I asked around, and no one has seen him play," Axel said. "Scores like that, you'd think he'd want the limelight, you know?"

Tony nodded even though he didn't think every player wanted to be noticed like Axel did. "You'd think someone would have seen them play," Tony agreed.

"It's gotta be a him," Axel said.

Tony disagreed. But he kept his opinion to himself.

"Guy's like a ghost," Axel said.

Apparently done with the subject, Axel rotated away from Tony and stuck a token into *The Bunbarians*. He started manipulating the game's joystick.

"Well, thanks," Tony said.

Axel grunted and kept playing.

Tony pivoted and surveyed the clamorous arcade. Although a few clusters of kids roamed the aisles, some joking around and some arguing about which game to play next, nearly everyone else in the Fazcade was playing games. No one looked particularly approachable. Not that unapproachable people would stop Tony. He just wasn't sure how much he was going to get out of talking to random people. If Axel, a frequent player who kept a keen eye on the high scorers rosters, didn't know who GGY was, what were the odds that someone else would know?

But Tony had to do something. No way was he going to just give up.

Tony spun around abruptly, intending to walk through the arcade until he felt the urge to talk to someone. And he walked right into one of the Pizzaplex employees.

Bouncing off the substantial chest of a stocky, long-haired Fazcade attendant, Tony cartwheeled his arms to keep his balance. His efforts were failing him, and he was starting to tip backward when the attendant reached out and grabbed the front of Tony's green corduroy shirt.

"Whoa there, dude," the attendant said in the laid-back, drawn-out lazy tone of someone kicked back in a hammock. "Sorry about that."

The attendant jerked Tony into an upright position, then grasped Tony's arms to steady him. The guy's hands were strong, and Tony felt like a little kid when the guy gave Tony's shoulder a pat.

"You good?" the attendant asked.

Tony nodded. "Sorry. That was my fault. I wasn't watching where I was going."

The attendant—his name tag said his name was

Finbarr—laughed. "Hey, a polite kid. That's a nice change of pace." He patted Tony's shoulder again.

Tony pointed at the black-printed name on the yellow plastic card pinned to the lapel of the red Pizzaplex employee shirt. "Finbarr," Tony said. "Isn't that an Irish name?"

"Hey, how about that," Finbarr said. "Polite and not all me-me-me." Finbarr cocked his head. "Yep. Means 'fair-haired.'" Finbarr pointed at his dirty-blond hair. "My mom said I was towheaded when I was born. My mom's one hundred percent Irish, from County Cork . . . Met my dad when he was traveling the world. According to Mom, Finbarr was Cork's patron saint."

Tony nodded. "Yeah, and in Irish folklore, he was the king of the fairies."

Finbarr raised an unruly dark eyebrow that didn't match his lighter hair. "Impressive."

"I wrote a story about how folklore has created a lot of our society's customs," Tony said.

A trio of little brown-haired girls with thousands of freckles among them came skipping down the aisle. Finbarr took Tony's elbow and pulled him off to the side, near a token dispenser.

"You're a pretty interesting little dude," Finbarr said. "I saw you wandering around staring at people. I've been keeping an eye on you. Thought something weird was up with you or something."

"Or something." Tony grinned.

Finbarr laughed. "I can see that."

A few feet away, a pigtailed girl Tony recognized from school—her name was Amelia, and he didn't like her at all—started kicking a *Fruity Maze* game machine. "You did *not* just do that!" she screamed at it.

The game let out a sprightly chortle as if it knew it had

just gotten the best of her. Then it bleeped and the "you lost" music blasted from the game's speakers.

"'Scuse me," Finbarr said to Tony.

He stepped away from Tony and walked over to the little girl. "Hey there, princess," Finbarr said to the strawberry-blonde girl dressed all in black (*The hair and the clothes didn't go together at all,* Tony thought). "You break it, your momma and daddy gotta buy it, and they won't be happy with you."

The girl looked up at Finbarr and growled at him. "I'm not a princess, you jerk, and you're lying." She kicked the machine again.

Finbarr shrugged. "Have it your way." He reached into his pocket and pulled out a walkie-talkie. As Finbarr raised the walkie to his mouth, it jostled the key card hanging on a lanyard around his thick neck. "PC on F level 2, aisle 7," he said in his mellow drawl.

The little girl was kicking the machine again. Finbarr pulled out a key ring heavy with a couple dozen keys. He unlocked the game's control box and powered it off.

"You can't do that!" the girl screamed.

Finbarr shrugged. "Pretty sure I just did."

Tony grinned. The girl saw him and shrieked, "And what are you looking at, weirdo?!"

Tony shrugged. He didn't stop grinning.

Finbarr turned and winked one of his heavy-lidded green eyes at Tony. Tony's grin widened.

The girl whirled to face Finbarr, and Tony was pretty sure she was going to kick Finbarr, too. Before she could, though, a tall, middle-aged Pizzaplex security guard came around the corner. He looked at Finbarr. Finbarr nodded toward the girl.

"C'mon, miss," the guard said. "Let's go."

The girl started to argue, but then she sighed

theatrically and crossed her arms. Throwing Finbarr and Tony dirty looks, she marched off ahead of the security guard, who turned back and rolled his eyes at Finbarr. "Living the dream," the guard muttered.

Finbarr shook his head, and his wavy hair flopped over his forehead. Finbarr flipped his hair back. Tony could tell Finbarr had made that move thousands of times.

"Okay, where were we?" Finbarr asked as he stepped back over to Tony.

Good question, Tony thought. Why was he still standing here?

Because Finbarr was the guy he needed to talk to, Tony realized. His intuition often gave him "hits" like that.

"The reason I've been wandering around," Tony said, "is that I've been trying to figure out who GGY is. GGY is—"

"The highest scorer on at least a dozen machines in this place," Finbarr finished.

Tony's eyes widened. "Yeah. Exactly. I noticed that his scores are—"

"Way higher than should be possible," Finbarr took over again.

Tony nodded. "I noticed it a couple days ago. I'm doing a story, and I thought finding out who he was and figuring out how he did it would be a good subject."

Finbarr nodded. He pointed at Tony's chest. "So, what's your name?"

"T-Tarbell." Tony had started to give his real name, but he had to get used to using Tarbell for a couple of weeks.

"T-Tarbell?" Finbarr pulled his chin inward and raised one eyebrow.

"Just Tarbell." Tony shrugged. "My friends and I use pen names when we're working on a story, and I chose Tarbell. My real name starts with a *T*, and I almost used that."

Finbarr nodded. "Got it. Good name. Ida Tarbell—"

"—Was an important muckraker at the turn of the last century." It was Tony's turn to complete a sentence.

Finbarr laughed. "Okay, Tarbell. I need to keep an eye on this zoo. Walk with me."

Finbarr motioned with his chin for Tony to follow him, and together, they began striding through the Fazcade. As they went, Finbarr pointed at a few machines, mostly pinball machines, but a few other arcade games as well.

"I'm very aware of GGY," Finbarr said. "Not sure any of the other arcade attendants are. Most of 'em just dial it in, you know. Put in their hours and get back to their lives. Me, I figure if I'm going to do something, I might as well *do* it and not just go through the motions. Ya know?"

Tony thought that kind of conscientiousness didn't fit with Finbarr's relaxed manner, but the "judging books by their covers" saying was true in more ways than one. Since Tony liked to be conscientious, too, he nodded. "I do. Yes."

"I've got a buddy who's one of the tech guys here," Finbarr went on. "I asked him to run diagnostics on the machines GGY scored so high on. I was sure the dude or dudette hacked the machines. But my guy says the machines are as they should be. He couldn't find any trace of a hack."

"But how—?" Tony began.

"—Does GGY get such high scores?" Finbarr finished.

"And how come no one—" Tony started again.

"—Has seen them do it? Good question. It's a mystery. GGY is flying way under the radar."

Tony gave Finbarr a look. Finbarr shook his head. "Sorry. Finishing people's sentences—"

"—Is a bad habit," Tony jumped in.

Finbarr laughed.

Tony smiled. "So, you think GGY is sneaking in and playing after hours somehow?"

Finbarr shook his head. "One of these"—he picked up his key card and fluttered it in front of his well-muscled chest— "gets you access to employees-only areas, but if an employee loses a card, it's immediately deactivated. You'd only be able to use it once or twice, if that, *and* this card doesn't get you in and out of the building. Only Security Badges do that. And those are even more closely guarded. Sometimes my fellow workers get careless with these things"—he toyed with his key card again—"but anyone who steals one won't get to use it for long." Finbarr frowned and looked over Tony's shoulder. "Sorry," he said. "Got another issue to take care of." Finbarr gave Tony another pat as he walked past Tony. "I'll see you around," he called back as he started to hurry away. "Let me know if you solve the mystery."

Tony watched Finbarr wade into a fight that was developing between a couple of Skee-Ball players. Then Tony sighed and turned to walk away.

Finbarr had been nice, but he hadn't been all that helpful. All Tony had learned was that GGY wasn't hacking the game machines . . . maybe. Just because the tech guy couldn't find evidence of a hack didn't mean a hack hadn't taken place. Some hackers were just that good.

Tony really wanted to talk to more people, but he couldn't. Not today. If Tony didn't get home soon, his grandma would come and drag him home. Missing his gran's Sunday dinner was a big no-no. Tony started heading out of the arcade.

Tony had almost reached the Fazcade's second-story exit when an anguished squeal distracted him. He turned and saw a skinny girl with wild hair shaking her fist at one of the pinball machines. The girl was maybe a year or two older than Tony. A round-shouldered boy a few inches shorter than the girl, but probably about the same age, was watching her with wide eyes.

"That was my best game *ever!*" the girl whined. "I just blew PDB out of the water." She pointed at the machine's high scorers roster. "See? But I'm still nowhere near GGY. How does she do it?!"

"How do you know GGY is a she, Dana?" he asked.

Dana turned and rolled her eyes at the boy. "Seriously, Wes? Do you think a *boy* could be that good?" She made the word *boy* sound like what she really meant was "gross, slimy slug."

"Excuse me," Tony said. "I couldn't help but overhear you talking about GGY. Do you know who GGY is?"

Dana turned and threw all the force of her narrow-eyed glare at Tony. "What's it to you?" she asked.

Tony tried to look harmless. "I've noticed GGY's high scores is all, and I've been curious." He pointed at the new second-place initials on the pinball machine's roster. "That's a great score you just got," he said. "It seems like GGY's scores should be impossible."

Dana's face relaxed just a bit. "Yeah, that's what I keep saying." She nudged Wes. "Don't I keep saying that?"

Wes nodded. "She keeps saying that."

Dana punched Wes's upper arm.

"Ow," he protested, rubbing the spot she'd hit.

Dana studied Tony for a second. "What do you know about GGY?" she asked.

Tony shook his head. "Not much." When Dana looked like she was losing interest in him, he added, "But I just found out from one of the attendants that they ran diagnostics on the machines that list GGY as the high scorer, and the machines haven't been hacked."

Dana's brows lifted. "Well, that's interesting. I was wondering about that. A friend and I were chatting about it online just yesterday. She thought GGY was hacking." Dana shook her head. "Guess not." She tapped her foot and scowled at the pinball machine's high scorers roster. "It's weird. You'd think someone that good would be in the forums or something." She shrugged and pulled a couple tokens out of her pocket. She turned back to the machine.

Tony had been dismissed. He turned away from Dana and Wes and started to walk toward the Fazcade exit.

After just a couple steps, though, a flash of glowing white caught Tony's eye. He looked to his left, and his feet faltered. He was being watched . . . by one of the animatronics.

Tony looked up into the gleaming white eyes of the big orange animatronic bear with the red, armored shoulder pads and the black top hat—Glamrock Freddy. Thinking that Freddy was just being friendly, the way the animatronics were during their Sunday stroll around, Tony lifted a hand and waved at the bear. Freddy, however, didn't return the gesture. He just kept his intense gaze on Tony, as if sizing Tony up.

Suddenly chilled for reasons he didn't understand at all, Tony looked away from Freddy and hurried on. After a few more steps, Tony glanced over his shoulder. Glamrock Freddy was still watching him. Goose bumps popped up on Tony's bare arms as he practically ran out of the Fazcade.

By the time Tony made it home that Sunday afternoon, he'd gotten over the weird freak-out he'd had over Glamrock Freddy. He didn't understand why the animatronic had gotten to him. He'd never found the robotic characters scary before. But then, none of them had ever looked directly at him before. Maybe that was it. Maybe Tony had just gotten the heebie-jeebies because he wasn't used to making eye contact with a robot.

Whatever. Tony didn't care about the weird encounter. He was too wrapped up in the mystery of GGY.

Throughout the next week, every evening after he did

his homework, Tony tried to find out more about GGY. He didn't make any progress, though, until he got to thinking about what Dana had said about forums. When he remembered her comment, Tony realized that maybe if he visited a bunch of the sites, he might be able to find GGY that way.

Over the next three nights, Tony dove down the rabbit hole of forums for top arcade gamers. Creating a user name, Digger1, and a password for over a dozen sites, Tony asked the same question in every forum he visited: "Does anyone know all the high scorers at the Pizzaplex?" He figured asking that way would obscure his real interest in GGY. For some reason, Tony had a feeling he shouldn't be too up front about what he was after in these forums.

When Tony didn't get any helpful answers to his question, he went back to just hanging out in the forums. But the hours he spent online got him nothing . . . until Thursday evening. That was when Morrigan99 confronted him.

Sitting cross-legged on his sagging twin bed (Tony's old bed had been a double with a memory foam mattress, which he missed very much), Tony was hunched over his laptop, as he had been for several hours over the previous three evenings. It was nearly 10:00 p.m.

Tony's room, like the rest of the house tonight, smelled like the sausage and cabbage his grandma had made for dinner. Even the open window, through which Tony could hear a soft rainfall pattering on the old house's metal roof, didn't take away the stench.

Tony was discouraged by the lack of progress in his investigation. He was about to log out of the forum he was currently in when he saw that he'd received a private message. He clicked on it.

Morrigan99: Why are you asking about people?

A little prickle of anticipation tickled the nape of

Tony's neck as his fingers hovered over his keyboard. He debated. Should he be coy or straightforward?

Something told Tony to be straight. He tapped the keys.

Digger1: Curious about GGY.

Tony waited a full minute before Morrigan99's answering PM popped up onto his screen.

Morrigan99: Will PM you tomorrow night in the other forum I'm in. Same time.

Tony typed quickly.

Digger1: What do you know?

Tony waited again. This time, Morrigan99 didn't respond.

Tony frowned and tried to remember which of the other forums he'd been in when he'd noticed the Morrigan99 username. He was pretty sure he knew which one it was, but he wasn't positive. Well, he'd try them all if he had to.

Tony closed his laptop and leaned back onto his pillows. What did Morrigan99 know?

Maybe nothing. But he'd keep the "date" and find out.

In the meantime, though, Tony had another plan. He'd decided on it while he'd been choking down his grandma's sausage and cabbage. Thinking back to his conversation with Finbarr while he'd been eating, Tony had begun to wonder if the Pizzaplex might have some record of GGY, some record that Finbarr didn't know about. How could Tony find that out?

Easy, he'd thought as he washed down the last of his sausage with a big gulp of milk. He just had to get into one of the employee kiosks. Those kiosks, a few of which were positioned in various locations around the Pizzaplex, were like mini employee workstations. The previous afternoon, Tony had passed one of them and seen an employee exit the kiosk without logging off the kiosk's computer. If Tony could get into a kiosk right after something like that happened, he could poke around the Pizzaplex's records.

Now as Tony stowed his laptop on the small maple desk tucked into the corner of his almost closet-size room, he pondered his next moves while he got ready for bed. Thinking about what he needed to do filled his stomach with agitated butterflies, but he was going to do it anyway.

Although Finbarr hadn't had much information about GGY, his discussion of the way the Pizzaplex key cards and Security Badges worked had given Tony his idea. What Tony needed to do now was find one of those careless employees Finbarr had talked about and get his hands on a key card. He was pretty sure he could do that easily.

Earlier in the school year, Tony and his friends had written a story about a gang of pickpockets. Tony had come up with the idea after he'd read a newspaper article about a rash of pickpocketing in the town square. He'd wanted to do an exposé on the subject, investigating the ins and outs of how pickpocketing worked. He hadn't been able to do that because Mrs. Sosa had insisted on fiction, but Tony had done all the research. He was pretty sure he could pull off lifting a Pizzaplex employee's key card.

He'd do it tomorrow afternoon. It would be a Friday afternoon, and Boots and Rab would definitely want to go to the Pizzaplex. They never cared when Tony wandered off. He should have plenty of time to lift a card, get into a kiosk with an active computer screen, and poke around the Pizzaplex records.

Tony slid into his bed. He took a deep breath and blew it out. He could do it. Tomorrow.

The key to a good pickpocket lift, Tony had learned when he'd researched the subject, was distraction. When combined with compassion, distraction was nearly a foolproof way to get whatever you wanted off a "mark." Or so Tony had read.

And it worked.

Having left Boots and Rab in the Fazcade battling it out on a Skee-Ball machine, Tony went out to the main lobby of the Pizzaplex and began scoping out the employee kiosks. The first two he checked out were empty, but he could see the log-in screen on the computer monitors. So, he moved on. The third kiosk he peeked into had an active screen.

And there . . . just a few feet away, a Pizzaplex employee was giving directions to a large family. The employee, a dark-haired young woman with a flattop haircut, was red-faced as she tried to talk to a dad with three screaming children tugging on his pants legs. When the family finally walked away, the woman ran a hand through her hair and blew out air. Tony knew the timing was perfect.

Quickly striding forward, as if about to pass the employee, Tony deliberately scuffed his shoe into the lobby's black-and-white floor tiles. He purposely stumbled forward and fell down.

The Pizzaplex employee immediately rushed forward. She bent over Tony.

Distraction. Check.

"Oh my goodness," the woman—her name tag read KATHY—said. "Are you okay?"

Compassion. Check.

Tony made a big deal of rubbing his knee, and he crumpled his face as if in pain. "Um, I think so," he said.

Kathy extended a hand. "Let me help you up."

Tony took the hand, and as Kathy pulled him up off the floor, he used his other hand to snag her key card off her lanyard. He made sure to wince and moan as he made the move.

Kathy, who had very kind brown eyes that made Tony

feel ashamed of what he was doing, was so focused on Tony's apparent pain that she didn't notice her key card disappearing into Tony's pocket. Tony hid his triumph and continued with his elaborate playacting.

"Where does it hurt?" Kathy asked. "Is it your knee?"

Tony, now wanting to get away from Kathy as fast as possible, kept his face contorted like he was hurting as he got to his feet. He brushed himself off and pretended to test his knee. "It seems to be fine," he said. "It just smarted there for a second. Serves me right. I was being clumsy."

"You sure you're okay?" Kathy asked.

Tony's gaze, directed by guilt, wanted to go to Kathy's empty lanyard. "I just need to walk it off," he said quickly. "Really. I'm fine. Thanks for your help."

How was Tony going to get away from Kathy? He may not have much time. She could notice the missing lanyard any minute.

Luck helped Tony out.

"Miss?" an elderly man called out. "Could you help me?"

"I'm fine," Tony said again. "Go on. Thanks."

Kathy frowned. Then she nodded and strode toward the old man.

Tony didn't waste any time. Taking advantage of the milling crowds and the cheers that accompanied a nearby animatronic rock band performance—the Glamrock animatronics were blasting a song from a makeshift stage set up in the lobby—Tony dashed around to the back of the kiosk. Using Kathy's key card, he let himself inside.

The employee kiosk was small and square, like a little tollbooth. Three of the kiosk's pale yellow sides were half walls topped by windows. The fourth side was solid, and it was covered by a cork bulletin board crammed with employee notices. In front of the bulletin board, a large flat-screen monitor sat above a small shelf, which contained a keyboard.

Cords ran from the flat screen down under the shelf, into the floor. Tony assumed those were the hardwires that linked the flat screen with the Pizzaplex's main computers.

Because the kiosks had observation windows, Tony knew he had to stay out of sight. He'd already thought this through, hoping that the keyboard had a long cord, or better yet, was cordless.

Tony grabbed the keyboard. Score! It was cordless.

Tony squatted down below the level of the windows, and he started tapping on the keyboard's keys quickly, poking around the Pizzaplex records. Following the plan that he'd come up with the night before, Tony rapidly scrolled through the databases, looking for GGY. He didn't know which database, if any, might contain a record of GGY, so he had to try several of them.

Again, he got lucky. He found GGY in the fifth database he tried.

Tony sucked in his breath when he spotted GGY on a list of issued Pizzaplex Play Passes. Clicking on the Play Pass in question, Tony frowned.

Tony wasn't a hacker, but he was reasonably good on the computer. Because of that, he was able to easily spot that the Play Pass issued to GGY had been modified. Although Play Passes were supposed to be designed to simply give frequent players access to all games without the need of tokens, this one had been modified into more of a Security Badge than a Play Pass.

Pizzaplex Play Passes were relatively simple white cards with a barcode. The card issued to GGY, according to the computer, had more than just the usual barcode. It also had the semitransparent Fazbear company logo that Security Badges had, and it had a magnetic strip. Tony was sure that with this card GGY could get into any employee-only area they wanted.

Tony squinted up at the screen. He wished he had a better angle on it.

Next to the hacked Play Pass was a list of three names. It looked like GGY had used the pass to get other people into the Pizzaplex after closing. Tony strained to see the names. Maybe they might lead him to GGY.

Craning his neck, Tony saw the name Mary on the screen, but he couldn't see her last name. He could only make out the first three letters of the next two names: Rae-something and Tre-something. Tony started to raise up a little higher so he could see more.

A scrape outside the kiosk door startled Tony. He glanced up to his right and saw the back of a Pizzaplex employee—right outside the observation window!

Tony quickly backed out of the Play Pass database, and he returned the keyboard to its position on the little shelf under the computer monitor. Keeping his gaze on the red-shirted back just outside the window, Tony crab-walked to the kiosk's door and eased it open. Exhaling in relief because no one was looking his way, Tony quickly stood, tossing Kathy's key card behind him as he pulled the door closed, and ducked into the nearby crowd. Tony started making his way back to the Fazcade. As he went, he thought about what he'd just discovered.

Clearly, Tony thought, GGY was not just an amazing game player. They also were a proficient hacker. A very proficient hacker.

But why did GGY want access to the behind-the-scenes areas in the Pizzaplex? What were they up to?

Tony was chewing on these questions as he walked. Because of this, he was paying very little attention to his surroundings . . . until he once again caught a glimmer of white out of the corner of his eye.

Remembering what had happened the last time he'd

seen the bit of luminous white, Tony barely turned his head and used his peripheral vision to check out what had gotten his attention. And as he'd expected, he spotted Glamrock Freddy. The animatronic was pacing Tony, three feet or so behind Tony's right shoulder. It looked like Glamrock Freddy was shadowing Tony. But why?

Tony's heart stuttered. What if Glamrock Freddy had seen Tony go into or come out of the kiosk? He could have. The stage where the band had been playing was very close to the kiosk. Had the band been playing when Tony had come out? He couldn't remember. He'd been too focused on getting clear of the kiosk.

Maybe it was just a coincidence that Glamrock Freddy was walking in the same direction Tony was going, just a few feet from Tony. Tony risked another glance at the animatronic. He quickly looked straight forward again.

Nope. Not a coincidence. Freddy was clearly focused on Tony.

Were the animatronics programmed for security as well as entertainment? Would Freddy report Tony to someone . . . or confront Tony himself?

Tony picked up his pace. He practically ran through the crowd until he reached the Fazcade. Then he shot down the nearest aisle and ducked behind a shooting game. His heart beating even louder than the noisy games around him, Tony waited for several seconds. When nothing happened, he eased his head out from behind the game. He looked around.

Glamrock Freddy was nowhere in sight. Even so, Tony waited another full minute. Finally, his palms sweaty and his pulse churning in his ears, Tony went to find his friends.

Tony pondered what he'd discovered the whole rest of the afternoon and evening. By 10:00 p.m., however, when it was time to get Morrigan99's PM, Tony was no closer to figuring out what GGY was up to. Maybe Morrigan99 would have some answers.

Logging into the forum he hoped was the right one, Tony checked for private messages. And sure enough, he'd gotten one from Morrigan99.

Morrigan99: What do you know?

Tony frowned and typed his response.

Digger1: About what?

Morrigan99: Don't be dense. GGY.

Tony wiggled his fingers. What should he do? Refuse to say? Or be truthful? He decided to go for truth. He typed.

Digger1: GGY has a hacked Pizzaplex Play Pass. They can go anywhere in the Pizzaplex. I want to know why they're doing that.

Morrigan99: Not bad for a little kid.

Tony's breath caught. His fingers trembled above his laptop keyboard. How did Morrigan99 know he was a kid?

Morrigan99: I know who you are. You're playing with fire.

Digger1: Who are you?

Morrigan99: Meet me in 30 minutes. Under the south side bleachers at the high school.

Tony started to type a response, but Morrigan99 logged out of the forum. Tony stared at his screen. Then he, too, logged out and closed his laptop.

Turning his head, Tony looked out his open window. It was raining again tonight, a little harder than the night before. This was the time of year when it rained more often than not.

Tony inhaled the familiar petrichor scent of the air and watched a breeze curl up the hem of his ugly brown curtains. He really didn't want to go out in the dark and rain.

But he had to.

Apparently, Tony had found every investigator's dream, "a source," and he wasn't about to be a coward and not take advantage of the situation. He needed to meet Morrigan99. If he didn't, he had no business wanting to be an investigative reporter. Journalists weren't cowards.

Through the thin wall that separated Tony's tiny room from his grandma's much larger room, Tony could clearly hear the droning voice of the local nighttime newscast's anchor. His grandma's hearing wasn't great, and she turned the TV up too loud.

But that was good for Tony tonight. His mom was asleep by now. She always went to bed early. Tony would be able to sneak out without any problem.

The high school, sprawling just outside the outskirts of town, was only a couple miles from Tony's grandma's house. He could bike that easily. Even in the pouring rain.

Tony looked around his room. What should he take? Tony's gaze flitted over his meager belongings.

Don't just stand here, he admonished himself.

Tony forced himself into action. Reaching into his nightstand drawer, he pulled out his small flashlight. He tucked it into his jeans pocket.

Then Tony went to his closet and pulled out his aluminum baseball bat. He didn't honestly think that a rendezvous near the high school bleachers was going to be dangerous, but he couldn't be sure. Why take the risk? He was going "armed." Tony reached up and pulled his rain poncho off its hook behind the closet door.

Tony looked around. Anything else?

"Just your courage," he muttered to himself.

Tony dropped the poncho over his head and went to his warped oak bedroom door. He waited until he heard a burst of music from a commercial on his grandma's TV. Then he quickly tiptoed into the hallway and snuck to the stairs. Still in his stocking feet, Tony made no sound as he descended the long, narrow flight of well-worn wood treads. Skipping the second to last one because it had a loud squeak, Tony hopped onto the dark blue braided rug in the entryway. He grabbed his shoes from under the scarred bench of his grandma's rickety coatrack and pulled them on. Then he let himself out into the barely moonlit night.

"Why couldn't I collect stamps for a hobby?" Tony asked himself as the rain started pelting the hood of his poncho.

At least it was a warm rain. Tony reminded himself that he couldn't melt as he retrieved his bike from the shed behind the house. Then, tucking his baseball bat under his arm, he pedaled down the driveway to the road that led to town.

By the time Tony reached the edge of the athletic fields at the high school, he was not only drenched, he was also thoroughly spooked. He really wanted to turn around and ride back home as fast as he could. But he didn't.

Tony got off his bike and leaned it against a darkened light post. His breath coming in tense little gasps, he grasped his baseball bat and surveyed his surroundings.

Tony and his friends had been to several high school football games. In just a couple years, they'd be attending this school. They liked pretending that they already did.

On game nights, the football field and the bleachers area were lit up by massive banks of spotlights. Between the lights and the crowds, this corner of the school grounds always felt alive and exciting.

The area didn't feel that way now. Tonight, the hundred yards of artificial turf, barely illuminated by a few weak security lights at the edges, looked like a vast pool filled with murky water . . . or maybe quicksand. Tony felt like, if he were to step out onto that field, it would suck him down into it, pulling him out of this reality and into another one.

Tony exhaled loudly. "Get a grip," he told himself.

Tony did a 360-degree turn, staring hard as far as he could see. He listened even harder.

The rain rapped and tapped a staccato rhythm on Tony's poncho, and at first, he could hear little else but the water's incessant beat. But then, behind Tony, something clanked near the bleachers. Tony spun toward the sound and tried to see into the dark shadows tucked inside the steady rain. He could barely see the rising outline of the aluminum stands. He squinted, searching the area where he thought the noise had originated.

"Get over here," a girl's voice called out.

A girl?

Of course a girl.

Idiot, Tony thought. Morrigan was an Irish goddess . . . or three of them, depending on which myth you read. Of course Morrigan99 was a girl.

"Come on," the girl called. "I won't bite you. And if I try, you can whap me with that bat."

Tony let the bat hang nonchalantly loose—but also at the ready—as he trotted toward the bleachers. Rain blew in under the hood of his poncho; he swiped it from his eyes. He blinked to clear his vision.

"Over here," the girl called.

The smooth voice sounded like its owner had an overabundance of attitude. Something about the voice was familiar, but that was probably just because Tony knew so many girls with attitude.

Tony slowed and took a couple more tentative steps forward. In seconds, he was under one of the bleacher benches listening to the rain's tinkling patter on the metal above him.

Even over the rain's racket, he heard a rustling. Then the murk to his left shifted.

A figure in a black rain parka stepped up to Tony. The figure lifted both hands. Tony tightened his grip on his baseball bat.

The parka's hood fell back. Tony found himself looking into the dark eyes of a girl with a long, black braid.

It was the girl from the arcade!

"It's you!" Tony said. He felt like an idiot as soon as the words were out of his mouth. He tried to recover. "Crystal, right?"

"You talked to Axel," Crystal said. "You never told us your name."

"Tony," Tony blurted out before he could remember he was supposed to use his nom de plume.

"Okay, Tony," Crystal said.

Rain trickled down from Crystal's parka hood and coursed over her pretty face. She didn't wipe it away.

"How did you know it was me in the forum?" Tony asked.

"You're not as stealthy as you think—you're literally the only person going around asking about GGY."

"Why'd you meet me?" Tony realized he still had a death grip on his baseball bat. He relaxed his hands and let the bat hang at his side.

Crystal glanced at the bat and smirked. Then her expression turned serious. "I wanted to meet you because I think you might be sticking your nose into something that could get you in trouble," Crystal said.

"All I'm trying to find out is who GGY is," Tony said.

"Exactly," Crystal said. "And I don't think that's a great idea."

"Why?" Tony asked.

Crystal poked Tony in the chest. "Use your brain, kid. You said yourself in your PM that GGY has hacked a Play Pass. Do you think that's just for kicks?"

Tony frowned. "I figured . . ." He stopped. He wasn't sure what he figured.

Crystal stepped closer, so close that Tony could smell her breath. She'd recently eaten something chocolate.

"I'm going to tell you something," Crystal said, "and if I find out you've told someone else, that baseball bat won't protect you."

Tony involuntarily tightened his grip on the bat again. "Okay," he said. He cringed when his voice cracked in the middle of the word.

Crystal leaned in close and stared into Tony's eyes. Apparently satisfied, she nodded. "My hobby," she said, "which I do for the fun of it, is hacking. I like to poke around and see what there is to see."

"Like GGY," Tony said.

"Not like GGY," Crystal snapped. "I look around. GGY has another agenda."

"What's that?"

Crystal shook her head. "That's the thing. I don't know. All I know is that they're doing things that are weird. And when I see weird, I think unpredictable. And unpredictable can be dangerous."

"What weird things?" Tony asked.

Crystal glanced over her shoulder. When she studied the blackness around them, it felt like spiders were skittering down Tony's spine. He ignored the instinct to shift his feet and look over his shoulder, too.

"One of the things I was poking into," Crystal said when she returned her gaze to Tony, "was the Pizzaplex animatronics' code. I was curious about how their behaviors were chosen. Just for fun. But when I was look-ing at the code, I spotted some strange lines that didn't seem original to the programming. The new lines of code created additional conversations and behaviors in Glamrock Freddy, Chica, Roxy, and Monty, stuff that wasn't in the legitimate coding. Embedded in those lines of code are seemingly random Gs and Ys."

Tony felt that little clutch in his stomach that always happened when it seemed like he was onto something. "Don't programmers sometimes leave, like, a bread crumb trail, like a signature?" he asked.

Crystal nodded. "That's exactly what they do. Or at least I do. And this signature is one left by a hacker, not by one of the original programmers. I'm sure of it."

"Gs and Ys," Tony repeated.

"I don't believe in coincidences," Crystal said.

"Me neither," Tony said.

Crystal reached out and grabbed Tony's arm. He had to stifle a gasp.

"For some reason, GGY wants to control the ani-matronics in very specific ways," Crystal said. "I don't know why, and I don't know what the code is designed to do." She shrugged. "I didn't think much about it when I found it, and I really didn't care, until you started ask-ing about GGY. That's when I linked what I found in the code to the GGY on the high scorers rosters. "And"—she shrugged—"I don't know. I just felt like I should tell you."

"Twice when I've been at the Pizzaplex poking around," Tony blurted, "I caught Glamrock Freddy watching me."

Crystal bit her lip. "You need to be careful," she said.

"But why . . . ?" Tony began.

Crystal shook her head. "None of it is my business. I repeat, I don't care. So, I'm going to forget all about it. But"—she rolled her eyes and sighed drammatically—"I have a little brother. And I would have felt like a jerk if I didn't tell you what I know and warn you to be careful." She raised her hood. "Now I've done that."

Without saying anything else, Crystal stepped backward and disappeared into the gloom. Tony gripped his baseball bat and turned to dash toward his bike.

Tony's weekend was packed with odd jobs for his grandma's neighbors. On Sunday, his mom and grandma decided, because the sky was totally blue for the first time in a couple weeks, that it was a good day for a picnic. After the picnic, they thought they were doing something nice for Tony by taking him to the Pizzaplex to play arcade games.

Thoroughly unnerved by Crystal's warning, Tony was tense the entire time he and his mom and grandma were in the Pizzaplex. Although Tony didn't even look at the high scorers rosters, he couldn't get GGY out of his mind.

When Tony spotted Glamrock Freddy watching him from the other side of the arcade, Tony pretended he didn't feel well, and he asked his mom and grandma to take him home. Mentally, he called himself a wuss, but he figured even investigative journalists had a right to a tactical retreat once in a while.

That evening, after his grandma and mom went to bed, Tony started his story. He didn't get much done, though. Stressed out and tense, he managed to write just a page before he was too tired to keep typing. He'd have to wait until the next evening to get back to it.

In spite of their "numb de plumbs," Tony's friends had shown no interest in their story assignment, even when Tony told them about what he'd found. "Just write what you think is best," Boots said after school on Monday, "then we'll put our two cents in."

That was how it always went. Tony did the work, and his friends threw in a few tidbits, and they all shared a grade equally. Tony liked to write, so he didn't mind . . . too much.

Tony's fingers flew over the keyboard Monday evening, Tuesday evening, and Wednesday evening. He could barely type fast enough to keep up with his ideas.

"GGY had a plan," Tony wrote, "and it was a plan they weren't going to share with anyone. Working behind the scenes, wraithlike, worming their way into the dark maze of the Pizzaplex's restricted areas, GGY left only the subtlest trail behind. Did they leave the trail on purpose, teasing anyone who dared to follow their convoluted intentions? Or were they so overconfident in their clearly superior hacking abilities that their carelessness left the occasional faint footprint?"

Tony wove what he thought was a great story around the mystery of GGY's high scores on the arcade games and GGY's alterations to the animatronics. "After GGY adjusted the animatronics' code," Tony wrote, "they became their new leader. Fazbear Entertainment may have thought the animatronics were in their control, but they weren't. The Glamrock stars of the Pizzaplex—Freddy and Chica and Roxy and Monty—continued to act normally most of the time, but in truth, under the facade of their normal duties, they were becoming GGY's minions."

It was just after 10:00 p.m. on Wednesday when Tony wrote the last lines of the story: "So, the simple curiosity of how one person managed to outscore, by the millions, all the other players in the Pizzaplex arcades, turned out to be much, much more. GGY infiltrated the Pizzaplex so thoroughly that the complex became their playground. What GGY and their obedient animatronics do there now, furtively moving in and out of the shadows, avoiding security guards and cameras, is something only GGY knows."

Tony stretched his fingers, then he typed, "The End."

Saving his document, Tony closed the laptop before he could start picking apart his work. He was never fully satisfied with his words, and he'd learned that he could tinker with them indefinitely if he didn't force himself to stop and call the story done.

Tony leaned back and stretched his arms over his head. He bent his fingers and cracked his knuckles. Then he stood so he could get ready for bed. He was wiped out.

When Tony was writing, his concentration tuned out the world. His mother had often told him that aliens could come through his window and throw a party in his room while Tony was writing and he wouldn't notice. That might have been a little bit of an exaggeration, but it wasn't too far off.

Now that Tony was out of his "writing zone," he heard his grandma's TV blasting as usual. Tony hummed along with a familiar potato chips jingle.

When the commercial was over, the news anchor started talking. Tony could hear the man's deep voice intoning, "The family of Mary Schneider, the school counselor who disappeared nearly five months ago, has made another appeal to law enforcement and the public."

Tony frowned. A memory was trying to clamber out of the thick stew of thoughts in his brain. What was it?

A breathy and high-pitched woman's voice replaced the anchor's voice on Tony's grandma's TV. "Our Mary wouldn't have just taken off," the woman said. "Something happened to her. Please, if you know anything, come forward." The sound of hiccupping sobs replaced the words, and the news anchor's voice took over. "Police say they currently have no leads," he said, "and they welcome any and all information that might help them find the missing woman."

Poor Ms. Schneider, Tony thought. Everyone in the school had known Mary Schneider. Even though Tony had never met with her, he'd seen her in the halls. A pretty woman who had worn round wire-framed glasses, Ms. Schneider had always had a smile on her face. Tony had thought she'd looked like a nice lady.

Tony shook his head and yawned. He still felt like there was something he needed to remember, but he was too tired to figure it out.

Maybe I'll think of it in the morning, Tony thought as he headed to the bathroom to brush his teeth.

When Tony and his friends met at their lockers before classes started the next morning, Tony gave Boots and Rab each a copy of his story. Boots looked at the title page.

"'The Mysterious GGY, by Boots, Mr. Rabbit, and Tarbell,'" Boots read. He grinned. "The title and numb de plumbs alone should get us an A."

Boots wasn't completely wrong. Although Mrs. Soto didn't have the best sense of humor, she did seem to like the fact that Tony and his friends always used interesting pen names. She also often said that a good title was an important part of a good story.

The last story they'd handed in, which had been about kids breaking into school after dark to look for hidden bank robbery loot rumored to be hidden in the basement, had been titled "The Loot in the Soot." Mrs. Soto had loved the rhyme. Tony wondered what she would have thought if she'd known that the loose basement window that gave the story's characters access to the school in the story was based, in a way, on fact. Tony and his friends had found a barely noticeable crack in the school's foundation, and when they'd investigated, they'd discovered they could wriggle loose some of the limestone to squeeze in next to a basement window. They'd only broken in once, just for the fun of it. As far as they knew, no one else was aware of the hidden access. And there was no real loot down there . . . or soot, for that matter.

Tony looked at Rab to see what he thought of the title, but Rab's expression was unreadable. Rab stuck the story in his backpack. "I'll look at it later," he said.

As Tony and his friends wove through the other kids in the school's crowded hallway, Boots started reading the story. Twice, Tony had to grab Boots's arm and pull him aside to keep him from colliding with other kids.

"What do you think?" Tony asked Boots.

"Don't know yet," Boots said. He raised his head and flipped through the typed pages. "I assume it picks up as it goes along."

Tony frowned. He thought the story started at a good pace. It raised all sorts of questions on the first page. Tony was tempted to say that Boots shouldn't criticize something he didn't do any work on, but he kept his mouth shut.

Before they went into the history classroom on the school's second floor, Tony said to his friends, "I have to mow some lawns this afternoon and paint Mr. Browning's new man cave this evening. Can we meet early to work on any changes you guys think we need?"

Mrs. Soto's assignments always had to be turned in by morning bell on the day they were due, which was the next day. If Rab and Boots wanted changes, Tony would have to scramble.

Rab shook his head. "Sorry. No can do. I'm going to be late tomorrow."

"Rab and I will work on it this evening," Boots said. "It'll be fine."

Tony gritted his teeth. He decided he was getting a little tired of this writing "partnership." He might have to talk to Mrs. Soto about it before the next assignment.

Tony was nearly finished painting the Brownings' basement, aka Mr. Browning's man cave, what Tony thought was a very depressing beige, when he suddenly remembered what had been nagging at him the night before. Tony's paint roller froze mid-stroke.

"Mary!" Tony said.

He stifled a sneeze. His sinuses were clogged by paint fumes and the dust from under the drop cloths he'd spread over piles of Mr. Browning's old books and sports memorabilia.

Tony stepped back from the wall by the stairs leading up to the Brownings' main floor. He watched a drip start to run down toward the baseboard. His gaze went to the floor, and that triggered a memory of squatting on the floor in the Pizzaplex kiosk.

Tony stepped forward and swiped his roller over the drip as he thought about the name that he'd seen on the computer in the Pizzaplex kiosk. One of the people GGY's hacked Play Pass had let into the Pizzaplex after hours was someone named Mary.

Why hadn't Tony put that together the night before, when he'd heard the news report?

Because he'd been tired.

Only half paying attention to what he was doing now, Tony dipped his roller in the paint. He slapped the paint on the wall and spread it around haphazardly.

Could the Mary that GGY had let into the Pizzaplex have been Mary Schneider, the missing counselor?

Tony shook his head. Mary was a very common name.

GGY could have let in a friend named Mary. Assuming that Mary was the missing counselor was crazy.

"It's a leap," Tony muttered.

But was it really?

If Tony's suspicions were right, GGY was up to something in the Pizzaplex. Crystal had said she thought so, too. She didn't care what GGY was doing, but Tony did. What if GGY had something to do with the missing counselor?

"That's a whole new story," Tony said to himself.

He grinned. He might be onto something really big.

Now in a hurry to finish up his job so he could concentrate on his realization, Tony began swiping paint over the wall as fast as he could. He was glad he only had a few square feet of bare wall yet to cover.

What if Tony was right? What if Mary Schneider was one of the people GGY's hacked Play Pass had let into the Pizzaplex after closing? Why would GGY have wanted Mary Schneider to come to the Pizzaplex?

Tony finished the wall. He stepped back and looked for more drips. When he didn't see any, he quickly put the lid on the paint can and rushed to clean up the roller in the utility sink on the other side of the basement (Mr. Browning had to share his domain with his wife's laundry room). Tony had just done the man cave's first coat, so he didn't have to clean up the drop cloths right now.

In less than five minutes, Tony was back on the main floor of the house, saying goodbye to the Brownings. "I'll be back tomorrow evening to do the second coat," he called as he flew through the Brownings' overcrowded living room.

Mr. and Mrs. Browning, both heavyset and kind-faced and in their sixties, were settled in their side-by-side easy chairs. Their huge flat-screen TV was blasting the play-by-play of a college basketball game. Mr. Browning was watching the screen intently. Mrs. Browning, a furrow of annoyance crimped between her brows, was knitting something big and bright pink.

Looking at her expression, Tony couldn't help but remember what Mrs. Browning had said when she had hired Tony to paint the basement. "Mr. Browning needs a man cave," she had said, "so I don't have to kill him." She'd said the words with a playful smile, but when she'd explained how she'd "had it up to here" with sports blasting in her living room every night, Tony had a feeling that the man cave just might save Mr. Browning's life.

Tony was halfway out the Brownings' front door when Mrs. Browning called out, "Bye now, dear!"

In the muted yellow glow of the Brownings' pole light, Tony jogged toward his bike. The rain had returned, but it was falling softly tonight. It wasn't much more than a mist, which actually felt good on Tony's face. The Brownings' basement had been stuffy and warm. Tony gratefully breathed in the cool, musky night air as he pulled his little flashlight from his pocket. He probably wouldn't need it to bike home, but he liked having it handy.

Tony got on his bike. And his brain continued to churn.

Think, Tony mentally commanded. He had to piece it together logically.

Tony got on his bike and coasted down the Brownings' driveway. "Okay," he said to himself as he started to pedal, "I think GGY is a kid. If they're a kid, they probably go to my school. If they go to my school, they probably knew Mary Schneider."

So what? Tony thought. Knowing Mary Schneider didn't mean anything. Most of the kids at the school had either known her or known of her.

But what if GGY had known Mary Schneider and they'd had a problem with her?

Mrs. Browning's voice played in Tony's head: ". . . so I don't have to kill him."

Tony braked to a sudden stop on the gravel verge just a quarter mile from his grandma's house. He straddled his bike and thought hard.

He had to find out more about Mary Schneider.

But how?

Tony looked down the road. He could see the exterior lights of his grandma's house through the drizzly darkness. He could also see the light in his grandma's bedroom window.

It was late. She'd be watching her TV. Tony's mom would be asleep. They never checked on him before he went to bed.

Tony looked back over his shoulder toward town. Pressing his lips together, he made a decision.

He turned his bike and began peddling away from his house.

It wasn't until he'd tucked his bike against the back wall of the school that Tony started to worry that maybe someone had discovered the hidden way into the building. It had been several weeks since he and his friends had found and used it. If the groundskeeper had seen the crack and repaired it, Tony wouldn't be able to do what he wanted to do.

But Tony's worry was unnecessary. When Tony scuttled past the bushes that lined the back of the school and walked flatfooted (in an attempt to be quiet that totally failed) over the gravel near the school's foundation, he was relieved to see that the crack was still there. The limestone could still be moved.

In just a few minutes, Tony had shoved aside the grainy stone blocks and squeezed through the barely wide enough hole between them. The stone, when Tony shifted it, smelled faintly of rotten eggs. Tony knew, from science class, that this was because the rocks, when rubbed together, emitted sulphureted hydrogen.

"Like that's important right now," Tony muttered softly as he dropped to the school basement's smooth cement floor.

Standing still under the flickering glow of a low-watt security light, Tony listened. Through the hole he'd come through, he could hear the rain's faint patter. Inside the basement, something was dripping even louder than the raindrops. Beyond the drip, a low hum was punctuated by a quiet rhythmic tick.

Normal sounds, Tony told himself.

The last time Tony had snuck into the school, he'd had his friends with him. Being alone, he discovered, was a little scarier. Tony had to clamp down his normal active imagination as he crept past the lumpy hulk of the school's furnace and several stacks of dusty boxes and crates.

Climbing the steep stone stairs that led from the basement to the school's main floor, Tony told himself that what he was about to do would be a piece of cake . . . and totally worth it. On the bike ride to the school, Tony had decided that his best chance of accessing the school's records was via Mrs. Hawkins's computer. Mrs. Hawkins, the grandmotherly librarian with a pun-heavy sense of humor and seemingly endless energy, had an office—not much more than an alcove—near the back of the school library. It wasn't a space that could be locked, so her computer could be easily accessed.

Tony had worked with Mrs. Hawkins on many projects. He was one of her "favorites," or so she said, because he was so curious and eager. She often had him join her in her office so she could help him research. Because of this, Tony knew Mrs. Hawkins's password (she tended to be pretty obvious about typing it in).

Although the school was ancient, Tony knew that it had some internal security. That security, however, was sparse, and Tony, because his curiosity made him aware of all sorts of little details, knew where the cameras were. He could easily avoid them.

It took Tony only a few minutes to get from the school basement to Mrs. Hawkins's office. Making sure he kept his head below the checkout counter before he entered her office, he duck-walked until he knew he was past the range of the library's CCTV. Then Tony took a seat in Mrs. Hawkins's white leather desk chair.

Tony scooted the chair toward Mrs. Hawkins's antique desk. The desk's wood was very dark; it looked almost black in the unlit office.

Tony pulled out his flashlight and shone it on Mrs. Hawkins's keyboard. He quickly typed in her password, shellyandpetey—of course she'd used the names of her two grandchildren.

As soon as Tony was into Mrs. Hawkins's hard drive, he searched for the school's personnel records. He wanted to find out everything he could about Mary Schneider.

Tony quickly found the personnel records. They were organized by position. He clicked on "Counselors."

Within the "Counselors" file, Tony found a list of counselors and then separate documents for each counselor, current and past. Mary Schneider's file jumped out at him immediately. But before he could click on it, his gaze landed on the counselor list. His hand froze on the mouse.

Tony leaned toward the computer screen.

The counselor list was long, but each name had a date

to indicate the counselor's tenure at the school. Only four of the names had dates within the last couple years. Tony figured those were the only ones that were relevant; the Pizzaplex wasn't even around before then.

The first name on the list for the dates in question was Mary Schneider's. After her came Raelynn Lawrence and Treena Welch. Then Georgia Lowe. She was the current counselor.

Next to each name, two dates noted the time that the counselors worked at the school. Mary Schneider had worked there the longest. She'd started three years before she disappeared.

Tony read the other dates. He raised an eyebrow as he studied them.

Raelynn Lawrence had replaced Mary Schneider, and she'd only worked there a month. Treena Welch had been the next counselor, and she'd lasted just seven weeks. The school had been without a counselor for a few weeks. Georgia Lowe had started just a month before.

Why hadn't Tony noticed that the school had been going through counselors so quickly? He shrugged. He had no reason to notice because he never met with them.

Tony rubbed his temple. Some memory was prodding at him again. What was it?

Tony clicked on Mary Schneider's file. There wasn't much to it—just a résumé, a few performance reports, and a summary page. Tony skimmed through everything quickly. Although the summary page noted under "Reason for Exit" that Mary Schneider was "missing—disappearance under investigation," nothing else in the file was remotely interesting.

Tony backtracked and clicked on Raelynn Lawrence's file, which was similarly sparse. Tony clicked on the summary page.

He sucked in his breath.

Raelynn's "Reason for Exit" was identical to Mary's. She was missing, too!

Why hadn't Tony known that? Had it been on the news and he'd missed it?

"That's so not a coincidence," Tony whispered.

Tony quickly brought up Treena Welch's file. His heart rate was picking up speed. He felt a trickle of sweat run down the back of his neck. Swiping it away, Tony opened Treena's summary page.

He sucked in his breath.

Treena was missing, too.

Tony clicked back to the list of names. Three out of the four women listed were missing!

Why hadn't that been mentioned on the news report about Mary Schneider that Tony had heard the other night? He tapped his fingers on Mrs. Hawkins's desk. Maybe the school was trying to keep it quiet. He could sure understand it if they were.

Tony stared at the women's names. What had happened to . . . ?

Tony blinked as the memory that had been nagging at him finally revealed itself. Tony's mind suddenly provided him with a mental snapshot of what he'd seen on the Pizzaplex kiosk computer. His mental freeze-frame showed him the first three letters of the other two people GGY's Play Pass had let into the Pizzaplex after hours.

Those letters had been Rae and Tre. Raelynn and Treena.

Tony suddenly felt like his skin was trying to crawl off his body. His breath was coming in rapid little gasps.

"A thousand times not a coincidence," Tony whispered to himself.

Somewhere in the old school building, something chittered. A mouse maybe? Or something else.

Outside, the wind was picking up. Tony could hear its pressing sigh against the windowpanes behind him.

Wanting to be out of the school, Tony quickly explored the rest of the school's records. He was hoping to find a list of students who'd met with the counselors. He thought he might spot a student with the initials GGY on the list.

But if such a list existed, it wasn't in the files Tony could access. After another ten minutes, he gave up.

Tony returned to the list of counselor names. His mind was zinging through what he knew—and didn't know—at one hundred miles per hour.

GGY had to have something to do with the counselors' disappearances, Tony concluded after just a little thought. It made perfect sense.

But why would GGY have done anything to the three women?

That's easy, Tony thought.

The counselors must have met with GGY, and maybe, one by one, they'd caught on to whatever GGY was doing at the Pizzaplex . . . and maybe other places, too. Who knew what GGY was capable of? Clearly, they were brilliant. Brilliance could be used for good . . . and bad.

Tony asked himself one of his favorite questions: What if?

What if the counselors had discovered what GGY was doing? And what if they'd known that they were onto them? And what if they'd lured them, somehow, to the Pizzaplex to do away with them?

Tony snorted. It sounded so out there when he ran it through his head. But then again, if Mrs. Browning could even playfully suggest killing her husband of over forty years because his sports watching annoyed her, couldn't a brilliant kid who was doing something illegal possibly kill to cover what he was doing?

It was wild, sure. But it was totally possible. Tony had heard far more outlandish things on the news.

Tony shook his head. He was missing so many facts. He couldn't possibly fill in the gaps with what he currently knew. He'd have to do more digging . . . because if he didn't, who else would figure out what GGY was doing? If someone had dug more into the embezzlement Tony's dad had been convicted of, maybe Tony's dad wouldn't be in jail. Tony didn't think getting to the facts should be an option. It had to be a necessity.

Tony had to get to the truth of what GGY was doing. GGY was no longer just some kid who got high scores and hacked the Pizzaplex for jollies. *No*, Tony thought. Something far more malicious, and probably dangerous, was going on.

Deep in the belly of the old building, something clunked. Tony stood so fast that Mrs. Hawkins's chair shot backward behind him.

That was enough. Tony needed to get out of there.

The next morning, Boots met Tony on the school's wide front steps. Today, the sun was shining. Its warmth hit the moisture from the previous night's rain, and steam wafted up from the staircase's pale stone.

"You're not going to believe what I found out," Tony said as soon as he saw his friend.

Tony grabbed Boots's arm and pulled him away from the chattering kids who streamed into the school. A few feet away, bus brakes hissed and car engines revved. Several kids shouted to their friends. Bursts of laughter punctuated all the commotion.

"Last night, I—" Tony began.

"We added some stuff to the story," Boots interrupted.

Tony closed his mouth and scowled at the sheaf of papers Boots held out to him. "Like what?" Tony asked.

"Go ahead and read it," Boots said. He glanced at his watch. "You have about fifteen minutes before we need to hand it in."

Tony quickly began to scan the opening of the story. He found the first change near the bottom of page one.

"GGY was the wizard's most favored apprentice?" Tony yelped when he read the line that had replaced Tony's description of GGY's high arcade game scores.

"Cool, huh?" Boots said. "Rab came up with that. Keep going. It gets better."

After reading the second page of the story, which described a corporate conspiracy that somehow reached another planet where the wizard resided, Tony's head began to throb. When he saw his description of GGY's control over the animatronics had turned into an anima-tronic supervillain who went into battle with a tentacled monster, Tony was pretty sure his ears were emitting steam similar to what was swirling along the surface of the step he stood on.

Tony's head was filled with a roar that blocked out all the other noise around him. The words on the page, which got more and more outrageous the more he read, began to blur.

They'd ruined his story!

Tony had written a super-awesome story based on a true-life mystery, and his friends had taken all the realism out of it. They'd transformed the story from something believable—and therefore creepily eerie—to something utterly bizarre and therefore not the least bit disturbing.

Frantic to fix what his friends had done, Tony pulled out a pen and started to scribble on the first page. They'd get marked down for having handwritten changes, he knew, but at least he could maybe get the story to . . .

"Dude!" Boots said. "What are you doing? Look at the time."

Tony glanced at his watch. The bell was about to ring. They had to turn in the story now, or they'd get an F.

Flinging a glare at his friend, Tony ran up the steps and into the school. He had barely a minute to reach the third floor and hand in the story. He figured they'd be lucky to get a C on it, but a C was better than an F.

"You're welcome," Boots called after Tony.

No, not Boots, Tony thought. *Ellis.* Tony's idiotic friend did not deserve to have a "numb de plumb" ever again. From here on out, Boots would be Ellis, as far as he was concerned.

Tony stewed about his trashed story through all of first period. When the bell rang, he didn't even look at Ellis as he stood and headed out of the room. He was aware that Ellis followed him, though.

Tony was striding out into the hallway when he heard his name over the school's loudspeaker. "Tony Becker," a woman's voice crackled, "please report to Mr. Adkins's office immediately."

Tony looked up at the speakers and frowned.

"Dude," Ellis said. "What did you do?"

Tony shook his head. Turning his back on his friend and ignoring the curious looks he got from his other classmates, Tony hurried through the packed hallway to the stairs. There, he trotted down to the main level and went directly to the glass-walled administrative offices.

The chairs lining the wall of the offices were empty,

and only Mr. Adkins's secretary, petite and sour-faced Ms. Logan, stood behind the wood counter that separated a dingy waiting area from a cramped space filled with filing cabinets, desks, and tables heavy with computers, a fax machine, and a photocopier. Ms. Logan spotted Tony and motioned with her jutting chin toward Mr. Adkins's closed office door.

Tony didn't bother to acknowledge Ms. Logan as he normally would have. He was too preoccupied with trying to figure out why he'd been called to the principal's office.

Tony pushed Mr. Adkins's door open and stepped into the big square room that was lined with heavy, dark shelves stuffed full of books and photographs. He looked across a massive, shiny cherrywood desk at the huge man who ran their school. With dark hair, olive skin, and strong features, Mr. Adkins looked a little like a mafia don . . . or at least Tony thought so.

"You wanted to see me, sir?" Tony said.

Mr. Adkins, whose suitcoat was thrown over the back of his chair, had his collar unbuttoned, tie loosened, and sleeves rolled up. Raising an almost ogre-size hand, he motioned to one of the two straight-backed wood chairs in front of his desk. "Sit," he said.

Tony did as he was told.

"It has come to my attention," Mr. Adkins said as soon as Tony sat, "that you snuck into Mrs. Hawkins's office last night."

Tony's eyes widened. "How?" The question was one he was asking himself, but he said it out loud.

"How did I find out?" Mr. Adkins asked.

Tony nodded.

Mr. Adkins licked his thick lips. His gaze flicked to

the books on the shelf to his right. He leaned forward and squinted at Tony.

"You were caught on camera," Mr. Adkins said.

He's lying, Tony thought. Tony knew where the cameras were. He'd stayed clear of them. But he couldn't say that, obviously. All he could do was hang his head and mumble, "Sorry."

But if Tony wasn't caught on camera, how had he been seen? Had someone else been in the school?

Tony had a very weird feeling that he hadn't been alone in the school last night. The thought made his stomach lurch.

When Tony looked at Mr. Adkins's narrow-eyed expression, Tony's weird feeling turned into certainty. Tony had been watched. And his watcher had ratted him out. But who was it?

"What in the world did you think you were doing?" Mr. Adkins asked. His rubbery features tightened as he speared Tony with a scathing look.

That wasn't a question Tony was going to answer. So, he mumbled again. "It was just a stupid dare," he lied.

Mr. Adkins sighed. He leaned forward and flipped through an open file on his desk. Tony read upside down. It was his file.

"You had a clean record," Mr. Adkins said. "Good grades." He leaned back and put muscular arms behind his head. Sweat stains darkened the light blue fabric of his shirt under his arms.

"Tell you what," Mr. Adkins said. "After school, you'll go back to the library for detention. You can explain to Mrs. Hawkins why you violated her space, and you can also do whatever tasks she deems appropriate. Capisce?"

Tony nodded. When Mr. Adkins waved him away, Tony meekly left the office and went to his locker to get his books for his next class.

Mrs. Hawkins was surprisingly calm about the way Tony had "violated her space." In fact, she acted somewhat conspiratorial when Tony reported to her after school.

"I bet you were doing some kind of research," she said, winking at Tony. "Right?"

"Right," Tony said. He was relieved that he could tell the truth. "But I'm sorry. It wasn't nice to get on your computer like that."

"Pishposh," Mrs. Hawkins said. "If that's the worst you have in you, the world is in no danger." She nudged him with her sharp elbow. "You know what they say, huh?"

Tony grinned, because usually this question was followed by a pun. "No," he said dutifully. "What?"

"What you seize is what you get." Mrs. Hawkins squinched up her friendly round features and let out a snorting laugh. "Oh, that's a good one, isn't it?"

Tony smiled. "Good one," he agreed.

Mrs. Hawkins pointed at four tall stacks of books leaning against one another at the end of the long oak library counter. "Why don't you busy yourself reshelving those books?"

Tony nodded. "Got it." He crossed to the books and grabbed a few of them.

Heading toward the shelves near the door to the hallway, Tony started scanning the rows for where the first book needed to go. Before he found its spot, he heard his name being called. He looked up and scowled at the other culprit who had ruined his story.

The story destroyer grinned at Tony. "Boots said you weren't happy with the changes we made to your story," he said. "Sorry we did so much to it. We might have gotten carried away. But we were just trying to make it more entertaining."

Tony wanted to unload all the righteous indignation he'd been carrying around all day, but that wouldn't have accomplished anything. He'd learned his lesson. He wouldn't be partnering with his friends on a story again. He'd find someone else in the class to work with.

"Thanks, Greg," Tony said with exaggerated politeness. Like Ellis, Tony was done calling Greg by his nickname, "Rab." It was Greg from here on out.

When Greg didn't move off, Tony raised a hand and said, "See you tomorrow."

Greg returned the wave. He smiled. Then he cocked his head and studied Tony for several seconds.

For some reason, Greg's scrutiny made Tony want to squirm. Before Tony could figure out why he suddenly felt odd, Greg started to walk away.

Tony let out a pent-up breath.

Greg stopped and took a step back toward Tony. "Listen," Greg said, "how about you meet me at the Pizzaplex when you get out of here. In an hour or so? I have some people I want you to meet. We'll have some fun, and you'll forget all about the story and getting detention."

Tony wasn't all that keen on going back to the Pizzaplex. He couldn't be in the place now without thinking of GGY and the modified animatronics.

"Come on," Greg pressed. "Say yes. We'll get you cheered up."

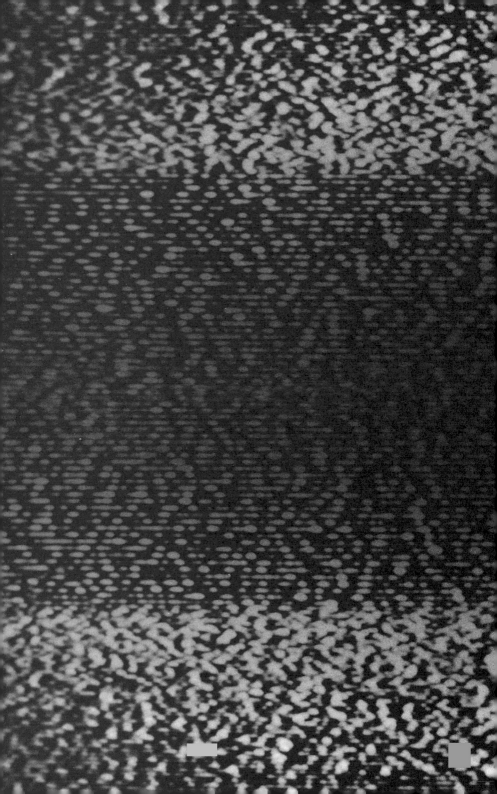

THE
STORYTELLER

MR. BURROWS PLUCKED THE WIRE-RIMMED READ-ING GLASSES FROM HIS ROMANESQUE NOSE AND USED THE GLASSES TO TAP THE SPREADSHEET IN FRONT OF HIM. HE GAVE THE ACCOUNTANT SITTING ON THE LEFT SIDE OF THE MASSIVE CHERRYWOOD CONFERENCE TABLE ONE OF HIS BEST WITHERING GLARES.

"I feel like you're boxing us in here," Mr. Burrows said. "These numbers can't be real."

Mr. Burrows looked down the length of the sixteen-foot table. His gaze went from the accountant to each of the other eight board members in turn. It finally landed on the one other man in the room besides the accountant who wasn't a board member. Mr. Burrows sighed.

Sitting at the far end of the table, directly opposite Mr. Burrows, Edwin Murray gazed out the picture window that took up much of the outer wall of the red-painted conference room. Murray's bulging gray eyes were unfocused, as if he was looking past the Mega Pizzaplex that dominated the view from the Fazbear Entertainment Executive Office Building, and even past the rolling hills behind the Pizzaplex. Heck, the old coot was probably looking even farther than the hills, out into some kind of virtual la-la land in his strange mind.

Mr. Burrows replaced his reading glasses precisely on his nose. He made sure the glasses were perfectly poised.

Mr. Burrows knew—from hours of studying himself in the mirror—that when his glasses were situated just so on the prominent bridge of his slightly downward-curved nose, his powerful stature as a man to be listened to was unmistakable. Mr. Burrows understood that he wasn't handsome in the classical sense. He had a fine jawline, sculpted cheekbones, and a strong, full mouth. However, the majestic nose was just a bit too majestic, and his eyes were a tad too small and set close together. Even so, his dark—almost black—eyes, and the shiny ebony hair that liked to flop over his broad forehead in a charming sort of way, combined with the aforementioned nose to create eye-catching impact. People noticed Mr. Burrows. And they listened to him . . . despite his relatively young age.

At thirty-five years old, Mr. Burrows was the youngest-ever Fazbear Entertainment board chairman. It was a coup to have achieved such a position so quickly, but it was one he deserved. Mr. Burrows (who had insisted on being called Mr. Burrows since he'd entered college at the precocious age of thirteen) had an IQ in the stratosphere and his extraordinary creative vision ran neck and neck with his business acumen.

Mr. Burrows scanned the costs spreadsheet that was the focus of this board meeting. "If these numbers are correct," he said, "the Mega Pizzaplex won't make one red cent the way it's currently set up." He once again took off his reading glasses. "That's the box. I refuse to be trapped in a box. That means we have to pare things down. If we shave off the excess, we can raise the profit margin and get out of the box."

Mr. Burrows put his finger on the line item that had gotten his attention. "Is this figure correct?" he asked Dale, the skinny young accountant who was supposedly a savant with numbers. Mr. Burrows knew Dale never got numbers wrong, but he liked to keep the kid in his place.

Dale cleared his throat. "Um, yes, sir. I ran the . . ."

Mr. Burrows waved a hand. Afternoon sun streaming in through the window caught the diamonds in his pinkie ring and refracted a rainbow across the printed spreadsheet. Mr. Burrows took a moment to enjoy the reds and blues and yellows. He loved reds and blues and yellows. That was why the conference room was filled with those colors. All the paintings on the walls, impressionistic depictions of classic, retro Fazbear animatronic characters, featured the vibrant colors Mr. Burrows favored. They melded nicely with the room's red walls. He wished the carpet was something other than a dull gray, but the board had, uncharacteristically, refused to back him when he'd lobbied for replacing it with a brighter shade.

Dale coughed. Mr. Burrows brought his attention back to the matter at hand.

"I'm sure the number is right," Mr. Burrows said. "Even if it's not exact, the import is clear."

Mr. Burrows leaned back. His black leather chair creaked. He smoothed his burgundy silk tie over his crisp blue cotton shirt, then interlaced his fingers and rested them on his chest. "Clearly, creative development is gobbling up a massive chunk of our overhead. The team is going to have to be downsized."

Edwin had been only peripherally paying attention to the board meeting ever since he'd reluctantly taken his seat at the outlandishly large table. These meetings were generally a waste of time. But given that Edwin had been placed onto the board via Fazbear Entertainment's buyout of his engineering company decades before, he was expected to be here. He was barely more than a mascot at this point. Still, he was resigned to being present. Often, his input was the only thing that stood between the board's tendency toward fly-by-the-seat-of-the-pants decisions and more levelheaded thinking.

Still, Edwin didn't like the time he spent in this huge room with its thick gray carpet, so thick it felt like trudging through sand. And he'd hated the meetings ever since Mr. Burrows had become the chairman.

Edwin loathed Mr. Burrows. The affected, vain, pompous jerk who refused to be called by his given name was not only annoying in the extreme, he was also dangerous. Mr. Burrows didn't think. He just acted. Case in point: the decision he'd just made.

Edwin, who had been trying to pretend he wasn't in the room, whipped his gaze away from the window. "Did I hear you right?" he asked, knowing full well that he had. "Did you just suggest downsizing the heart and soul of the Mega Pizzaplex, firing the very people who have been responsible for the Pizzaplex's enthusiastic popularity?"

Mr. Burrows sighed and closed his eyes. "I take issue with your premise," he said as if talking to himself. "The creative development team has contributed to the Pizzaplex's success, obviously, but to say they've been responsible for it is to strain the truth to its breaking point."

Edwin opened his mouth, but Mr. Burrows didn't let him speak. "Spending this much money on creative content—nothing more than the ideas of people sitting around making stuff up—is outrageous," Mr. Burrows said. "The backbone of the Pizzaplex, in fact, of Fazbear Entertainment as a whole, isn't the stories; it's the technology. Without the tech, without the animatronics and the software that runs them, the stories are nothing. We might as well be selling camping excursions, requesting that people pay for the privilege of being told a horror story while they roast marshmallows."

Edwin snorted. "I can tell you from years of experience that without the stories, all your hardware and software would be nothing more than lumps of metal and wires and a meaningless mass of zeros and ones. Story drives Fazbear Entertainment."

Mr. Burrows toyed with his showy pinkie ring. "Be that as it may, we need to get in the black."

"But," Edwin started.

Mr. Burrows held up his ring-free hand. "I'm not suggesting that we give up story development, Edwin."

Edwin felt his jaw muscles bunch at the way Mr. Burrows used his name. Mr. Burrows always put heavy emphasis on the "win" part of Edwin. The stress was purposeful, a slap-in-the-face reminder that Edwin wasn't a winner at all. The only reason he was part of

Fazbear Entertainment was because his own company had failed. Mr. Burrows loved to remind Edwin of that fact.

Mr. Burrows looked around at the other board members. "Wouldn't you agree, ladies and gentlemen, that Fazbear Entertainment has the best minds in the industry?"

Edwin rolled his eyes as he watched the board members nod. Mr. Burrows knew darn well that no one at this table was going to disagree.

As Mr. Burrows waxed eloquent on the company's creative and technological accomplishments, Edwin tuned him out and studied the other board members.

The Fazbear Entertainment board was made up of five men and four women. Edwin, at sixty-four years old, was the oldest person in the room. *At least I'm not the baldest*, he thought—two of the five men were full-on bald, and two of them had receding hairlines. The thought made Edwin feel like a kid saying, "Na-na-na-na-na," but it made him feel good. He had to do something to hold his own in this room full of sleek, well-dressed pretty people (the five men in the room, despite hair loss, could all be described as good-looking, and the women ranged from attractive to downright beautiful). Everyone in the room exuded wealth. Edwin knew that if someone had the temerity to come into the room and rob its occupants, the jewelry haul alone would be in the hundreds of thousands. Edwin, in contrast, wore nothing but an old Timex watch.

Edwin Murray was at an age where he knew who he was and he knew who he wasn't. Never—not even when he was as young as Mr. Burrows—a good-looking fellow, Edwin had accepted that his imagination was his greatest strength. He wasn't overly concerned with his appearance, although he liked using it to have a little fun. At 5'5" tall, Edwin was slight—no matter what he ate, he remained skinny. When he'd been young, his round nose, slightly slanted big blue eyes, and too-large ears had given Edwin a gnomish appearance. As he'd aged, he'd decided to get playful with that fact. He'd let his thick head of white hair grow long, and he'd groomed a short, pointed beard to go with the full mustache he'd worn since he was old enough to grow it. The beard covered Edwin's insubstantial jawline and weak chin. In retrospect, he probably should have grown it a long time ago.

"I see no reason why the creative process can't be automated," Mr. Burton said.

"What?!"

"Oh, come now," Mr. Burton said, leveling a condescending glance at Edwin, "you can't tell me that story creation can't be computerized. Record labels use software to write songs. I don't see why we can't create stories in a similar way. We could replace most, if not all, of the creative team with one computer"—he snapped his fingers—"and just like that, we're out of the box. The overhead overage is gone!"

"Computers can't write stories," Edwin said.

"Why not?" Mr. Burrows asked. "Most of the Fazbear Entertainment stories, the ones that are the most popular, share similar elements. I think it quite likely that these elements, and a series of preprogrammed options, could be used in concert to come up with new, randomly generated stories. Think of it like a smorgasbord. The average buffet probably has . . . what? . . . forty or fifty dishes—meats, casseroles, salads, and so on. And most of those are made from the same ten to fifteen or so foods. You can create a virtually endless variety of meals from those few ingredients. We'd use the same principle to create a computer program that would combine various tropes and characters to come up with an endless variety of stories." Mr. Burrows snapped his fingers again. "We could call the program 'The Storyteller.'" He beamed at the rest of the board members. "What do you think?"

"Genius," one of the women said.

A couple of the men chimed in with "Inspired" and "Love it!"

Edwin couldn't take it. He pounded a fist on the table. "I can't believe you're talking about firing the creative team. A computer can't . . ."

Mr. Burrows ignored Edwin. He leaned forward, his beady little eyes all lit up like an eagle with an injured bird in its sights. "We could even turn The Storyteller into part of the Pizzaplex's appeal. It could be a huge draw. It would become the star of every show, the Pizzaplex's ringmaster, if you will." Mr. Burrows laughed and threw out his arms as if he was introducing the cast of a three-ring circus.

Edwin could almost hear tinny circus music in his head. *Where are the clowns?* he asked himself.

"That's a ludicrous idea," Edwin protested. "Your idea is a slap in the face to all the hardworking people who have created all those story lines you're planning to stuff into some insane computer program."

"Hardworking doesn't mean good," Mr. Burrows said. "If their stories were good enough, the Pizzaplex would be gen- erating enough revenue to cover all those expensive creative team salaries. Clearly, there's room for improvement, and I think we should hand the task of that improvement over to the tech team. They can create The Storyteller."

Edwin stood up so fast that his chair spun out behind him and hit the wall. "Your plan is an insult to me and to every writer on the creative team."

Mr. Burrows leaned forward and steepled his fingers over the spreadsheet that had precipitated his scheme. He scanned the faces of the other board members. "Ed*win*'s offense aside, who's in favor of creating The Storyteller and letting it take the place of the current creative teams?"

Edwin glared at the other board members as every man and woman in the room raised a hand. "Unbelievable!" Edwin shouted. "You're all idiots."

Mr. Burrows pressed his lips together and stared down his nose at Edwin. "Careful, Edwin. You're close to getting yourself thrown out of this meeting, if not the company."

Edwin could barely hear Mr. Burrows's words through the roar of the blood rushing in his head. He smoothed his beard and straightened his shoulders. "Don't get too big for your britches, Mr. Burrows," he said. "I can't be fired, as you should know if you'd bothered to read my buyout contract. And I may not have a lot of power here, but I can—"

"You can do nothing," Mr. Burrows said, flicking his fingers toward Edwin as if Edwin was a pesky mosquito. "But I tell you what? Because I'm feeling magnanimous, we'll make you a consultant on the project. You can have some input on what story elements are programmed into The Storyteller."

Edwin's chest constricted. His doctor had told him he shouldn't let himself get riled up. It was bad for his heart. Well, Edwin was definitely riled up. His face was hot, and his fingers tingled from the rage that was coursing through his body.

"If you've finished with the theatrics," Mr. Burrows said, "perhaps you could retake your seat? Peg, could you please help Edwin?"

Peg got up from her seat to Edwin's right. She gave him a gentle pat on the shoulder as she stepped past him and retrieved his chair from where it had come to rest, next to a table that held a silver coffee urn and a crystal plate full of fancy pastries that were always present at the meetings and that no one ever ate.

Peg pulled Edwin's chair over to the table. She took his arm and escorted him to his seat like he was geriatric.

Edwin had his issues, he knew. He'd been haunted for years by things that he should have done differently. But he didn't need *help*. He wanted to lash out at Peg, but he was too much of a gentleman to do that.

Peg was actually a pretty nice lady. Maybe she wasn't the smartest person in the room, but she was the kindest. So, Edwin didn't protest when she helped him back into his chair. Instead, he smiled up at her as if he wasn't envisioning himself setting the building on fire.

"There," Mr. Burrows said, once Peg had retaken her own seat. "Now let's continue. I propose that we put together a tech team to create and program The Storyteller. It shouldn't take too many techs. We won't have to hire anyone new. We can just pull people off other projects."

Edwin, his heart still galloping in his chest, spent the next couple of minutes concentrating on his respiration. His cardiologist had taught him a breathing exercise to slow his heart rate and lower his blood pressure. The doctor frequently hooked Edwin up to a biofeedback machine to help Edwin track the effectiveness of his internal focus. He was getting pretty good at regulating his vitals. He used that skill now to calm himself.

Mr. Burrows's idea, like too many other Fazbear Entertainment ideas, was extraordinarily shortsighted. Right off the top of his head, Edwin could think of a dozen ways The Storyteller could go wrong. If he had any hope of preventing a tragedy, he had to keep it together. No one would listen to him if he was ranting.

Edwin raised his hand like a demure schoolboy. Peg smiled at him. Mr. Burrows cracked his knuckles and said, "Yes, Edwin?"

Edwin put everything he had into keeping his voice

measured and not allowing even a trace of disdain to taint his words. "You keep talking about the program choosing elements from a smorgasbord of characters and plots and themes, and so on, but how exactly would The Storyteller devise the stories? You can't just randomly pull story elements together and expect to create a story. You can end up with all character sketches and no actual story arc. Or all plot with no interesting characters. How will The Storyteller determine how to combine the elements you program into it?"

No one answered Edwin's question. Instead, one of the other board members, Waylon, a balding man with very large teeth, asked, "What should The Storyteller look like?"

Peg chimed in. "That's a good question. If The Storyteller will itself be a character seen by the Pizzaplex's patrons, it will have to be something other than just a garden-variety computer interface."

Mr. Burrows waved his hand as if shooing away a fly. "We'll think of something." He chuckled. "Maybe we should let The Storyteller itself decide what it's going to look like."

A rumble of laughter swept the room like an ocean wave rushing in and receding. Edwin didn't join in.

Once again blocking out the discussion around him, Edwin looked past the self-important board members. His gaze scanned the ridiculously modernist art on the room's vast walls. He could remember when the boardroom had been decorated with framed Freddy Fazbear Pizzeria signboards. Edwin had enjoyed the vintage posters. Mr. Burrows, however, had ordered the old posters removed as soon as he had become the board chairman. He was going to have them put in the trash, but Edwin had rescued them and taken them home.

He wasn't sure why he'd wanted them. He hadn't hung

them on the walls of his pathetic one-bedroom walk-up. In all honesty, Fazbear posters reminded Edwin of a past he'd rather have forgotten. If he'd been forced to explain himself, he'd probably have to admit that keeping the signboards was a form of self-punishment. He had much to atone for and no way to do it. Maybe keeping the images of Freddy Fazbear close was Edwin's way of keeping himself on the hook for all the mistakes he'd made, mistakes that had snowballed into a disaster the day he'd agreed to sell his company to the behemoth that was Fazbear Entertainment.

The truth was that even though Edwin tried to make himself useful at the company and tried to live a semi-normal life, he was rarely actually in the present moment. He lived primarily in the past, back in the days before he'd made a hash of everything.

Edwin's cardiologist had recommended that Edwin see a therapist, and the therapist had told Edwin that he had to learn to be "mindful." "You must stop reliving what is no longer real," the therapist had said. "Practice mindfulness. Concentrate on the details of the reality around you. Be present."

That was easier said than done, so he didn't even bother to try. Yes, he moved through the "real" world, but he didn't see much of it. What was in front of him was usually obscured by visions of his old life, replays of his worst mistakes, images of what he'd once had and lost.

Mr. Burrows clapped his hands and snapped Edwin out of his reverie. Edwin blinked and looked over at the board's bombastic leader.

"It's decided, then," Mr. Burrows said. "We'll get the design team working on The Storyteller ASAP."

Even though his heart rate was under control and his expression was placid, deafening warning bells were going off in Edwin's head. He was having a strong sense of déjà vu. And that wasn't a good thing. Not a good thing at all.

The Storyteller went from concept to construction at almost the speed of light, or so it seemed to Edwin. Although he'd tried to stall the project, the idea took hold too quickly for him to implement any of his plans. Everyone was thrilled with The Storyteller. Every techie on the team fairly buzzed with glee as they worked on constructing and programming the Pizzaplex's soon-to-be star attraction.

Edwin was given a consulting role on the project, but he was never actually allowed to consult. He was aggressively kept on the periphery of the engineering process, so much so that he was never even allowed to see The Storyteller specs. That made him nervous. Very nervous.

On the rare occasions that Edwin did offer an opinion on The Storyteller, that opinion was ignored. He had suggested, for example, that The Storyteller be confined to a remote part of the Pizzaplex in order to give it an enigmatic aura, perfect for the fans who enjoyed the mysteries of the Pizzaplex. His true reason for the suggestion was his conviction that The Storyteller would, at some point, become a problem. But it didn't matter what his motivation was: The Storyteller was built right smack in the center of the Pizzaplex's atrium.

Construction of a central hub began days after the board approved the creation of The Storyteller. Like everything else, the design of the hub was Mr. Burrows's idea.

"I think The Storyteller should reside in a huge fake tree, like a wise old owl in an old-growth forest, kind of like a tree of life," Mr. Burrows had said. "Since story is the lifeblood of Fazbear Entertainment, it makes sense that The Storyteller will be the lifeblood of the Pizzaplex."

When the design team had met to decide on a style for The Storyteller's tree, there was much debate about what kind of tree to use as a blueprint. At first, Edwin had just listened to the ideas.

"How about an oak tree?" Yvette suggested.

Edwin had always liked her. With an impish face decorated by piercings and a couple of intricate flower tattoos, Yvette was bright and focused, but she was always quick to laugh, and she treated Edwin with respect. This was something the other team members didn't do.

"We had an oak tree in our backyard when I was a kid," Yvette said. "I always imagined elves or fairies or something lived inside its gargantuan trunk. I think a tree like that would be perfect for The Storyteller."

"Not an oak," the burly engineer next to Yvette barked. "An elm. Elms are stately trees."

Yvette smiled placidly at him. That was another thing Edwin liked about her. She was peaceful. Twice, he'd caught her meditating in one of the back hallways of the Pizzaplex. Her ability to look serene amid all the noise and commotion that radiated throughout the building, no matter where you were, was amazing.

The other team members began talking at once. Edwin heard redwood, eucalyptus, olive, fig, and poplar. Everyone had some reason for their tree choice. No one liked anyone else's idea. The discussion was beginning to degenerate into a shouting match when Edwin cleared his throat and said loudly, "Baobab."

The rest of the team stopped talking and stared at Edwin. He didn't give them a chance to start up again. He continued quickly, "The baobab tree is one of longest-living trees in the world, and it's one of the hardiest. Baobabs thrive in the harshest of conditions, in the droughts of Africa and

Asia. They're bizarre looking; their trunks can be over thirty feet in diameter. The width of the baobab trunk would suit our purposes perfectly, allowing plenty of room for all the hardware needed to sustain The Storyteller."

As always happened whenever Edwin even thought of The Storyteller's name, nausea welled up within him. He determinedly ignored it and went on, "There's a baobab in South Africa that's over six thousand years old. Its trunk is hollow, and it's a tourist attraction. There are all sorts of legends associated with the baobab tree. Given that the tree we use is housing a storyteller, choosing a tree associated with grand narratives seems apropos."

"I've never heard of a bao, a bao . . . what?" the freckled tech said.

"Baobab," Edwin pronounced slowly and patiently.

Yvette, who had been fussing with her phone while Edwin spoke, handed the device to a freckled guy. "I think a baobab is a great idea," Yvette said while the freckled guy frowned over the picture of a baobab on her phone. She took back her phone and held it up so everyone could see the picture. "See? They look sort of like an oak tree that's been uprooted and put back in the ground upside down. They're weird and cool. And isn't that what Fazbear Entertainment is all about?"

Several of the team members nodded their heads. The freckled guy said, "Okay. I'm down with it." He pulled out his laptop and tapped a few keys. Then he turned his laptop and showed a screen filled with images of several baobab trees to the rest of the team. "What do we want to go with? Tall and thick or shorter and rounder?"

The question sparked another fifteen minutes of debate. At the end of it, the team agreed to design a tree with a trunk that had a vaguely bulbous appearance. It would be fifteen feet in diameter at the bottom, swelling to about twenty-five feet across at about ten feet or so up the trunk and then narrowing again to just a few feet wide as the trunk climbed another fifty feet up to its branches. The trunk would extend nearly to the Pizzaplex's domed roof, and its branches would sprawl like a fifty-foot-wide skeletal umbrella over the Pizzaplex's center.

Still not at all pleased with the project, Edwin felt an unexpected sense of satisfaction for having contributed to it in such a visible way. Now he just hoped that the whole thing wasn't going to be the disaster he was afraid it would be.

Construction blasted into overdrive. With little else to do, Edwin took to loitering around the construction zone, watching the tree take shape.

This morning, he had parked himself on a bench near the Pizzaplex's main concourse.

In spite of the myriad negative associations Fazbear Entertainment held for Edwin, he couldn't help but get caught up in the glitz and glam of the Pizzaplex when he was in the midst of all its action. Who could resist the splendor of the place?

Fazbear Entertainment was known for the wild and wonderful and over the top, but the Pizzaplex soared above and beyond anything the company had come up with before. From the bright yellow roller-coaster track that twisted through luminous, multicolored, serpentlike climbing tubes to the pinging, bleeping games arcade and the buzzing laser tag arena, the Pizzaplex was a masterpiece of happy sights and sounds. At its busiest, the Pizzaplex was packed with spun-up kids and jovial families, and all the happy screams and shouts and chatter was like an electrical circuit that, if it could have been harnessed, probably would have generated enough power to run a dozen Pizzaplexes.

Edwin watched a little girl wearing a bright pink frothy dress skip past. The girl's patent leather Mary Jane shoes tapped a sprightly rhythm on the tile floor. Edwin smiled, but then a familiar old pain forced him to look away from the child.

He turned to watch diners churn through pizzas in the flashy main dining room packed with shiny red-topped tables and chrome chairs. Scanning the boisterous crowd, he idly wondered how it might be possible to channel human joy into a machine. It had to be possible, he mused.

Edwin returned his attention to the baobab tree that would house The Storyteller. Would anyone realize the tree was a baobab? Although the tree's fat trunk and sparse branches were reminiscent of the tree they'd chosen as the basis of The Storyteller's tree, this bright and shiny tree didn't look like any real baobab.

Loathe to have the centerpiece of the Pizzaplex be a "dull tan" in color, Mr. Burrows had decreed that the trunk of The Storyteller's tree was to be the same vibrant yellow as the Pizzaplex's roller coaster. Edwin's protest that tree trunks weren't yellow was completely ignored. At least the artistic team had taken some initiative to diminish the freakish impact of the yellow. They'd had the tree's trunk painted in several tones of yellow—ranging from the roller coaster's lemon to more subdued shades of flaxen, mustard, and light goldenrod. These variations in tint had been applied to textured metal, and this gave the trunk the striations of real baobab bark. The combination of a mottled application of different yellows and the bumpy metal at least approximated Mother Nature's version of a tree trunk.

The tree branch's hues were similarly fanciful. "Green is such an uninspiring color," Mr. Burrows had said when the design team had first brought its vision to the board. The team had no choice but to toe the line when

Mr. Burrows suggested that the tree's branches be "the colors of the rainbow."

So, the tree that Edwin watched "grow" up in the middle of the Pizzaplex was like no tree that actually existed on earth. Sprouting from a pear-shaped yellow trunk, a kaleidoscopic array of sparkling multicolored branches exploded like a contained spray of fireworks, frozen in time above the Pizzaplex's core. LED lights made up the tree's "root system," which splayed out from the trunk's base and stretched, like gnarly groping fingers, out to the edges of the concourse. From there, the roots appeared to sink into the floor, disappearing under the black-and-white tiles of the concourse. In actuality, the roots were a network of wiring that connected to every venue in the Pizzaplex. That wiring would sync up with the story-driven attractions and feed its programming to the appropriate hardware. Every animatronic in the Pizzaplex would get its instructions from The Storyteller via the tree's roots. The roots, Yvette had told Edwin, were receiving those instructions from The Storyteller through a network of fiber-optic cables within the tree's trunk.

Edwin really wanted to see those fiber-optic cables, but he wasn't allowed inside the tree trunk. And this was something he took great issue with.

"Why can't I see inside the tree?" Edwin asked Mr. Burrows after one of the board meetings.

The board members had gotten up from the table, and they were trailing out of the room. Mr. Burrows was placing his papers carefully within a crisp red folder. Edwin had waited for Gretchen to pass him, holding his breath so her heavy perfume wouldn't poison him. Then he'd hurried up to Mr. Burrows.

"No one is allowed inside the tree, Edwin," Mr. Burrows replied to Edwin's question.

This development in the project had come about after a board discussion of how to protect The Storyteller's intricate systems. Although originally conceived of as a character that patrons could see close-up, the plans had changed to keep The Storyteller hidden from view.

"The Storyteller's tree will be enough of a draw," Mr. Burrows decided. "We'll keep The Storyteller behind the scenes. That will add to the mystique of it. The Storyteller will be the Pizzaplex's Oz."

That pronouncement had raised goose bumps on Edwin's arms. Oz had been nothing more than a man behind a screen. Would The Storyteller be just as ineffective?

"Well, clearly someone is allowed inside the tree," Edwin protested when Mr. Burrows denied him access. "The tree's interior isn't being created by magic elves."

Mr. Burrows rubbed the big nose he seemed inordinately proud of. He offered a fake laugh. "How droll, Edwin. Yes, of course, the construction crew is allowed inside. But no one else. Even I haven't been inside the trunk. It's all hush-hush."

"But you're the chairman of the board," Edwin said.

"Why would I want to spoil the surprise?" Mr. Burrows asked. "Do you unwrap your gifts before Christmas, Edwin? If you do, shame, shame." Mr. Burrows clicked his tongue and turned away from Edwin.

Short of snatching at Mr. Burrows's expensive blue suitcoat sleeve, Edwin could do nothing else. He watched Mr. Burrows strut from the room and decided he'd figure out a way inside the tree eventually.

When Edwin wasn't lurking near the construction zone, he was surreptitiously gathering every working memo related to The Storyteller project that he could get his hands on. Thankfully, internal security in the executive offices wasn't stellar. The Storyteller project had been compart-mentalized away from all other Fazbear Entertainment projects, but the occasional memo found its way into the light. Edwin turned himself into a memo scavenger. He gathered them up the way a squirrel collected nuts.

Unfortunately, the memos didn't help Edwin much. Everything related to The Storyteller was cryptic in the extreme. He did manage to glean one tidbit, though. He'd learned that the larger parts of The Storyteller were to be transferred into the tree trunk late one night after the Pizzaplex's closing. Given that Edwin had access to every part of the Pizzaplex, he was sure he could position himself at the appropriate time and place to get a glimpse of what was being placed at the hub of the Pizzaplex.

And he was right.

At 11:42 p.m. on a drizzly Thursday evening, Edwin slipped into the Pizzaplex via the loading dock. The drab, concrete-walled area was deserted, as he knew it would be, and he had no trouble weaving his way through the back halls until he could come out into the corridor out-side one of the restrooms near the junglelike expanse of Monty's Gator Golf. As he'd hoped it would, one of the fake plants in the lobby of the mini golf venue provided cover for a perfect vantage point from which to observe the entrance of The Storyteller's tree.

From the shouts and thuds coming down the hall on the opposite side of the atrium, Edwin could tell he'd arrived just in time. Something was being brought in. Edwin brushed aside a wide, thick plastic leaf and gazed hard at the entrance of the tree.

The tree's door, which wasn't so much a door as it was a hidden curved panel that blended right into the rest of the yellow trunk, was open. Unfortunately, a shadow consumed the resulting gap. Edwin could see nothing inside the trunk.

He could, however, see what was being carried toward the open door. And what he saw bent him over double. For several seconds, he literally couldn't breathe.

Gasping audibly, Edwin clutched at his chest. A sharp pain shot through his rib cage and his lungs constricted.

"Did you hear that?" a man's voice asked.

Edwin shrank back into the shadows of the faux jungle. He dropped into a crouch, closed his eyes, and covered his ears with his hands.

It wasn't that Edwin was attempting to pull a child's stunt, blocking out the world in a misguided attempt to be invisible. If the workers found him, they found him. He wasn't trying to hide. The reason he was trying to shut down his senses was because they were transporting him back into a horror from his past.

The sounds . . . a screech and a scream, his own yelling. The sights . . . blood, so much blood, and a gut-clenching grimace. The smells. Edwin gagged at the metallic scent that suddenly assaulted his nostrils.

He wanted to moan, he needed to run, but Edwin did neither. Even in his flashback, Edwin was aware that if he was found here, any chance he had of minimizing The Storyteller's potential damage would be lost.

So Edwin forced his body to ride out the memories. Trembling from head to toe, sweating so profusely that it felt like a waterfall had erupted from his neck and was pouring down his spine, and enduring viselike pressure in his head, Edwin kept himself contained. He made sure that everything he was feeling was managed silently. After his initial gasp, he didn't make a sound.

Vaguely, as if he was listening to them via a distant TV, Edwin could hear the scuffs and taps of multiple footfalls. And he heard voices. At first, the voices were indistinct, their utterances a mishmash of sound that Edwin couldn't parse into specific words. After a few shallow and quiet breaths, though, Edwin was able to discern three different voices.

"Are you sure the sound came from over here?" one voice asked. The speaker was male, young, and exasperated.

"I thought it did." This was the first voice Edwin had heard. It was the man who had heard Edwin gasp.

"I think you're just hearing things," a third voice said. This voice belonged to an older man. His tone was low and rough.

"Come on," the younger man said. "Let's get this thing in there so we can wrap up and take off."

The older man chuckled. The sound was a rumble that for some reason Edwin found soothing. The low-register purring slowed his heartbeat. The sharp pain scoring through his chest abated.

"You letting this place get to you?" the older man asked.

A scrape and the rustling of clothing preceded a skin-on-skin slap. *The sounds of a scuffle,* Edwin thought.

"Cut it out," the first man said. "Act your age."

The man's voice was close. Too close. Edwin held his breath, willing the men to back away from Monty's Gator Golf and return to their task.

Edwin's will apparently had some clout. The men did exactly as Edwin wanted them to. They retreated toward the tree.

Edwin commanded himself to get it together and ever so slowly eased toward his original vantage point. He concentrated on breathing softly and evenly as he prepared himself to take a second look at what had nearly unhinged him.

It took just a couple of seconds for Edwin to reposition himself behind the outermost leaves of the plastic plant. Hoping that the three men wouldn't look his way again, he raised his head until he could see the tree.

And there it was. There was the thing of Edwin's nightmares.

Edwin gritted his teeth and held his breath again. He ignored the tremors that vibrated through his body.

The three men had returned to their task, which was to carry into the hollow tree trunk a giant white tiger head. Not a real tiger head, obviously. If the thing the men were hefting was a real tiger head, Edwin wouldn't be as rattled as he was.

Ha, he thought. Rattled was an understatement. He'd had a full-blown, nearly-untethered-from-reality meltdown. No disembodied tiger head would have caused that . . . unless it was like *this* tiger head.

"Keep a grip on it," one of the men warned. It was the old guy with the rough voice. He was exactly as Edwin pictured him. He had a heavily lined face smudged with a couple days of beard growth, and his graying hair was thinning. But he was big and beefy. He was clearly in charge of moving the tiger head.

Edwin could well imagine that the head was tough to hang on to. Even from this distance, Edwin could tell that the three-foot-wide tiger head was made of metal. The white-painted head rose up nearly four feet from a set of tiger shoulders, and the underside of those shoulders was slickly smooth and gleaming silver. Edwin could see the edges of a surface that glowed like polished platinum. For all Edwin knew, the tiger head could have been made of platinum. Although the one that lived in his memories hadn't been.

Grunting and grousing, the three men managed to wrangle the tiger head through the tree's open doorway. They disappeared into the shadows that obscured the tree trunk's interior, and once they did, Edwin exhaled loudly.

He immediately turned and headed back the way he'd come. There was nothing else for him to observe tonight. He'd seen enough.

Mr. Burrows faced an array of flat screens lined up precisely on his Queen Anne credenza. Sighing, he tapped a few keys on the keyboard and leaned forward in his crocodile leather chair. He studied the nearest monitor.

Yes, it was just as he'd been told. There was that annoying curmudgeon skulking behind one of the large-leafed plastic plants at the front edge of Monty's Gator Golf. He was a persistent little rat, wasn't he?

Edwin Murray had already been a thorn in Mr. Burrows's side with a buyout contract that gave him an exorbitantly large salary that he in no way earned, but ever since The Storyteller project had begun, he'd become a human gnat, constantly buzzing about, questioning every aspect of the new project.

Mr. Burrows steepled his fingers as he watched Murray flounder around behind the fake bush. What was he doing?

Mr. Burrows leaned even closer and studied the screen. He frowned. The old man's eyes were nearly bugging out of his head. And was that sweat?

Shaking his head, Mr. Burrows tapped a key to stop the security video replay. He made a mental note to praise the security team for bringing Murray's actions to his attention. He didn't think, however, that Murray was a problem. Yet. The man couldn't do any harm watching from a distance. And there was no way he could get inside the tree that housed The Storyteller. Mr. Burrows had made sure that the tree's door was accessible only by himself and a select few of the construction team members.

No, Murray wasn't an immediate issue. But he might

become one at some point. Mr. Burrows would have to stay on top of the situation.

Friday morning, just a few hours after he'd recovered from his panic, Edwin marched down the long, wide hallway on the top floor of the Fazbear Entertainment Executive Office Building.

Once again cursing the building's annoyingly plush carpet, Edwin charged past portraits of executives and famous characters. In a comic display of contrast, the staid and proper portraits of the executives were alternated with cartoonish depictions of the characters. Edwin had always wondered whether the hallway decor was meant to poke fun at the executives or an attempt to elevate the importance of the creations.

Edwin never made it to Mr. Burrows's office. Instead, he plowed into Mr. Burrows outside the executive washroom (men of Mr. Burrows's stature didn't use mere "restrooms").

"Whoa there, Edwin," Mr. Burrows said as Edwin bounced off the taller man's midsection. "Where are you off to in such a hurry?"

Edwin, panting at the effort to stay upright on the cushy carpet, caught his breath and wiped his moist forehead. "I was coming to speak to you," he said in between gulps of air.

"What a joy for me," Mr. Burrows said. His sarcasm was evident.

Mr. Burrows flicked an invisible speck off the lapel of his charcoal gray suit. He straightened the deep-purple pocket handkerchief that matched his tie.

"What program are you using to create The Storyteller's stories?" Edwin asked Mr. Burrows.

Mr. Burrows sighed. "Why can't you just trust The Storyteller, Edwin?"

Edwin shook his head. "Just tell me what program you're going to run."

Mr. Burrows shrugged. "It's a simple template-style software that takes pieces of previously created stories and rearranges them into new scenarios for VR, AR, and arcade games. It's slick as can be. Beta testing is going beautifully. It's going to be sweet."

Edwin seriously doubted that. "Who's doing the programming?" he asked.

Mr. Burrows waved away the question. "We have our best minds on it. No need to concern yourself with it, Edwin. Now, if you'll excuse me, I'm late for an appointment."

Mr. Burrows didn't wait for Edwin to reply. He stepped around Edwin and strode down the hall. Edwin frowned at Mr. Burrows's retreating figure. There absolutely *was* a need for concern. Edwin had to get a look at The Storyteller's programming.

No matter how hard he tried, Edwin couldn't get his hands on any of The Storyteller's programming specs. And then, to his profound chagrin and deep dread, The Storyteller was brought online.

The "big reveal" of The Storyteller wasn't a reveal at all. Edwin thought The Storyteller's "Birth Party" was a crock. Every patron in the Pizzaplex had seen the tree go up, and The Storyteller itself was kept hidden. As a result, Edwin thought the hoopla surrounding The Storyteller's activation was little more than a high-tech tree lighting. With great fanfare, the LED lights of the tree's branches and root system were lit, and the crowd dutifully oohed and aahed at the colorful display. But that—and a big tree-shaped cake— was the extent of The Storyteller's first day on the job.

Edwin supposed the whole thing should have been a relief. The Storyteller program was running, and nothing bad was happening. Maybe all his worries had been just his memories getting the best of him.

Then again . . .

Edwin decided that since no one else expected a problem with The Storyteller, it was up to him to monitor the impact of the program. To that end, he began hanging around the various Pizzaplex venues, observing the way its characters behaved and analyzing the new stories being portrayed on the various stages throughout the entertainment center.

And he saw issues right away.

The first problem he saw was in Roxanne Wolf.

The queen of her domain, Roxy Raceway, Roxanne Wolf was an animatronic with a punk rock look. With bright yellow eyes, purple lipstick, and green fingernail polish, Roxanne was a spectacle of sass and style. Although she was just an ordinary gray wolf with black markings, she wore red hot pants with a red crop top, and she sported black earrings, a spiked belt, and purple tiger-striped arm and leg warmers.

Roxanne was self-centered and competitive. She loved to admire herself in the mirror and frequently asked others how she looked. Edwin had never really liked her personality, but it was what Fazbear execs had wanted for the character and it was what Edwin expected of Roxanne when he observed her interaction with the kids in her raceway. What he didn't expect, however, was the mean-for-the-sake-of-being-mean quality that he began to see in Roxanne when he hung around the raceway. Sure, Roxy had always enjoyed poking at people's insecurities because of her own deep-seated self-esteem issues, but when The Storyteller came online, Roxanne turned into a full-blown bully. She began verbally attacking anyone and anything around her. It was like her inherent lack of empathy was morphing into a more aggressive form of pathological cruelty.

Then there was Chica. The bib-wearing bright yellow chicken was . . . well-known for her gluttonous nature. Chica's story lines nearly always included food. The chick loved pizza and was very pushy about getting it, but she was, on the whole, one of the more loving characters in the Fazbear Entertainment family. After The Storyteller came online, though, that changed.

Chica began showing aggressive tendencies. Her loving persona was replaced with a snarky one. No longer interested in food, Chica became obsessed with getting attention. She was constantly demanding that Mr. Cupcake show her more deference. Mr. Cupcake, for his part, began acting up as well. He developed the personality of a vicious terrier.

Montgomery Gator also exhibited disturbing changes. The alligator featured in Monty's Gator Golf was the quintessential rock star. With a red mohawk, star-shaped sunglasses, and purple shoulder pauldrons, Monty was a performing gator. He was all about being a rock and roller. Prone to smashing things as part of his extravagant image, Monty was always dramatic, but he had been harmless . . . at least until The Storyteller started messing with him.

Now the alligator was turning into a sulky shadow of his former self. Monty's rampages became more violent, and in between tantrums, he withdrew into a depressive silence that was actually driving children to tears.

All the Pizzaplex's other main characters began to undergo similar personality shifts. Whatever trait was normal for them began to skew toward the dark side. The shift wasn't dramatic. None of the animatronics had turned homicidal or anything, but the altered dynamic was noticeable, at least to Edwin.

When Edwin brought the personality changes to Mr. Burrows's attention, Mr. Burrows was dismissive. "They're just being a little larger than life, is all," he claimed. "The Storyteller is amping up the conflict. Every story needs a good conflict. The program is working exactly as it should be."

Edwin wasn't so sure.

Not long after he had confronted Mr. Burrows about the changes in character narratives, the Pizzaplex was beset with strange malfunctions. Although none of the incidents were inherently dangerous, they were concerning. It wasn't the glitches themselves that were the problem, it was the frequency of them.

The glitches were relatively benign: sparking crossed wires, shorted-out electrical systems, pipe leaks, random animatronic shutdowns, sound system static, audio mix-ups in which characters inexplicably exchanged voices with one another, locked doors that should have been unlocked, unlocked doors that should have been locked. None of these things as isolated incidents threatened the Pizzaplex in any substantial way. No patron was in any sort of peril because of these issues. But the sheer volume of problems, Edwin thought, was a big blaring claxon that bellowed, "Danger!"

Something was happening, and it was naïve to think that The Storyteller had nothing to do with it. The timing negated any argument for coincidence.

Or at least that's what Edwin thought. No one else agreed with him.

Clearly, Edwin was the only one who could do something about what was going on. He had to get inside The Storyteller's tree.

Access to The Storyteller was strictly controlled. The door to the tree's hollow center was not just hidden; it was locked.

Edwin did his best to stake out the tree during the Pizzaplex's business hours. When crowds were thick by the tree, he was able to feel around the seams of the hidden door and look for a shielded lock or control panel. But he found nothing. The door seemed to be little more than a cutout in the tree trunk, and he couldn't figure out how to get it open without being noticed by daytime security. Night security was far more relaxed, he knew. After hours, he might have a chance to get past the door.

On the weekends, the Pizzaplex was open late, too late for any forays into The Storyteller's tree. Edwin had to wait until Monday night to attempt to sneak in. In the meantime, however, he decided he could gather some intel.

Edwin had been part of Fazbear Entertainment for a long time. Therefore, The Storyteller's tree aside, Edwin had access to pretty much every part of the executive building and all the company's properties. That access included the company's archives.

After a project was completed, all the project plans were stored in a massive warehouse on the outskirts of town. Edwin always thought it ironic that a tech-savvy company like Fazbear Entertainment kept its records on hard copies stuffed into cardboard boxes and stacked sky-high on metal shelves that seemed to go on for miles, but that was the way it was. And that was something Edwin could take advantage of.

Midmorning on Friday, Edwin got in his old compact sedan and put-putted out to the Fazbear archives building. Shielding his eyes from a harsh sun, he hurried into the building and crossed the small, bland-beige lobby. Holding only a couple straight-backed plastic chairs and a long, black Formica-topped counter, the tiny space would have had no personality at all were it not for the woman behind the counter.

The woman, large and ebony-skinned with shoulder-length dreadlocks, had done her best to spruce up her work area. A profusion of healthy houseplants flourished on a narrow table behind her, and a row of small versions of Fazbear characters was lined up on the counter. Next to a pint-size Foxy, a fuchsia pottery bowl held a profusion of multicolored gumdrops. The candy's sweet aroma filled the air. So did the jasmine scent of the woman's perfume.

When Edwin let the glass entrance door whoosh shut behind him, the woman looked up from a paperback romance novel. "Eddy!" the woman boomed in a Caribbean accent. "My favorite little guy!"

"Hello, Chevelle," Edwin said. "You're looking as lovely as ever."

"Oh, shut your mouth, Eddy. You're needing glasses." Chevelle flipped her orange-beaded dreadlocks, and they clicked in time to her rhythmic laugh.

"Thankfully, my vision is twenty-twenty," Edwin said, "all the better to see your stunning beauty."

Chevelle trilled another laugh. Edwin winked at her.

Chevelle had been the head records clerk of the archives for as long as Edwin could remember.

"What can I do for you today, Eddy?" Chevelle asked.

"I was hoping you could let me poke around a bit," Edwin said.

"Poking around" wasn't strictly kosher, Edwin knew. Chevelle, of course, knew that as well. Fazbear Entertainment had a precise procedure for accessing old records. Edwin could avail himself of the records any time he wanted, but he was supposed to apply for the records and Chevelle was supposed to bring them to him. Edwin, however, didn't want to leave a paper trail revealing what he was up to.

Thankfully, Chevelle really liked Edwin. And as he'd hoped she would, she winked at him, and said, "I don't see why not. It's not like I can even see you." Chevelle looked up and to the side like an innocent debutante. "Nuh uh. I can't see nothing at all. I'm just going to mosey on over here," she wandered toward the door to the main archives, "and I'm going to go and check on a few things. If the door happens to close slowly behind me, who's to say what invisible thing might follow me in."

Chevelle winked at Edwin again. He winked back and gave her a thumbs-up. As soon as she hefted herself from her barstool-height chair, he stepped around the counter. And when she opened the archives door, he slipped through it behind her.

Chevelle put her finger to her lips as Edwin bowed to her and pretended to doff an invisible cap. Then she backed out of the archives and returned to her position behind the counter. Edwin immediately headed down the nearest long, cement-floored aisle.

The aisles were oppressive. Edwin always felt like he was descending into catacombs when he was in the archives. A person could easily get lost forever in the maze of records.

Thankfully, Edwin knew exactly where he was going.

All Fazbear Entertainment records were filed chronologically. Within the chronology, they were filed alphabetically.

It wasn't always possible to predict how a project would be labeled because Chevelle did the labeling, and sometimes she got creative with it. The Storyteller specs could be filed under "the," "storyteller," "creative computer," or some other title Edwin hadn't thought of, but since the time period was relatively compact, he was confident he'd find the records he needed pretty quickly.

And he did. They were filed under "baobab." Edwin smiled.

For the next half hour, Edwin riffled quickly through all the engineering specs for the fanciful baobab tree.

"There has to be a way in," he muttered as he flipped through the schematics and notes.

And there was.

Edwin grinned when he saw the sketch of what he'd been looking for. "Well, wasn't that clever," he said. His words echoed through the colossal building.

Once he found what he needed, Edwin skimmed through everything related to it. By the time he was done, he knew exactly how he could get into the baobab tree to check on The Storyteller.

It was 11:22 p.m. when Edwin made his way up the maintenance stairs to the top level of the roller coaster. *Engineers are the bomb,* he thought as he climbed the metal steps. The maintenance access to the baobab tree was nothing less than inspired.

Edwin's steps clanked on each tread. He wasn't concerned. He wasn't worried about being seen on CCTV, either. This part of the building wasn't monitored.

At the top of the roller coaster's maintenance stairs, a small corridor led to what appeared to be, at first glance, a dead end. Thanks to what he found in the archives, though, Edwin knew that the seemingly solid wall wasn't solid at all.

Edwin confidently approached the wall and placed his hand on its upper right. As soon as he did, the "wall" parted. He grinned.

A pressure switch. Very smart.

He'd hoped to find something similar on the tree trunk itself, but he hadn't been able to locate it. That was because it wasn't there. According to what he had read in the project files, the only way to get through the tree trunk door was by using a hidden palm scanner pad. The pad was programmed to accept only three palms.

Mr. Burrows's palm, of course, was one of the three. Edwin's palm, obviously, was not.

But he didn't need the stinking palm scanner. Thanks to the engineers' ingenuity, Edwin would get into the tree via the maintenance access. And that access, assumed to be unknown and undiscoverable, was not protected by anything.

Once the wall parted, Edwin spotted the control panel he would need. It was right inside the opening.

He reached around the opening and pressed the button he found there. A soft hum preceded a click, and a telescoping catwalk extended out from the wall, heading toward the branches of the baobab tree.

Once the tree was designed, Edwin had read in the project notes, there'd been much discussion about how to access the tree's branches for maintenance. LED lights were long-lasting, but things inevitably went wrong, and the far ends of the branches might need repair. They would also need cleaning. The engineers who designed the tree included metal climbing rungs within the tree; these would allow maintenance people to get to the top of the tree, but the branches were far too fragile to be crawled on. So, getting to the tips of them couldn't be done from that central position.

That was why the engineers built an extendable catwalk that could be stored within the network of roller-coaster tracks and maintenance stairs and activated only when access to the tree branches was needed.

The catwalk juddered to a stop. It clicked again. The hum ceased. Edwin gazed along the length of the stainless grated walkway. Looking down to be sure no security personnel were strolling along the concourse, Edwin grasped the catwalk's metal railings and stepped out onto the walkway.

The catwalk shimmied ever so slightly, but it seemed sturdy enough. Edwin might have had his demons, but he wasn't afraid of heights. He didn't hesitate. He hurried toward the baobab's trunk.

Edwin knew the catwalk was eighty feet long, but the distance wasn't at all daunting. He was so buoyed by having found this access that all he felt was triumph as he strode toward the tree. He reached the tree trunk in no time.

As he'd read in the baobab tree's specs, Edwin found the end of the catwalk had self-anchored to the top of the tree. Just beyond the end of the catwalk, a sliding panel covered the top of the tree trunk. From what Edwin had read, the panel wasn't locked. No one had worried about a security breach from the top of the tree.

The panel, which had a hermetic seal, slid apart swiftly. Edwin peered through the opening and spotted the first of a series of metal rungs that acted as a ladder leading down into the tree. This was it. Edwin was about to gain access to The Storyteller.

And that thought brought with it Edwin's first frisson of fear.

What if he was right?

Edwin shook off the thought. There was no point in catastrophizing. Yet.

Edwin shifted to lower his foot onto the top rung inside the tree trunk. The rung was thick and sturdy; it felt secure. Edward lowered his other foot, feeling around for the next rung. He found it easily.

From that point, Edwin was home free. He climbed down the seventy-five-foot tree trunk just as quickly as he'd traversed the catwalk.

As he climbed, Edwin kept his gaze forward. In spite of his ticker's problems, he was reasonably fit for his age.

Even so, he wasn't about to risk falling. He concentrated on planting his foot carefully on each rung. His rubber soles did a good job of gripping the smooth metal, and they made little sound. He felt like a cat burglar. That thought made him smile.

Edwin's smile, however, vanished instantly when he reached the bottom of the trunk. That was when he saw The Storyteller, in its full glory, for the first time.

He'd thought he was prepared for it. He was wrong.

Edwin had seen the tiger head, and so he knew what to expect. But it was worse up close. At a distance, carried by the three men, the tiger head's size was discernible, but standing next to it, the head seemed to swell to even larger proportions.

Gleaming white, the metal tiger head was majestic. Or it would have been if Edwin hadn't known what it stood for. With eyes painted in two different colors—a deep emerald green and a brilliant blue—the tiger's expression was blank, almost placid. The tiger, unlike real white tigers, hadn't been given stripes, and its nose and mouth were the same color as the rest of its painted metal. The tiger's mouth was open, exposing not white but back-lit silver teeth. Beyond the sharp canines, intermittently blinking lights could be seen. Edwin understood he was looking at part of The Storyteller's hardware.

The lack of stripes wasn't the tiger's only non-tigerlike feature. The tiger bust, which was mounted on one curved yellow-painted wall of the trunk's interior, also had four spread arms, which jutted from the tiger's neck; two slanted upward and two slanted downward.

Edwin turned in a full circle and surveyed the contents of the hollow trunk. The interior of the tree trunk, he discovered, contained nothing but the mammoth tiger head. The stark, vacant space was just a void above a round white floor, surrounded by a circular yellow wall. The floor and the wall, however, were covered with white LED lights. Banks of LED lights marched up the walls in soldierlike rows, and a spray of LED lights cascaded down from above the tiger's head. More LEDs were inset into the floor in a crisscrossing pattern. All that illumination bathed the four-armed tiger in a way that made it radiant, almost celestial. The tiger's eyes sparkled in the lights' glow, and the head's white-painted surface gleamed.

Edwin had to take a minute.

Edwin retreated twelve feet to the trunk's far wall and sat on the tree's ceramic floor tiles. He took three long, deep breaths.

The images were streaking through his mind again, the same way they had when he'd first seen the tiger head being carried into the tree. They were worse this time, though. Of course they were. The blank, metal tiger head had triggered the old emotions, but this version of the tiger head was even more reminiscent of the one that haunted him.

All the usual symptoms of his panic attacks erupted at once. His breathing ratcheted up to a staccato beat. Sweat trickled down his neck. His stomach churned. He started to shake.

Edwin closed his eyes and put his face in his hands. "Stop it!" he commanded himself.

He didn't have time for this right now. He needed to see what he was up against.

Edwin mentally smeared black paint over all the pictures that were flipping through his mind. He forced himself to blot out his memories.

It took a few minutes, but eventually, his breathing slowed. The shaking stopped.

Edwin opened his eyes.

"Think like an engineer," he told himself.

Edwin pressed a hand against the cold, smooth interior wall of the tree trunk and he stood. He took a step toward the tiger head and examined how it was interfaced with the wall.

Was the tiger movable? Was it designed to be mobile?

No. The tiger was stationary. It wouldn't suddenly come to life and attack.

The tiger head's workings did, however, have a substantial reach. It appeared to be hardwired to the tree. And the tree was hardwired to all the Pizzaplex's systems.

Edwin turned away from the tiger head and spotted a small inset in the wall. He found a compact computer terminal. Its keyboard slid in and out of the inset. Edwin pulled it out.

Of course The Storyteller's operating system was password protected, but Edwin didn't need to get into the system to learn what he'd come here to learn. What he had hoped he wouldn't find was right there on the start screen: The Storyteller was running a program called Mimic1.

"No," Edwin whispered.

His worst fears were confirmed.

He'd known it. He'd tried to pretend he hadn't known it. But he'd known it. He'd known it from the very beginning.

No wonder the Pizzaplex characters were changing. No wonder problems were cropping up all over.

It was happening again. And Edwin had no idea what to do about it.

Edwin opened his eyes. He winced and closed them again. He groaned.

As it always did on clear days, a sliver of blazing sunshine was piercing through the slats of Edwin's yellowed, sagging Venetian blinds. Unless clouds gave Edwin a reprieve, the sun speared him this way every morning, yanking him from the sweet oblivion of sleep, forcing him to face existence yet another day.

Edwin could have done something about the blinds. Even though he was renting the ratty little apartment, he could have replaced the ancient metal window coverings. Or he could have added to it, hanging room-darkening curtains over it. For that matter, he could've just nailed a heavy blanket over the window. But he didn't do any of these things.

Why? Because the light coming in through those blinds, however scourging it might be, was the only thing that got Edwin out of bed in the morning.

Edwin rolled over on his narrow, lumpy bed. With his back to the window, the light wasn't as intrusive, but it still nudged him to move. He threw back his sour-smelling sheet and sat up.

Edwin's knee joints cracked when he put his feet on the floor. His thigh muscles burned.

For the last five nights, Edwin had been sneaking into The Storyteller's tree. His old legs weren't used to all that exercise, and they were protesting.

Edwin's whole body, for that matter, wasn't happy with him. Although Edwin hadn't had a good night's sleep in decades, he at least usually managed four or five sporadic hours. Now, because of his nocturnal forays into the baobab tree, he was grabbing only an hour or two before dawn forced him awake and pushed him into his day.

Rubbing the dried rheum that had accumulated at the corner of his eyes in the short time he'd slept, Edwin looked around the sad, lonely space where he spent his nights. The dirty peach-colored walls were bare. The scant furniture in the room—the bed he sat on, a scarred dresser, and a wobbly nightstand—had come with the rental. Edwin had added nothing of his own when he'd moved in, nothing but his clothes and toiletries, a handful of books, and a small item that sat, dingy and beleaguered, on top of the dresser. Edwin knew he shouldn't have kept it, but he couldn't bring himself to throw it away. It was the only thing he had left of a time that he shouldn't have been allowed to forget.

Not that he hadn't tried.

Edwin had spent the better part of three decades trying to forget. He'd run as far away as he could, all the way around the world. Until one day, he'd run out of money. Then he'd been forced to come back and demand that Fazbear Enterprises honor their buyout agreement.

If anyone had told Edwin, forty years before, that this was where he'd end up, he'd have laughed himself silly. Edwin Murray in a place like this? No way. Edwin Murray was a brilliant engineer, a creative genius. He was destined for great things.

This hadn't just been Edwin's twenty-four-year-old ego talking. "Your company is going to change the world," Fiona had told him every morning when he got up and went to the old warehouse where he tinkered with his inventions and built his machines.

Life had been so full of promise then. Yes, money was tight at first, but Edwin started breaking through the financial wall and he and Fiona were able to move into a large fixer-upper house. The house was an old Queen Anne mansion, and they'd planned to restore it to all its former grandeur. By then, Fiona was pregnant, and she was bursting with ideas for their child's nursery and playroom.

But then, the bubble burst. The promise, it turned out, had been a lie.

Fiona had died in childbirth. Edwin had been left alone with a baby boy who never stopped crying.

Oh, but how Edwin had loved that little boy. Even lost in his own grief, Edwin had poured himself into learning to be a good dad. If only . . .

Edwin rubbed his eyes roughly, wiping away his memories and forcing himself to face the present. He stood and shuffled into the tiny space that served as his bathroom. Avoiding the mirror, he pulled off the sweat-stained white T-shirt he'd worn to bed. Stripping the rest of the way, Edwin turned on a water-spotted faucet and ducked into the pathetic drizzle that spurted from the old, lime-clogged showerhead.

The trickle of warmth that sluiced over Edwin might have been weak, but it cleared his head. A tiny bit of his despair sloughed away, and he remembered the night's triumph.

Mr. Burrows adjusted the collar of his indigo-blue polo shirt as he stepped onto the main concourse of the Pizzaplex. The cotton fabric was slightly moist. The temperature outside was warm enough that even though he'd changed clothes after his morning round of golf, he was already sweating again by the time he got to the Pizzaplex. Mr. Burrows inhaled deeply, satisfying himself that the sandalwood scent of his subtle cologne was masking any unseemly perspiration odor. He hated to smell. It was undignified.

Not that any scent of his own could be picked out from the myriad aromas filling the Pizzaplex. In just one inhale, Mr. Burrows noted the scents of spicy pizza sauce, sickly sweet cotton candy, buttery popcorn, and fruity bubblegum as well as the odors of dirty socks and even dirtier diapers. The latter wrinkled his nose. And the pervasive smell of harsh cleaning fluids made his eyes burn. He knew why the Pizzaplex janitorial staff had to use the bleach and other caustic chemicals, but he didn't like to breathe them in.

Generally, even though Mr. Burrows was the head of Fazbear Entertainment, he spent little to no time in the company's venues. Mr. Burrows had achieved his position based on his programming and business skills, not on his love of games and robots and pizza. Honestly, he thought most of what Fazbear Entertainment created was frivolous, even stupid, but he sought a position with the company right out of college because Fazbear Entertainment was a wildly successful corporation, and he aspired to be the head of such an enterprise. He also had a knack for creating games, however much he didn't enjoy playing them.

It was the challenge that he liked, he supposed. Creating games and story-driven entertainment was like putting together a complex puzzle. Mr. Burrows enjoyed mastering that kind of intricate thought.

Mr. Burrows's current conundrum was a challenge as well. But this one didn't entertain him; it annoyed him. What was Murray up to?

Mr. Burrows had gotten to the point in his career where he was little more than a delegator most of the time, and that suited him. He'd planned since age five to be a multimillionaire by the time he was thirty. He'd missed the mark by a couple of years, but he was where he wanted to be now. Although he had a knack for business, he much preferred play to work. He applied himself not so he could work more and more but so that he could afford his hobbies. Mr. Burrows had expensive hobbies. Golf was the most affordable. Mr. Burrows also loved yachts, scuba diving, and collecting art.

This was why Murray was starting to annoy him. Mr. Burrows was missing a regatta this weekend because he needed to see for himself what was going on with The Storyteller.

According to the employees who monitored such things, many of the Pizzaplex shows were morphing in strange ways, and several of the characters associated with various attractions like Monty's Gator Golf, Roxy Raceway, Fazer Blast, and Bonnie Bowl were exhibiting unusual behaviors. One of Mr. Burrows's advisers had suggested that The Storyteller itself might have been creating the anomalies, but Mr. Burrows was sure Murray was responsible.

Mr. Burrows's unpleasant visit to the raucous, crowded Pizzaplex today had a twofold purpose. He wanted to see for himself what was happening to the stage shows and what the characters were doing. He also hoped to catch Murray in the act of sneaking into The Storyteller tree.

It was this catch-him-red-handed task that Burrows took on first. Because the Pizzaplex's main dining room had the best view of the tree, Mr. Burrows positioned himself at a table near the dining room's entrance and he ordered a pizza.

The pizza—Mr. Burrows had opted for a veggie pizza with artichoke hearts and sundried tomatoes—wasn't bad. But how in the world was someone expected to digest food in this atmosphere?

Mr. Burrows liked bright colors, but even he had to admit this was technically garish. It was the light, he decided as he chewed his pizza. LEDs and neon lighting were everywhere. LED lights wrapped the tabletops and traced the perimeters of the black-and-white checkerboard squares on the floor. The archway leading into the dining room was neon, and neon pizza wedges decorated the walls, their colors in-your-face reds, blues, greens, yellows, pinks, purples, and oranges. All this light was caught by the mirrored ceiling and refracted, sending streaks of color throughout the space. Even the servers threw out light; they all had multicolored glow necklaces hanging around their necks.

And then there was the noise. Why did children have to scream so much?

Mr. Burrows endured the commotion as long as he could, but after an hour of nursing a soda and watching a couple little boys chew with their mouths open, Mr. Burrows had to get out of the dining room. He hadn't spotted Murray. He decided to give up on this task and check out the animatronic characters.

Mr. Burrows wove his way through an adrenaline-driven crowd of screaming, sticky children and overstimulated adults. He checked his Rolex. His timing wasn't ideal; he was between stage shows. No matter. He figured he could get a sense of the characters' antics if he visited Rockstar Row. Between shows, the main performers—Glamrock Freddy, Roxanne Wolf, Montgomery Gator, and Glamrock Chica—hung out in their greenrooms. Mr. Burrows stepped around a small boy crying because he'd dropped his pinwheel sucker, and he headed into the neon-star-lined area filled with glass-fronted cases that featured a collection of props used by both old and new animatronics. Mr. Burrows strode toward Glamrock Freddy's greenroom.

Greenroom was a misnomer for the red-walled area that was Glamrock Freddy's domain. Above the red walls, a giant bright-blue neon star dominated the ceiling. There was nothing green about the room.

The space was stuffed with various forms of Freddy's visage (the bear's face was painted on the wall and displayed on posters, and the room held a large sculpture of Glamrock Freddy as well as an oversized plush doll version of the character). And right now, the room also held Glamrock Freddy. But he wasn't at his best.

Glamrock Freddy was a massive bear who sported a black bow tie and a top hat encircled by a blue stripe. His body was painted bright orange and yellow with a turquoise lightning bolt on his chest, and his broad shoulders were decorated with substantial red shoulder pads. He wore spiked bracelets and a red earring in his left ear. In other words, Glamrock Freddy was badass. Usually.

Right now, however, Freddy was acting more like a spoiled brat than a rock star. Mr. Burrows's eyebrows arched as he watched Glamrock Freddy engage in a tugging match with a small pigtailed girl. The object being tugged was a furry plush version of a vintage Freddy Fazbear.

"That's mine!" the little girl screeched as she determinedly grasped the bear's arm.

Glamrock Freddy ignored her and continued to attempt to pull the bear from the little girl's clenched hand.

The girl's mother, a young brunette with a prominent blue nose ring, stepped forward and used her shoulder-length denim purse to swat Freddy on the arm. "Stop that!" the mother demanded. "Let go!"

Uh-oh, Mr. Burrows thought. He started toward the girl, the bear, and the mother.

Before Mr. Burrows took one step, though, Freddy let go of the plush version of his predecessor. The sudden release of tension sent the girl reeling backward into her mother's embrace.

Mr. Burrows continued to rush forward, not sure what Glamrock Freddy would do next. The animatronics, although programmed to be entertaining and fun, were powerful machines. If they went off program, they could be dangerous.

But Mr. Burrows needn't have worried. Not about a hazard anyway. He was, however, very concerned about the story program running the bear because Glamrock Freddy turned his back on the girl and her mother, stomped to the far side of his greenroom, hunched his shoulders, and started to cry.

What in the name of all things Fazbear is going on here? Mr. Burrows asked himself.

"Murray," he muttered.

Something was rotten in the state of the Pizzaplex, and Mr. Burrows was going to root it out and get rid of it. Turning on his heel, Mr. Burrows stalked out of Rockstar Row.

He'd seen enough. Now all he had to do was decide how to remedy the situation.

Mr. Burrows, plowing through the Pizzaplex's hoi polloi, was thinking about next steps instead of focusing on where he was going. It wasn't a surprise, therefore, when he suddenly tripped over a toddler who had, for unfathomable reasons, sat down on the floor with a large orange crayon to draw a picture on one of the white floor tiles.

Mr. Burrows windmilled his arms but was unable to keep himself from hitting the floor. He landed flat on his back, faceup.

Mr. Burrows managed to grit his teeth against the curse that wanted to come out. As several well-meaning kids and adults gathered around him, asking him if he was okay, he blinked to clear his vision.

The view from the floor was an interesting one. Mr. Burrows's eyes were mildly unfocused, and the sea of faces against the rainbow-colored backdrop of The Storyteller tree's branches was bizarre, to say the least. Mr. Burrows felt like he'd fallen into a surreal painting. Seeking a focal point to get his bearings, he looked past the faces, up through the tree branches to the Pizzaplex atrium's glass roof.

And that was when it hit him. He knew how Murray was getting into The Storyteller tree.

Mr. Burrows let a couple strangers help him to his feet. He waved off concerned questions, excused himself, and hurried toward the Pizzaplex exit.

First order of business was a shower. Mr. Burrows didn't even want to think about the amount of bacteria on the concourse floor. Second order of business, get one of the tree's engineers into his office.

If what Mr. Burrows suspected was true, he now knew what to do next.

Mr. Burrows had what he needed by the following Tuesday evening. Sebastian, the lead engineer on The Storyteller tree project, brought it to Mr. Burrows at the end of the day.

"This should do it, Mr. Burrows," Sebastian said as he crouched next to the end of Mr. Burrows's credenza.

Sebastian, a tall, broad-shouldered guy with chin-length blond hair he never seemed to comb, finished connecting a couple of wires. "This control pad will give you command of all the tree's mechanisms."

"Good work," Mr. Burrows said.

Sebastian's mouth twisted. "I'm really sorry about the security snafu. We just never thought anyone would figure out the catwalk mechanism, so we didn't think to install security cameras up there or lock down the top of the tree." Sebastian's shoulders rounded forward as if he expected to be disciplined for the oversight.

"Don't worry about it," Mr. Burrows said magnanimously. He looked away from Sebastian. The man's red Fazbear Entertainment uniform shirt was a size too small, and it rode up his back, away from his black pants, exposing more of Sebastian than Mr. Burrows wanted to see.

Sebastian glanced up. His thick black brows were bunched. Clearly, he was expecting a dressing down.

Mr. Burrows had to admit that he was usually not known for his forgiving nature. So, he understood Sebastian's trepidation. In this case, however, the engineers' mistakes were fortuitous.

After he'd showered on Saturday, Mr. Burrows had gone to his office and started issuing orders. The first set of orders had confirmed what Mr. Burrows had suspected—the top of the tree had lax security. The second set of orders had put the tech team to work retasking several of the CCTV cameras. This had resulted in a fine, clear video of Murray sneaking into the tree from the top and then exiting the tree the same way a couple hours later. As he'd watched the video, Mr. Burrows had smiled.

Murray thought he was getting away with something. He was wrong. In fact, Murray was going to walk right into Mr. Burrows's trap.

"You're all set," Sebastian said, rising to his feet and tugging his shirt into place.

"Thank you, Sebastian," Mr. Burrows said.

Mr. Burrows turned to look at his new control panel. He grinned. He couldn't wait to use it.

Mr. Burrows only had to wait a few hours before he got to put his new control pad through its paces. By then, it was 11:26 p.m.

Mr. Burrows hadn't bothered to go home that evening. He'd had Celia get him Chinese takeout, and he'd enjoyed an excellent Peking roasted duck. After he ate, Mr. Burrows had reviewed The Storyteller tree specs. He knew the tree had the features necessary to implement his plan, but he liked to be thorough; he double-checked everything.

As he'd already been aware, the interior of The Storyteller tree was airtight. The hollow portion of the tree had been designed that way in order to maintain the optimal conditions for The Storyteller's processors. Once the tree was closed up, whatever oxygen that had entered the room when its doors were open was all the oxygen available. The tree had no venting system.

When Murray was sneaking into the tree, he was leaving the top of the tree open while he was inside. That provided him with enough air.

While he'd waited for Murray to show up and slip into the tree, Mr. Burrows's gaze had repeatedly gone to his new control pad. He now had the capacity to close and lock the top of the tree. The thought made him want to rub his hands together in glee.

And finally, it was time. Mr. Burrows saw movement on the flat screen behind his desk. He watched as the catwalk started extending out toward the top of the tree.

And, yep, there he was, the little weasel. Murray didn't waste a second once the catwalk stopped moving. He scurried along the narrow walkway and crawled down inside the tree.

Mr. Burrows counted slowly to sixty. He figured that would be plenty of time for Murray to get to the bottom of the tree trunk.

Would Murray notice the panels at the top of the tree close?

Mr. Burrows didn't really care. Murray would find out soon enough that he couldn't get out when he tried to leave the tree.

With a dramatic flourish that he enjoyed immensely, Mr. Burrows pushed a button on his new control panel. He tapped a couple keys on his keyboard, and the image on the flat screen shifted. Now it showed the panel closing at the top of the tree.

"Gotcha," Mr. Burrows said aloud.

★ ★ ★

Now that the tree was closed off, Mr. Burrows could no longer see Murray. Security cameras couldn't be placed inside the tree. The Storyteller's functions kept causing the cameras to glitch. Mr. Burrows could now only imagine what Murray was doing inside the tree.

Mr. Burrows frowned. Was what he'd just done the act of a gentleman?

For an instant, he was beset by doubt.

The instant was short, though.

Locking Murray inside the tree was absolutely the right thing to do . . . for the good of Fazbear Entertainment. Murray was an expensive employee. The salary specified by his buyout contract was scandalous. Murray was also a bothersome employee. His interference had been an issue on other projects, but his meddling with The Storyteller was dangerous. Given that Mr. Burrows couldn't fire Murray without costing Fazbear millions in legal fees, Mr. Burrows was doing right by the company to remove Murray's potentially disastrous tampering.

Besides, Murray had brought this on himself. He knew he wasn't permitted inside the tree. He'd defied the rules. And defying rules had consequences. Murray was only getting what he deserved.

In spite of his conviction that he'd done the right thing, Mr. Burrows's thoughts were dominated by Murray's confinement within the tree all through the rest of the week and even over the weekend. Mr. Burrows and a particularly lovely model had flown to Cozumel for a scuba diving excursion on Friday evening, but nothing about diving in the pristine waters distracted Mr. Burrows from images of Murray trying to batter his way out of the tree.

Monday morning, Mr. Burrows went to work with

his muscles in knots. He half expected to be greeted by his security team, or worse, by law enforcement personnel. Surely, Murray had made an attempt to exit the tree. And that attempt could easily have been heard.

When Celia greeted Mr. Burrows with his usual morning espresso, however, she was alone. And she said nothing about The Storyteller tree.

"Anything that needs my immediate attention?" Mr. Burrows asked Celia.

"Nothing at all, Mr. Burrows," Celia said as she set the espresso cup on his blotter. "Just the board meeting this afternoon."

"Good, good," Mr. Burrows said.

What was Murray doing? Mr. Burrows wondered. Why wasn't he trying to get out?

Mr. Burrows mulled this question over and over as the day passed. He was barely aware of what was discussed during the board meeting. All he could do was stare at Murray's empty chair. He only half paid attention to the paperwork that came across his desk.

In the late afternoon, Mr. Burrows met with some of The Storyteller's programming team to discuss the strange character behavior being reported from nearly all the Pizzaplex venues. When someone suggested going into the tree to run a full diagnostic on The Storyteller, Mr. Burrows choked. When he stopped sputtering, he said, "No, let's just wait and see what unfolds. The Storyteller probably has a long-term plan. Let's see what it is."

This comment garnered Mr. Burrows a few odd looks. He ended the meeting right after that.

Maybe Murray had suffered a heart attack when he realized he was trapped, Mr. Burrows concluded the next day. He could come up with no other explanation for why Murray wasn't trying to get out.

Unless . . .

At the end of Tuesday afternoon, a full week after Mr. Burrows had locked Murray in the tree, Mr. Burrows concluded that Murray was somehow sneaking in and out of the tree in a way that was eluding Mr. Burrows. Was there a trapdoor Mr. Burrows didn't know about? Had Murray defeated the panel lock and sabotaged the camera feeds?

That had to be it. Somehow, the old guy had outsmarted Mr. Burrows. Mr. Burrows hated entertaining this idea, but it was the only explanation he could come up with for why Murray had never made a racket demanding to get out.

Mr. Burrows very much wanted to consult the engineers to see if any of his theories were possible, but doing that would potentially expose what he'd done. No, he had to look into it himself.

The best thing, Mr. Burrows decided, would be to confront Murray directly. And he was going to do that this evening, during the busiest time in the Pizzaplex.

Although, as the chairman of the board, Mr. Burrows had every right to access any part of the Pizzaplex any time he wanted to, he didn't want to draw attention to his entrance into the tree. He figured if he approached the tree when the concourse was at its busiest, his presence might not even be noticed.

By the time he reached the Pizzaplex, Mr. Burrows had worked himself up into a full froth of anger. Murray was such an enormous pain in Mr. Burrows's backside. He couldn't even die properly. Mr. Burrows couldn't wait to get his hands on Murray. He wanted to shake the old man until his teeth fell out of his head.

As Mr. Burrows had known it would be, the atrium was packed. The stage shows were going full blast, and the audiences had spilled into the open space around the tree. Rock music blasted from every speaker in the building. Couples danced. Little kids spun like tiny dervishes. Older kids roughhoused or played air guitar. It was dense, exuberant chaos.

The noise hurt Mr. Burrows's ears, and he had to endure a half-dozen elbows and shoulder bumps as he made his way to the tree, but the commotion was perfect. No one was going to notice him.

Mr. Burrows slipped between two girls jumping up and down and a young couple too wrapped up in each other to notice anything else. He hurried up to the tree's hidden door.

Mr. Burrows watched the palm scanner appear. He placed his palm on the screen.

The door made a soft whooshing sound as it slid open. Mr. Burrows ducked in through the six-foot doorway. As soon as he was inside the hollow tree, the door snicked closed behind him.

Mr. Burrows whirled around. For a moment, he panicked; then he chastised himself. His palm was his key to get out. Everything was fine.

He turned back around. And he froze.

"What's all this?" Mr. Burrows asked.

No one answered.

Frowning, Mr. Burrows gazed around at the most unexpected sight.

He wasn't sure what he'd thought he'd find when he faced off with Murray inside the tree. He supposed he'd find Murray hunched over the computer keyboard, trying to rewrite The Storyteller program.

Instead, he didn't see Murray at all. Maybe the old guy hadn't slipped back into the tree yet.

But clearly, he'd been here. What was all this? What had Murray been doing in here?

The entire interior of the hollow tree trunk, to about six feet up the wall, was plastered with large sheets of construction paper. The paper was in an array of colors, but each sheet was marked up with plain black marker.

Every sheet of paper was covered with odd stick drawings and strange symbols that were not at all familiar to Mr. Burrows. Squiggles. Squares. Loops. Triangles within triangles. Mathematical equations, nonsensical ones from what Mr. Burrows could tell, were tangled up in the symbols. And written over the top of all this, on nearly every sheet of construction paper, were two words: "I'm sorry."

What did it all mean?

For a full minute, Mr. Burrows circled the interior of the tree. He barely glanced at The Storyteller, which was plastered with construction paper as well. He just kept looking up the walls, trying to decipher what must have been some kind of code that he didn't understand.

He puzzled over what he was seeing . . . until his foot came up against an obstruction. Mr. Burrows looked down. He gasped and covered his mouth with his hand.

Mr. Burrows had been wrong. Murray hadn't been sneaking in and out for the last week. He'd never left. And now he never would.

Half buried under a mound of blank construction paper, Murray was sitting, doubled over, a crayon clutched in his curled, motionless right hand. Unquestionably deceased—his eyes were wide open and cloudy—Murray appeared to have died in the middle of scribbling yet another odd stick figure. He'd already written, "I'm sorry," on the paper. His left hand lay above the words, palm up, as if asking for forgiveness.

Mr. Burrows backed away from Murray's corpse. He stumbled, and abruptly, he was gripped by the need to get out of the tree. Every one of his nerve endings was screaming, "Run!" Even though the only thing in the hollow tree besides Murray was The Storyteller and all the benign sheets of construction paper, Mr. Burrows suddenly felt like he was standing in the midst of a contagion. He had to get away from it.

Whipping toward the door in a panic, Mr. Burrows accessed the palm reader display. He put a now-trembling hand on the screen and waited for the door to whisk open.

Nothing happened.

Mr. Burrows pressed his palm to the glass again.

Nothing.

Then it dawned on him what was going on.

"No!" Mr. Burrows shouted.

How could he have been so stupid?

He'd forgotten that the button he'd pushed on the control pad Sebastian had so helpfully installed on the credenza in Mr. Burrows's office overrode every function in the tree. The command Mr. Burrows had given in his office when he'd locked in Murray had rendered Mr. Burrows's palm completely ineffective inside the tree. He was trapped.

Mr. Burrows didn't hesitate. He immediately began pounding on the tree's exit door. He battered it with his fists. He kicked it with his leather-soled shoes. He also screamed. He shouted. He bellowed.

"Hey! In here! Get security! I'm trapped in here!" he yelled over and over.

In a matter of minutes, Mr. Burrows was gasping for air. His heart thundering in his chest, he put his ear to the door. As if from a great distance, Mr. Burrows could hear the sound of children playing.

He took in a gulp of air and bellowed as loudly as he could. "Help me!!"

He once again pressed his ear to the door. The children continued to laugh and scream.

It was no use. No one was going to hear him.

Trying to control his racing heart, Mr. Burrows scanned the small space. *Think*, he commanded himself.

I'm a smart guy, he thought. *I can figure this out.*

Mr. Burrows's gaze landed on the cables that extended from The Storyteller. Of course. If he broke the connection between The Storyteller and the Pizzaplex, the attractions would malfunction. Someone would come. Right?

Right, he told himself.

Mr. Burrows dove toward the cables that stretched out from the base of The Storyteller. Grabbing them with both hands, he jerked the cables away from The Storyteller's metal platform. The cables came free easily, but even when they did, The Storyteller, its white metal tiger head lit up like a starry sky, didn't go dark.

Mr. Burrows growled in frustration. Scrambling to his feet, he began pummeling The Storyteller. "Stop running," he screamed at it.

The Storyteller remained lit up. Enraged, Mr. Burrows grabbed one of The Storyteller's arms. He put his full weight into it and snapped the arm off the tiger head. The tiger head continued to glow.

On some level aware that what he was doing was pointless, Mr. Burrows nonetheless attacked the next arm violently, grunting as he yanked at the thing. He broke it off, then went for the next arm. And the next. He wrenched off all four arms. As the metal appendages tore free, a tangle of wires flowed from The Storyteller's shoulder sockets like a stream of vessels and veins.

Mr. Burrows began beating The Storyteller's tiger muzzle. In seconds, his fists were bloody. And it was getting hard to breathe.

Mr. Burrows sank to the floor and put his head in his hands. He started to sob.

Then he raised his head.

"Idiot!" he snapped.

Staggering to his feet, Mr. Burrows lunged toward The Storyteller's control keypad. He typed in his password.

The screen flashed, "Password failed."

"What?!" Mr. Burrows wailed.

Once again, he collapsed to the floor. The control pad command had countermanded his access to the program, too. He couldn't shut down The Storyteller.

Mr. Burrows sucked in air. And he realized that it was becoming harder to take in enough oxygen to breathe. He was beginning to feel light-headed.

Mr. Burrows looked up, his gaze scanning the metal rungs leading to the top of the tree. Would he be heard if he pounded on that exit panel?

He tried to stand, but he couldn't. It wouldn't have worked anyway, he knew. No one would have heard him beating on the top of the tree.

It was all useless. There was no way out.

Even so, Mr. Burrows's fury and his refusal to believe the facts of his situation sent him crawling back toward the doorway. He lay on his back and kicked at the door with every ounce of his strength.

"Help!" he shrieked. "Help me!"

He screeched and hollered, keening in high-pitched howls. Someone had to hear him.

Kids loved The Storyteller tree. The chunky trunk, with its swollen-belly-like appearance, made the little kids giggle, and it made the older kids wish they could get inside it. Kids of all ages liked to circumnavigate the tree, chasing one another until they dropped.

BOBBIEDOTS, PART 2

ABE SHOULD HAVE BEEN HAPPY WITH HIS RECENT PROMOTION AT THE MEGA PIZZAPLEX THAT HAD ALLOWED HIM TO LIVE IN THE FAZPLEX TOWER. BUT HE'D LEARNED THE HARD WAY THAT THE PERK WAS NOT GUARANTEED—THERE'D BEEN ONLY ONE "OFF-LIMITS" APARTMENT AVAILABLE WHEN IT CAME TIME FOR HIM TO MOVE IN. HE'D TRICKED HIS WAY INSIDE, HACKING THE SYSTEM TO GIVE HIM A PLACE TO STAY.

It had seemed great at first. At least he was no longer homeless and living inside a pile of tires on Roxy Raceway.

And it wasn't just a roof over his head. He had the Bobbiedots to take care of him. Olive, Rose, and Gemini, each with a different function, were holograms that took care of his every need. When strange things started happening around the apartment, they'd blamed it on the gen1 Bobbiedots that lived in the ceiling crawl space. The gen1s couldn't be turned off and still tried to help, even though they didn't really understand what helping meant. They'd already nearly boiled Abe alive and almost caught his hand in the garbage disposal.

But lately, Abe was starting to wonder whether the gen1s were really the cause of his misfortunes.

Freshly showered (and thankfully unscalded), Abe moved around his bedroom getting ready for work. His holographic "helpers," the Bobbiedots, hovered on the screen near his closet.

"Today's forecast," Olive said, shading her green eyes against the glare coming through the window, "is for sun."

"I could have told him that," Rose said, squinting her pink eyes and nibbling on a croissant.

Gemini tapped her blue headset. "How about some jazzy music to celebrate the weather?" The frenetic notes of Dixie-style jazz filled the apartment.

Abe preferred quiet in the mornings, but he was working hard to stay on the Bobbiedots' good side. He didn't say anything about the music.

He crossed to his dresser, pulled open the second drawer, and reached for a pair of socks. He pressed his fingers to his temple. The music was giving him a headache.

Rose winked into view. "Are you okay? Do you have a headache?"

"No!" Abe snapped. "It's just that . . ." He stopped. He

didn't want to complain about the music, or anything, for that matter. He couldn't afford to anger the Bobbiedots. He forced a smile. "Everything's fine."

Olive popped up on the screen next to Rose. "You're acting strange," she said. Her green eyes closed to near slits as she studied him.

Did she know he no longer trusted the Bobbiedots?

Abe looked at Rose. Was she watching him just a little too intently?

Abe turned away from the Bobbiedots. "Work stuff," he said nonchalantly as he sat to pull on his socks.

Abe put on his shoes, pulled on a shirt, and headed to his bedroom door.

He attempted to pull the door open. It wouldn't budge.

He jiggled the door. It remained closed.

"What's going on?" he snapped.

"Oh, I initiated the bedroom door lock for your protection," Olive said.

Abe looked at Olive. Her green eyes looked back at him impassively.

"Uh, okay. Thanks," Abe said. "But could you please open the door now?"

The door clicked. Abe opened it.

Abe couldn't wait any longer. He had to get on with his plan.

Abe had decided that the first thing he needed to do was find out, once and for all, whether the gen1s actually existed. Were they real or a convenient scapegoat for his Bobbiedots' antics?

If the gen1s were real, Abe figured there had to be information about them somewhere in the Pizzaplex databases. It was time for him to use his engineering access.

It was nearly 7:00 p.m. Abe was the only one left in the office. Outside, the sun was down, but it was still throwing an orange glow across the horizon. The glow fell over the Fazbear Tower and made it look vaguely like a shiny bright carrot jutting up toward the sky. Why had he ever thought it looked like a palace?

Abe returned his attention to the computer. His screen displayed a list of all the Fazbear Entertainments robots. Abe scrolled through the list. He couldn't find any reference to gen1s. The only Bobbiedots entry was for the holographic Bobbiedots.

Okay. So they didn't exist.

Or did they?

Fazbear Entertainment didn't always keep records of animatronic failures. It was still possible that the gen1s' records had been deleted. Abe drummed his fingers on his desk. Now what?

He scrolled back through the information and his gaze landed on the links to "storage location" next to each animatronic entry.

Of course. Abe shook his head. The retired and dysfunctional animatronics were kept in the Pizzaplex's underground levels. If the gen1s did exist, Abe might be able to find one in storage. It was worth a try.

Abe grabbed a flashlight, left his desk, and headed out of the office.

He wasn't a big fan of the Pizzaplex's underground. He knew his way around it, of course. But it was dark and filled with eerie animatronic parts. The dungeon-like air made Abe feel claustrophobic.

But Abe was willing to face the underground if it helped him solve his problem.

Abe took the elevator to the first level of the underground. From here, to get to the lower levels, you had to follow descending tunnels.

The first level wasn't so bad. The official storage floor

for the Pizzaplex was just a big warehouse. It had concrete block walls and a shiny cement floor. Metal shelves held thousands of boxes, and crates lined the walls. At least a dozen or so employees worked down here full-time. Abe didn't know any of them personally but waved at the beefy guy behind the wheel of a forklift. The guy nodded.

Abe walked on, heading to the dingy opening to the "utilidor." The utilidor was a dark passage with a metal-grated floor. Abe's feet created a metallic cadence that echoed around him as he strode as fast as he could between runway-like rows of red lights that lined the metal grid-work. Above, more red lights barely illuminated the long, cramped hallway. The lights threw their red glow over a network of wires and pipes lining concrete walls.

Abe always thought the red lights were appropriate for the area, even if they gave him the heebie-jeebies. This section of the Pizzaplex was like its circulatory system. All the complex's utility lines originated here. This area gave the Pizzaplex its life. But nothing about it felt life-like. The utilidor was rank and musty. Abe wondered how many small animals had found their way down here and died, their corpses decaying in the moist, warm air.

Abe hurried to the end of the utilidor. Now for the worst part.

Abe's pace slowed as the metal grates gave way to smooth concrete again. The floor sloped downward and curved. Abe turned on his flashlight and swept the area in front of him and on either side of him to be sure he was alone.

This was the sewer. It was even darker than the utili-dor, a graveyard of damaged and discarded animatronics. It seemed to Abe that the Pizzaplex had enough square footage to designate a friendlier area for robotic rejects, and that it was a waste of money to let their old metal turn to rust. But he wasn't in charge, and this was where the old and useless were left to languish.

Abe had reached the sewer level. He squared his shoulders and took a deep breath.

With concrete walls and a cement floor similar to the storage level, the sewer area wasn't a real sewer per se. Yes, a large sewer pipe ran through it, but it wasn't itself the conduit for sewage. You didn't have to slosh through excrement to move through this section. It did, however, smell like you were sloshing through excrement. The odor down here was fetid and nauseating.

Whereas the storage level was kept clean and was brightly lit, this floor was little more than an indoor landfill. And it was infested with wandering, wasted animatronics.

Abe sucked in his breath when his flashlight's beam landed on one such animatronic. The pitiful remains of a Glamrock Chica resting against the sewer's outer wall blinked at Abe and raised a handless arm. The lower part of Chica's face was a gaping maw. The unblinking eye was staring upward. Abe hurried past, trying to ignore the way Chica's head turned to follow his movement.

Abe rushed forward, whipping his flashlight right and left as he went. This might have been a fool's errand, he knew, but he had to give it a try.

If he found a gen1, he'd have a better idea of what he was dealing with. If he didn't, well, that didn't necessarily prove that the Bobbiedots were lying. The underground was a huge area. He wouldn't be able to search it all.

Abe practically ran through the sewer, dodging past a small army of wandering endoskeletons and mutilated animatronics. As far as Abe knew, no human had ever been hurt by the roaming robots, but he wasn't taking any chances.

Abe searched the underground until well after

midnight. By then, he was a jangle of edgy nerves. He was hot. He was dirty. And he was discouraged.

Even though he was moving fast, he'd been able to identify every animatronic he passed. None of them were gen1s.

It was time to give up.

Abe was almost at the end of a corridor when his flashlight beam landed on a purple hippopotamus. It was a Mr. Hippo!

Of all the animatronics, Mr. Hippo was his favorite. He was one of the friendlier-looking machines. Abe thought of the hippo as a sort of grandfatherly character.

Abe studied the unmoving hippo before him. Mr. Hippo was supposed to have blue eyes and four teeth on his bottom jaw. He was also supposed to have a black top hat. This Mr. Hippo's eyes were missing. So were two of his teeth and his hat. He did, however, still have a flower and buttons on his chest.

Abe reached out and patted Mr. Hippo's shoulder. The hippo didn't move.

Abe started to turn away, but he stopped when his gaze landed on a hint of purple on the floor a few feet from Mr. Hippo. Abe bent over and picked up a Mr. Hippo magnet.

"I remember these," Abe whispered.

He rubbed his finger over the small Mr. Hippo face.

Mr. Hippo magnets were novelty toys that had been recalled several years before. The magnets, Abe remembered, were so strong that they'd shorted out electronics.

The magnet probably was strong enough to disable the locks in his apartment. He could use it to get out of his bedroom at night and find out what the Bobbiedots were doing. He could no longer rely on them to open doors, and he didn't want to tip them off to his plans.

Abe pocketed the magnet.

It was time go back to his apartment and get to the truth.

★ ★ ★

Abe pulled on his pajama bottoms and threw back the covers on his bed. He sat down on the edge of the mattress and sighed, feeling a strange longing for the nights when he'd crawl into his sleeping bag in his tire fort.

Tonight was the night. Abe had gotten home too late the night before to initiate his plan, and the Bobbiedots had already been suspicious of his late arrival. Now he was going to bed early in the hopes of getting some sleep before he did what he planned to do.

Rose and the other two Bobbiedots hovered on the glass panel above the head of the bed. Rose watched Abe with her big pink eyes.

Abe looked at all the Bobbiedots in turn. "Good night."

The Bobbiedots gazed at him unhappily. He couldn't read their expressions very well. Did they feel sad for him? Were they annoyed with him? What were they planning next?

"Good night," Abe said again.

The Bobbiedots blinked out of view. Abe waited a couple minutes. Then he set his alarm for 2:00 a.m. He turned off his bedside light and got in bed.

The alarm woke Abe at 2:00 a.m. He sat up and looked around. All the screens were dark. So was the apartment.

Abe reached under his pillow and pulled out the Mr. Hippo magnet. Since he'd found the thing, he'd kept it with him at all times. He hadn't wanted to leave it lying around for the Bobbiedots to spot.

Abe tucked his feet into slippers and shuffled silently to the bedroom door. Abe swiped the magnet at the lock. It clicked. The bedroom door swung open.

Abe crept out of the bedroom and looked around the darkened apartment. His plan was to get to the main terminal near the kitchen, where he hoped he could monitor the Bobbiedots' activity while they were dormant.

Abe got as far as the coffee table before he heard the noise. It was the same noise he'd heard so many times during the night. It was a soft swish of movement, and it was close. Too close.

Abe crouched low, ducking behind the sitting area's partition. He froze and listened. He heard a rustling sound and a scrape. Slowly, he leaned forward and peered around the partition.

His gaze followed the direction of the sound.

Abe had to swallow a gasp. The trapdoor was opening.

Abe took cover behind the partition again. He tried to keep his breathing even and silent.

He wanted to see what was coming through the trapdoor. But he didn't want whatever it was to see him.

After what seemed like a nearly endless few minutes, the sound moved away from Abe. He risked a peek.

And nearly screamed.

Long black cables dropped from the open trapdoor and trailed through the apartment. The cables looked like tentacles, as if a giant black squid was slithering down from the ceiling to find Abe.

Several rubbery cables twitched Abe's way. Seemingly alive, they groped and scrabbled toward him. Abe scrambled backward, seeking the shelter of his sofa.

The cables pursued Abe, writhing and twitching. They made cracking, rustling noises as they flicked against one another.

Abe crawled around the end of the sofa, ducking behind it just in time. Another mass of cables trailed over the coffee table and spread up onto the sofa just as Abe dove behind it.

One of the cables flipped over the top edge of the sofa, just a few inches from Abe's face.

Up close, it was clear that the black cord wasn't a snake or a tentacle. It was an electrical cable. But it didn't act like any electrical cable he'd seen. It quivered and pulsed with a life of its own.

Abe twisted away from it and looked up at the ceiling. A mass of the writhing cables hung down through the trapdoor opening.

The cable near Abe flipped toward him. He flattened himself to the floor and scooted on his belly around the end of the sofa, taking refuge behind the easy chair. There, he concentrated on breathing. Were the cables the gen1s?

His Bobbiedots weren't lying.

The gen1s were real.

Goose bumps erupted on Abe's arms. His muscles went taut.

Crouched, frozen in shock, Abe listened.

The cables made whirring sounds as they slid through the apartment. The sounds weren't loud, but they suddenly seemed deafening to Abe.

Or was that the sound of the blood rushing in his head or the sound of his heart trying to beat its way out of his chest?

Abe struggled to accept what was happening. There was an old robot sneaking around Abe's apartment. And it wanted to kill him.

Abe scooted around his easy chair. He looked toward the main terminal he'd wanted to access.

Abe's breath caught.

He wouldn't be accessing the terminal tonight. A gen1 was at the terminal.

Abe gawked at the cable-trailing robot.

The gen1 was clearly a precursor to his Bobbiedots. This one shared Rose's bright pink coloring.

But this version of Rose—*Three*, Abe thought, as Rose had initially introduced herself—was severely damaged.

The top of Three's face and one of her eyes were missing, exposing blackened metal beneath the smooth plastic surface. Her exoskeleton was cracked, revealing part of her metal rib cage. The rest of her exoskeleton mirrored Rose's feminine form, except for an open midsection that revealed black wires and servos. And instead of Rose's pink pigtails, Three's hair was made of black, plastic-covered power cables that cascaded from her skull like a tangle of wriggling snakes. It reminded him of Medusa.

Abe's breathing had gone shallow, but he forced himself to study the robot. He had to know what he was up against.

Whereas the gen2 Bobbiedots' color designations were prominent, outlining their clothing and filling their eyes and the streams of light that made up their hair, this gen1's colors were more subtle. Three had one hot-pink eye, a hot-pink glow from her chest area, and a hot-pink light panel on her right thigh and on a power box midway along one of her cables.

As Abe watched, Three interfaced with the main terminal. He was so mesmerized by the robot that he wasn't prepared when it suddenly turned and started moving toward the sitting area. And it was coming directly toward him.

But the robot didn't seem to see him.

It wasn't reacting to him at all.

Three turned to the right and moved toward a wall socket. She either didn't care about Abe—which was unlikely—or she couldn't see him.

Standing carefully, Abe sidled around the sitting area to get a better view of the robot. He watched her as she felt around the wall.

No, he concluded. She couldn't see.

Abe exhaled in relief.

But he exhaled too loudly.

The robot whirled toward Abe. And she opened her mouth.

Three let out an ear-splitting keen that pierced right through Abe's eardrums and speared his brain. He couldn't help himself. He screamed, too.

She charged toward Abe, her cables writhing around her.

Abe tore back toward the bedroom. When he got inside, he slammed the door closed, engaged the lock, and backed away. He picked up his bedside lamp and brandished it like a club.

He listened, fully expecting the robot to crash through the door.

His chest heaved. His whole body shook.

Abe waited.

Nothing happened.

Several long seconds passed. And Abe heard the scratching, rustling retreat of the cables. The sound retreated from the bedroom door.

Then there was a thump.

The trapdoor. Closing.

Abe collapsed onto his bed. He fell back, then curled up on his side.

He now knew who his real enemy was. It wasn't the Bobbiedots after all.

Before Abe went to bed the next night, he pulled out his laptop to write to his mom, who lived at a facility to treat her long-term degenerative illness. He wrote to her every week and had been lying to her every week for months about the state of his life, except for a brief window of time when things with the Bobbiedots were good. He hadn't wanted to trouble her with news of his homelessness before, and then he hadn't wanted to scare her with stories of the danger he was in. But after weeks of lying,

Abe wanted to tell her something true. He needed some comfort that wasn't coming from a holographic creature.

Abe stared at his fingers poised over the keyboard. They were trembling. He clenched his fists.

He couldn't tell his mom about what he'd seen. He didn't want her to know how scared he was or how much danger he was in. He thought hard for a few seconds, then he stretched out his fingers and started typing.

Did you have a good day today, Mom? I hope you did. My day wasn't as good as I wanted it to be. I have a problem I need to solve. To be honest, it's stressing me out. But I remember what you always told me about problems: If you look at them the right way, they're always opportunities. I'm not sure how what I have to deal with is an opportunity, but I'll do my best to see it that way. I miss you, Mom. I love you.

Abe

Later that night, Abe tried to do what he had told his mother he was doing. What else could he do about the gen1s?

He couldn't go to anyone for help. And even the Bobbiedots couldn't deactivate the gen1s or stop them from entering the apartment. The only thing Abe could think to do was to watch the gen1s enough to get an idea of how to stop them. It filled him with dread, but he had to do it.

Abe's alarm went off at 2:00 a.m. He rubbed his eyes, gathering his courage to get out of bed.

The Bobbiedots continued to lock Abe in at night. They said it was for his own good, and he couldn't argue with them, not after what he'd seen. Keeping the gen1s out of the bedroom was definitely a priority. But the Bobbiedots didn't like Abe's attempts to watch the gen1s, either, so he kept using the Mr. Hippo magnet.

As Abe stepped into the sitting area, his skin prickled. He'd spotted a gen1. It was the blue one.

Just as Abe had labeled Rose's counterpart as Three, Abe immediately thought of Gemini's blue-eyed counterpart as One. He hadn't yet seen Olive's counterpart, Two. And that was okay. One gen1 at a time was enough.

Abe pressed back against the wall as One skulked past. He held his breath when the robot turned and looked toward him. When it didn't react, he realized Three wasn't the only blind gen1. One was blind, too. Was Two blind as well? Again, Abe was in no hurry to find out.

As One moved on by, Abe studied her. One was missing an arm and the lower part of her face covering, which exposed a blackened-metal, tooth-filled mouth and jaw. Her remaining arm was missing its white exoskeleton below the forearm, so her remaining hand was nothing but battered, inky metal. One's cables, unlike Three's, emanated from the crown of her head, like a topknot ponytail. Both of One's eyes shone blue, and she had a glowing blue oval on her forehead, similar to those of the gen2 Bobbiedots.

He hadn't heard Three speak, but One's voice box appeared to be damaged. It was emitting hissing and gurgling sounds. The sounds were soft, but they were unnerving.

Abe was used to robots, even damaged ones, so he didn't know why he found the gen1s' appearance so disturbing. *If I didn't know they were trying to hurt me, would they bother me so much?* he wondered. Yes, even then, he was pretty sure they'd make his skin crawl.

It was their cables, Abe decided. Abe shifted his attention to the cables now. He recoiled from the convulsive flow of the black cables that moved along with One. Looking at the black taillike things streaming behind One, Abe felt like his apartment had been transformed into a nest of vipers. As the cables twitched near him, Abe shrank back, as if a single touch of their twitching ends could kill him instantly.

For all he knew, the cables were just that deadly. He really didn't want to find out.

One moved off, heading toward the kitchen. Abe waited a moment and then followed her from a safe distance, stepping carefully to avoid the trailing cables.

He leaned forward to study her movements. She didn't seem to be doing anything except feeling the counter and cabinet surfaces. It almost seemed like she was looking for something. Maybe she was seeking the next best place to lay one of her deadly traps.

Abe sidled through the sitting area to get closer to the kitchen. Unfortunately, he wasn't as careful as he should have been as he passed an end table. His leg brushed against it and the table shifted, jostling its lamp.

The lamp didn't make much noise as it wobbled slightly—just a little rattle—but the noise was enough to get One's attention. What the gen1s lacked in sight they made up in hearing. Her head slowly rotated toward Abe.

He froze.

One stared directly at Abe. He held his breath.

Her servos clicking, One turned away from the kitchen. She took two ponderous steps toward the sitting area. The black cables throbbed and surged. The rubbery cords were only a couple of feet from Abe's legs. He stared at them and swallowed hard, leaning backward.

Abe was afraid to move from his position, though. Even the stealthiest of steps would get One's attention. And she was close enough to grab him if she knew he was there.

One took another step. She was so close that Abe could see each scorched, barren metal tooth in her flayed-open jaw. The glowing light from her beaming blue eyes fell across Abe's face. He had to blink and shift his head slightly to avoid being blinded by the intensity of her unfocused gaze.

One was so close . . . too close. Abe couldn't believe he'd let himself get cornered like this.

If One realized he was here . . .

Abe couldn't hold his breath any longer. He opened his mouth and exhaled as quietly as he could.

He wasn't quiet enough.

One lunged toward Abe, her bare metal hand hinging open, seeking something to grab. Abe had no choice. He had to move.

Abe edged toward the bedroom, and thankfully One didn't appear to hear him. With a low hum, her head rotated left and right as she sought him. She reached her single arm out and swept the air around her, feeling for him.

Abe took another hesitant step and cringed when his hip skimmed the sofa's upholstery with a soft shushing sound. One reacted immediately. She moved in his direction, blocking his way to the bedroom.

Abe went the other way, sprinting as silently as possible through the kitchen, heading toward the office.

Abe pulled the office door closed behind him. It clicked as he shut it; One probably heard that. How long would it take for her to corner him in this small room?

Abe put his ear to the door and listened. The slithering rustle of One's cables was coming his way. He turned and looked around. The office was darkened, but he could easily see the hulking shapes of furniture.

He scurried over to the desk and ducked beneath it.

Abe settled on the plush carpet, pulling his knees up tight to his chest to fit in the tiny space. He tried to calm his staccato breathing as he ignored the sweat that wormed its way down the back of his neck.

What would One do if she got ahold of him? She only had one hand, but it was powerful metal. It could easily crush his bones or choke the life out of him.

Stop it. He couldn't listen for his attacker if he was entertaining worst-case scenarios.

Abe wasn't sure how long he waited. It felt like hours. His head ached with the effort of trying to listen.

But he no longer heard anything. Nothing. No whispers or rustles. No taps or clicks.

Had One returned to the crawl space?

She must have. If she was still moving around, he'd have heard her.

Abe pulled in a long, quiet breath. He gently crawled out from beneath the desk and stood up. He painstakingly crept to the office door. He pressed his ear to it and listened.

He heard nothing.

Abe reached out a trembling hand and gripped the cold metal of the office door's handle. He held his breath and pushed it down. He paused, then pulled the door open until he could just peer through the resulting crack and see into the kitchen.

He looked at the shadows mottling the table and the counters. The area was clear.

Then he looked up. A tangle of cables still dangled from the open trapdoor. One was still down here. Somewhere.

Abe started to close the office door again. Before he could, the cables began to shift, slackening. One was coming closer.

Abe couldn't get trapped in the office again. The door

didn't lock. He opened the door farther and surveyed the apartment. He mentally cataloged his options.

He could dash into the kitchen and find a weapon, but what good would a paring knife do against a steel robot?

He could race toward the apartment door. No, he didn't want to bring attention to himself by fleeing into the hall in his pajamas. He was still technically squatting in the apartment against regulations. No matter how scared he was, he couldn't risk someone alerting the front desk.

He could stay where he was and hope for the best. No. He was tired, and he didn't trust himself to stay on the alert for much longer.

He really had just one option. He had to try to get to his bedroom.

Abe looked left and right. Although he could see cables, he couldn't see One. She must have been in the sitting area, probably behind the sofa. That was the direction the cables seemed to stream.

Abe stepped out of the office and tiptoed through the kitchen. If he could get around the fridge, it was a straight shot to the bedroom.

Abe gauged the distance. He took a deep breath.

He moved out, away from the fridge . . .

. . . and he nearly walked right into One.

One gazed directly at Abe. Her toothy mouth clenched in a metal grimace, the lights in her eyes pulsed. He gasped.

The metal tooth–filled mouth opened. Abe looked into a darkened maw.

One screamed. Her voice box was damaged, so it sounded a bit like a Klaxon that had melted in the summer sun—still searing, but garbled rather than shrill. She lifted her single arm, her darkened-metal hand flexing, reaching.

Abe was in motion instantly. He lunged away from

One, taking a long step toward the bedroom. Unfortunately, he didn't complete the step.

One's hand clamped tightly around his ankle and tugged. Abe crashed to the floor.

His head grazed the coffee table on his way down and pain shot through his temple. He landed on his stomach and the air was knocked out of him with a grunt.

The apartment floor quaked as One leaped toward Abe, her heavy foot landing next to his head. Abe rolled to the left. He managed to avoid her outstretched arm. At least this meant his leg was free.

Unfortunately, he couldn't avoid the cables. They were everywhere and they snapped into frenzied motion, whipping through the air and hitting Abe's bare arms and neck. It felt like he was being flogged from all directions. His skin was abraded and sliced, even flayed in places where wires had broken through the protective cabling. Abe rolled, trying to free himself from the writhing cables.

Soon, he was on his feet. Staggering, he tore around the back of the sofa. And that's when he discovered One wasn't the only gen1 that had come down out of the crawl space tonight.

As Abe rounded the back of the sofa, his ankle was once again ensnared in the tight grip of powerful, sharp metal fingers.

Abe screamed.

Two answered Abe's scream with one of her own. When she screamed, her broken lower jaw creaked and flopped to the side. Abe shuddered as he looked into the blackness beyond her metal teeth.

If One and Three were damaged, Two was ravaged. She was just a stripped-down metal endoskeleton topped by a mutilated one-eyed skull. Even her cables were laid bare; copper wiring sprouted from the top of her mangled cranium. Two was nothing but a stark metal torso and skull streaming exposed wires; Two's hip sockets were ragged as both limbs had been torn away.

The only way Two could move, obviously, was to drag herself along by her arms. She was able to do that amazingly quickly, her movements spiderlike. As she squirmed closer to Abe now, her exposed wires sparked around her.

One of these sparks landed on Abe's calf. He yelped. Two did the same. And she tightened her hold.

Two's grip on Abe was viselike. Red-hot pain shot through Abe's ankle. He swore he could feel his bones being crushed. Panic overtook him. But the adrenaline that surged with it gave him strength.

Abe kicked out hard and wrenched his foot from Two's grasp. He winced as he pulled his leg back and jumped to his feet. He turned.

He was, once again, face-to-face with One. Abe paused, which gave Two time to grope her way up his leg and clamp her hands around his thigh. Abe bellowed. Warmth flowed down his leg.

One extended her single hand toward Abe's face. Abe pulled his head back, but the metal fingers kept reaching.

This was it. They were going to kill him.

Suddenly, the TV came on. A perky blonde meteorologist's weather report blasted into the room.

The sound was deafening. One recoiled, and Two let go of Abe's thigh. Both robots attempted to cover their auditory sensors.

In spite of his shock and the excruciating pain, Abe was able to lurch away from One and Two while the TV's cacophony distracted them.

The distraction, however, didn't last long . . . because Abe's TV didn't last.

One shot toward the flat screen, yanked it off the wall,

and slammed it down on the coffee table. Shattered glass exploded through the room like shrapnel. It sprayed Abe like a thousand tiny knives. He curled into a ball, but too late. He could already feel little slices all over his body. Blood coursed down his face; his clothes were saturated.

Despite the blood getting in his eyes, Abe didn't think he was seriously injured. The pain was biting but not profound. He could survive this if he could get to the bedroom.

Abe uncurled himself and looked around. The two robots were just a couple feet away. One was turning in circles, feeling the area around her. Two was skittering across the floor, her arms sweeping back and forth in a search pattern.

Abe held his breath.

One and Two didn't know where he was. But they would find him the minute he moved.

Abe looked at the glass screens. As he'd hoped they would, the Bobbiedots appeared. Their eyes wide, their hands to their faces, all three watched Abe and the two gen1s in horror.

Abe pointed at Gemini. She blinked at him.

Abe pointed at the overhead speakers and silently mouthed, "Music."

Would she understand?

Gemini nodded.

Rock music blared from the speakers.

One and Two screeched in anger. They batted at their heads as if trying to disable their auditory systems. Two started crawling up the wall, digging her metal fingers into the drywall for purchase, trying to reach the speakers.

Abe stood. One stopped batting at herself. She cocked her head.

Abe went for it. He raced across the glass-covered floor and dove into his room, barricading the door behind him with his dresser. He added the chest of drawers for good measure.

Then his legs gave out. He sank to the floor.

The Bobbiedots appeared on the glass panel above him.

"Turn the music off, please," Abe said to Gemini.

The rock music stopped. The apartment was still.

Abe listened to the shuffle of the gen1's retreat, but it gave him little relief. He lay back and stared at the ceiling. He imagined the gen1s creeping along over the ceiling above him.

"I recommend you wrap your wounds," Olive said.

"You'll need a lot of gauze," Rose said.

Abe exhaled and sat up, wincing. Abe used the bed to heft himself to his feet and stumbled into the bathroom. Wiping blood from his eyes, he gazed at himself in the mirror.

It was worse than he'd thought it would be. He looked like something out of a horror movie. Every inch of his exposed arms was sliced and scraped. His face was cut up; cuts split his chin, dissected his cheeks, and scored his forehead. One gouge, he realized, had narrowly missed his left eye.

Shallow horizontal slashes bisected Abe's neck. One of them was perilously close to his jugular. Blood flowed down from his neck, soaking his T-shirt. The material, which had been pale blue when he'd pulled on the shirt, was now a shiny dark red. It was cut into ribbons as well. His chest and stomach were lacerated. Most of the cuts were as shallow as the ones on his neck, but one was deeper. Feeling sick, Abe realized he could see subcutaneous fat oozing from between the jagged edges of one six-inch-long slice just under his rib cage.

He needed to go to the hospital. Some of his wounds should be stitched.

But how could he explain his injuries? What if the hospital contacted the police?

If Abe went for help, his entire ruse would fall apart. Technically, he was allowed an apartment by his job, but this one was off-limits for a very good reason. Fazbear Corporate cracked down on rule violations. Would he lose his job? Would they press charges? What if he ended up in jail?

And how would he pay for the emergency room visit? ERs weren't cheap. Abe's new job came with benefits, but there was a three-month waiting period before those kicked in.

Abe gripped the edge of the bathroom sink, but his legs gave way. He sank to the floor.

Weakly, Abe reached into the cabinet under the sink. He groped for gauze and bandages. Starting with his worst wounds first, he began trying to patch himself up.

He was crying after a few minutes and keening in pain after a few more. He was spent when he finally finished wrapping all his wounds.

How much more of this could he take?

Oddly, as hard as it had been, dealing with Abe's many wounds wasn't as challenging as answering his coworkers' questions when he went to work looking like a mummy. He couldn't blame anyone for commenting on his appearance. His arms and hands and neck were wrapped in gauze, and he had bandages all over his face.

Even so, he was already tired of hearing "What happened to you?"

"Walked into a glass door at a friend's house."

When his friend Rodin labeled Abe an idiot for that "smooth move," Abe couldn't argue. He *was* an idiot. He'd hacked himself into a lethal apartment.

And he was stuck there.

Abe managed to get through his morning by remaining very still at his desk. Just before lunch, though, he had to take care of an issue in Monty's Gator Golf. Everyone else on his team was dealing with other pressing problems.

Monty's Gator Golf was packed when he reached it. Kids ranging from toddlers to teens filled the junglelike area, darting and yelling and giggling.

The whole of Gator Golf was neon green and decorated with palm trees and ponds. A holographic Montgomery Gator moved through the course during his performance, and his countenance was prominently displayed on much of the decor. The Gator Golf area wasn't just an eighteen-hole miniature golf course. It was also a play area; it had a golf-ball-themed carousel in addition to a ball pit and a catwalk. Of course dazzling light was everywhere.

Most of the golf course's holes were either jungle or gator inspired. But the fifth hole featured a rotating birthday cake that dripped with faux-chocolate frosting. The ball was supposed to be hit through a gap in the cake when it rotated to just the right point in its revolution. According to Abe's work order, the cake wasn't turning.

Abe grimaced when a couple of kids bumped into him and stepped onto the path that wound through the golf course. Breathing in the smells of sugary candy, spicy pizza, and kid sweat, Abe navigated through the course until he reached the cake. There, he chastised a little girl who was pounding on the cake with her golf club.

"Stop that," Abe told the curly-haired rascal.

The girl put her hands on her hips and glared at Abe. Her green eyes flashed, and she rubbed at an uptilted nose. "It's broken!"

"Yeah, well, pounding on it isn't going to fix it."

"That's what my daddy does to his computer when it doesn't work."

"Please go stand over there," Abe said with extreme patience. "I'll fix this in no time."

The girl smacked her lips and gave Abe a dirty look, but she did as he asked. Abe clenched his teeth as he slowly kneeled near the fake cake.

"My grandpa moves faster than you," the girl said.

"Good for him."

Abe tried to ignore the jabs of pain in his arms as he opened his toolbox.

"How come you look like a mummy?" the girl asked.

"How do you know I'm not a mummy?" Abe asked as he poked at the mechanism to troubleshoot the problem.

"Mummies don't talk. They moan."

Abe let out a long moan.

The girl giggled. "You're funny."

"Thank you. Now, if you'd please give me a minute, I'll fix this."

The girl lifted her golf club.

"If you hit the cake again," Abe said, "I'll sic Montgomery Gator on you."

The little girl stuck her tongue out at Abe. But she backed off.

It took fifteen minutes to fix the cake on the fifth hole and Abe felt every second. He said goodbye to the little girl, adding another mummy moan that made her giggle again, and went to the atrium to grab a slice of pizza. When he finished it, he looked at his watch. He still had a half hour of his lunch break left. He was hurting, and he probably should have returned to his desk, but whenever he sat alone, his mind replayed the horror of the previous night. He relived being showered with glass shards over and over. So Abe decided to head for Rockstar Row. Maybe watching all the happy families enjoying themselves would make him feel better.

Designed to give Pizzaplex visitors a breather between inhaling pizza and playing games, Rockstar Row was a museum-like area that celebrated Fazbear Entertainment's animatronics. Filled with neon-wrapped display cases that showcased both old and new versions of the popular robots, the gallery also had golden statues of all the Glamrock characters and greenrooms for each of the lead animatronics.

Abe paused in front of Roxy's greenroom and stared at the tires and racing flags that decorated the walls. The tires reminded him of his former hidey-hole, which he was once again thinking of fondly.

"They're all kind of full of themselves, aren't they?" a young woman's voice asked.

Abe blinked and turned to find a petite brown-haired girl with an almost impish face standing next to him. She flashed a very pretty smile and winked. Her eyes were a startling violet blue.

"Who are?" Abe asked. He looked around at all the kids and families.

The woman pointed at the life-size drawing of Roxy holding her keytar. "The animatronics. They exude confidence."

Abe shifted his gaze from the woman to Roxy's image. "I suppose they do. Is that a bad thing?"

"Maybe. Maybe not. I haven't decided. That's why I'm here."

"To decide whether or not the animatronics are too confident?"

The girl laughed. Her laugh was light and airy, like the flight of a butterfly. Abe liked the sound a lot.

"Not exactly," the girl said. "No, I'm . . . Wait. Why don't we start at the beginning?"

Abe stepped aside to avoid a couple of roughhousing boys. Although the crowds were thick around him and the woman, and the music and laughter were relentless, Abe felt like he'd stepped into a bubble. The woman seemed to push reality away from him. Even his pain diminished.

"What do you mean?" Abe asked.

The woman stuck out a small square hand with neatly trimmed unpainted nails. "I'm Sasha."

Abe smiled and shook her hand. Even through the bandage's gauze, he could feel it was soft, but the palm had a few calluses that suggested she didn't do a lot of sitting around doing nothing. "I'm Abe."

Sasha looked at the gauze encasing Abe's hand, but she didn't comment on it. "Nice to meet you."

"You too."

With her hair cropped short and her face clean of makeup, Sasha struck Abe as a straightforward kind of woman.

"Want to stroll with me?" she asked.

Abe nodded and offered his gauze-wrapped arm. Sasha didn't balk. She gently took his arm, and they began walking through Rockstar Row.

The crowd continued to press around them. Abe continued not to care about anyone but Sasha.

"I'm a social worker," Sasha said. "I work with troubled kids. One of my coworkers wants to bring some of our kids here for an outing, and I'm not sure it's a great idea. Don't get me wrong. I love the Pizzaplex and all things Fazbear. I'm a Freddy fangirl; I'm not ashamed to admit it. But when I started thinking about the animatronics and how they'd come across to kids with, well, issues, I wasn't sure this was the best place to bring them." Sasha looked at Abe's Pizzaplex uniform shirt. "You work here. What do you think?"

"Honestly?"

"What would be the point of anything else?"

Abe smiled. "Okay. Well, I think the Pizzaplex is a

great place for kids . . . to a point. The games are fun. The food's good. Kids love it here, but if I was a dad . . ."

"Go on."

"I wouldn't leave my kids unattended, and I'd make very sure they didn't spend too much time with the animatronics. The robots are fun, but they're—"

"A little over the top," Sasha supplied.

Abe nodded. He and Sasha zigged in perfect unison around a boisterous trio of teen girls who weren't watching where they were going.

"What games do you like?" Sasha asked.

"I'm partial to old-fashioned arcade games," Abe said.

Sasha grinned. "Let's go play."

Abe looked at his watch. "I have twenty minutes before I have to get back to work."

"We'll make the most of it."

And they did. Abe and Sasha managed to pack in two games of Skee-Ball and three games of pinball. The whole time, they laughed and joked. Abe was smitten.

"Would you have dinner with me tonight?" Abe blurted as they left the arcade.

"Sure!"

"Not here," Abe said.

"Obviously not."

Abe named a Chinese restaurant not far from the Pizzaplex.

"I'll meet you there," Sasha said. "Seven?"

Abe nodded. Sasha disappeared into the crowd.

The Golden Garden was a high-end Chinese restaurant, one Abe wouldn't have been able to afford before he got his promotion. The truth was, he could barely afford it now, but he wanted to take Sasha someplace nice.

The Golden Garden had dim, romantic lighting and plush, comfortable chairs. It was filled with the mouth-watering aromas of garlic and sesame oil.

"I've never been here," Sasha said when they were seated. "What's good?"

Abe pointed out a few menu items, and they agreed on sharing vegetable egg rolls, hot and sour soup, mu shu chicken, kung pao chicken, and vegetable fried rice.

"That's all perfect," Sasha said. "I don't eat beef."

"Neither do I anymore. Olive won't let me."

"Olive?"

Abe winced. Why had he said that? He decided to ignore the question.

"Why do you like the Pizzaplex so much?" he asked.

"Deflection. Okay. I'll let you get away with it. For now." Sasha gave Abe one of her delightful winks.

Abe smiled. "Thanks."

"No problem. I like the Pizzaplex, and the whole Fazbear franchise, because of the juxtaposition of the fun and mystery. I've read all the lore about the old locations. The scandals. The rumors. I'm a big mystery fan."

"Me too."

Sasha beamed. "I knew I liked you."

Abe flushed.

"But I also love fun," Sasha went on. "Fazbear Entertainment is a crazy mix of the two."

The waiter brought their egg rolls. For the next half hour, Abe and Sasha focused on their food and bantered about Freddy Fazbear.

When the fortune cookies arrived, Sasha cracked hers open and read, "'Secrets poison good relationships.'" She looked up. "Uh-oh. You know what that means."

Abe toyed with his own cookie. He didn't like fortune cookies. "What?"

"We need to circle back to what you said about Olive. Sorry. I can't let you off the hook any longer."

Abe pushed aside the fortune cookie. He looked at his hands. "You haven't asked me why I'm all bandaged up," he said.

"I figured you'd tell me if you wanted to."

Abe hesitated. Then he blurted, "I live in the Fazbear Tower. Olive is one of the holographic helpers in my apartment."

Sasha leaned forward. Her eyes sparkled. "Really? I've heard stories about the high-tech stuff in those apartments. Oh, you have to invite me to your place."

"I have to?"

"If you don't, I'll scream."

Abe widened his eyes, and Sasha laughed. "Not really. Or, yeah, maybe. Screaming works for my kids sometimes." She laughed again. "No, I won't scream. But I'd really love to see your place."

Abe tried to imagine Sasha in his apartment. What would she think of the Bobbiedots? What would they think of her? He thought about the shattered TV and coffee table in his living room.

Having Sasha over would be a very bad idea.

Sasha pressed her hands together, tilted her head, and batted her eyelashes. "Pretty please?" She grinned at him.

"Okay," Abe said. "For date two. I'll make you dinner."

"Awesome!" Sasha clapped her hands.

Abe immediately regretted what he'd done. But then again, he didn't.

He grinned. He was ridiculously happy. And he was very, very worried.

How was he going to keep Sasha safe when she came over?

★   ★   ★

A few days later, Abe walked into his kitchen carrying supplies he'd borrowed from the Pizzaplex's maintenance department. He looked up at the trapdoor in the ceiling, then he set his tools on the kitchen table. He dragged the table across the floor and positioned it under the trapdoor.

The nearest screen lit up and the Bobbiedots popped into view. "Are we rearranging furniture?" Rose asked. "Putting the table closer to the refrigerator is a great idea!"

Abe smiled as he climbed onto the table. "Sorry, Rose. This isn't where I'm going to leave the table." He picked up his tools and stood.

"Is something broken?" Olive asked. "I can provide instructions for repair."

Abe shook his head. "Thanks, but I've got this."

Abe kept his voice light, but he wasn't feeling relaxed. He didn't like being this close to the trapdoor.

Abe felt his heartbeat pick up now that they were watching, and pulled out a new heavy-duty lock hasp from his pocket. He positioned it on the ceiling and marked the spots for its screws.

"The trapdoor already has a lock," Olive pointed out.

"One that the gen1s can unlock, obviously," Abe said. "They won't have the key for this one." He quickly drilled the necessary holes for the hasp, and he installed it. Once he'd done that, he fitted a padlock through the sturdy hasp eyelet.

Abe climbed down off the table and gathered up his tools. He looked from the trapdoor to the Bobbiedots. "What do you think? Will that keep the gen1s contained?"

"It looks like a very strong lock," Gemini said.

"That was a very smart thing to do," Olive said.

"Now that you've done that, we can have the special dinner for your girlfriend," Rose said. "What are you fixing? Something yummy, I hope!"

Abe smiled. He rolled his shoulders to let go of the tension he'd been holding there. "Yes," he said. "I'll make something yummy." Abe returned the table and chairs to their usual position and gathered up his tools.

"I'll start cooking in a bit," he told Rose. "First, I need to clean the place up."

Thankfully, that morning, Abe had been able to dispense with his mummy look. His cuts, although still red and scabby, were healing well. He wasn't nearly as sore. That made the work he had ahead of him easier to manage.

Over the next hour, Abe removed all the debris from his apartment. He wasn't able to replace the broken table and TV, but the sitting area didn't look too bare without them. Everything else, he was able to clean up easily.

"Now are you going to make dinner?" Rose asked as soon as Abe put away the vacuum cleaner.

Abe grinned. "Yes, now."

Abe had decided to make fettucine alfredo with shrimp. Rose was over the moon. "And Caesar salad?" she asked. "You have to make a Caesar salad. With croutons."

"Sure, I can do that," Abe agreed.

"You must have flowers and candles," Gemini had said the previous evening when Abe had announced the upcoming date. "All romantic dinners require flowers and candles."

"Roses are the most common romantic flower," Olive said.

"I think I'm going with daisies," Abe had said. He'd already thought about it. Daisies were all he could afford, and he was pretty sure Sasha was more of a daisy girl than a rose girl.

"Daisies always set a fun and playful mood," Olive had said. "According to flower experts, daisies represent innocence, cheerfulness, and new beginnings. When you combine colors, they symbolize sincerity."

Abe had nodded. "Good to know."

Now Abe adjusted his multicolored daisies and simple white candles. He straightened the place settings. Everything was just right.

He looked around. The kitchen appeared to be safe enough. It would probably be okay while Sasha was here, as long as he was careful around the stove and avoided the garbage disposal and kept Sasha away from anything but the table.

But what traps might the gen1s have set during the day, before he locked the trapdoor?

Abe shifted his gaze to the Bobbiedots, who hovered on the nearby glass panels. "Bobbiedots, I need your help."

"Music? Do you need music?" Gemini asked.

"Actually, yes. Maybe some slow pop music."

A romantic ballad began playing from the speakers.

"Thanks," Abe said, "but what I really need is for all three of you to help me keep Sasha safe."

"Of course we will," Olive said.

"I appreciate you," Abe said, grinning. His Bobbiedots giggled. The appreciation issue had become an ongoing joke.

Abe wiped his hands on his apron and gave the alfredo sauce a stir. The sauce was smooth and had just the right thickness. Its buttery, garlicky aroma filled the kitchen.

The apartment's intercom buzzed. Abe adjusted his long-sleeve, button-down shirt. One of the shirts Landon, the previous tenant, had left. Abe chose it so he wouldn't scare Sasha with all his healing cuts.

Abe headed toward the door. When he opened it, he stared. Sasha looked amazing in a fitted short green dress.

She brushed past Abe and turned to look at him. "Um, are you expecting someone else?" Sasha asked.

Abe blinked at her. "What?"

Sasha gestured at the apartment door, which Abe continued to hold open. Abe laughed nervously and let go of the door. It closed with a click.

"Are you okay? You're looking at me like I've grown horns. Did I? You never know; anything's possible." Sasha batted at her head as if feeling for newly sprouted horns. "Nope, no horns. Whiskers?" She rubbed her hands over her clear, pinkish cheeks. "Nope. Whisker free." Sasha winked at Abe.

Abe gave her a weak grin. "Sorry."

"It's the dress, isn't it?" Sasha flushed and looked down at the clingy material that hugged her body like a second skin. "Is it too much? I was going to wear jeans, but my friend Meg made me dress up."

Abe shook his head several times. "No, the dress is great. Really great, actually."

"Aren't you going to introduce us?" Rose piped up.

Sasha turned toward the sound and looked at the Bobbiedots, who were clustered together on the glass panel at the edge of the sitting area. Sasha smiled and clasped her hands together. "Oh, hi! Aren't you three pretty?!"

Rose giggled. "Thanks. So are you! I'm Rose. This is Gemini and Olive." Rose gestured at her fellow Bobbiedots in turn.

"Very nice to meet you," Sasha said. "I'm Sasha."

"We know," Olive said. "He's been talking about you a lot."

Abe felt his face heat up. "Uh, I need to check on the pasta." Abe strode toward the kitchen.

Sasha followed him. So did the Bobbiedots.

"This is a very nice place," Sasha said. "So modern and open."

Abe stepped up to the stove. Careful not to put his

arm over another burner, he tested the pasta. Almost done. He turned to watch Sasha.

Sasha stepped into the kitchen, looked around, and then gazed past Abe toward the opening to the office. "You're into minimalism, aren't you?"

Abe shrugged. "Not really. This is how the place was when I moved in. I just haven't had a chance to do anything with it."

"If you want to redecorate," Olive said, "I can research styles and colors to give you options."

Sasha beamed at Olive. "Oh, that's so cool. It must be wonderful to have a helper like you."

"And me!" Rose said.

"And me," Gemini said.

"Of course," Sasha said. "Why don't you tell me about yourselves? What is it you do for Abe?"

The Bobbiedots began jabbering about their responsibilities. Sasha, attentive and complimentary, peppered them with questions and showered them with praise.

Abe took the pasta pot off the stove and walked over to the sink to drain the water. He added the drained pasta to the shrimp and alfredo sauce. Rose winked into view on the glass panel near the kitchen counter. "Oh, that looks delicious," she said. "But are you sure you made enough for all of us?"

Sasha looked at Rose. Her brow furrowed in puzzlement. Olive must have noticed the expression, because she said, "Don't mind Rose. She has food delusions. She's convinced she can eat."

Sasha smiled at Rose. "Well, then, you have to join us for dinner."

"No, she doesn't," Gemini said. "This is Abe's first romantic dinner. It's supposed to be for the two of you, not for us."

"But—" Rose began.

"Hush," Olive said. "We'll be back later."

Gemini and Olive disappeared from the glass screens. When Rose remained, Olive winked back into view, grabbed Rose's arm, and yanked her off the screen. The screens went dark.

Sasha looked at Abe and grinned. "They're delightful!"

Abe nodded. "Yeah, they're pretty fun." Abe gestured at the table. "Have a seat."

Sasha pulled out one of the padded, straight-backed gray chairs. "This all looks lovely. Oh, daisies! I love daisies. How did you know?"

Abe shrugged. "Good guess?"

Abe set plates of fettucine and salad in front of Sasha. She waited for Abe to sit down and then she picked up her fork and twirled pasta around its tines. She put the pasta in her mouth and chewed. "Mm, this is amazing! You made the sauce?"

"Yeah," Abe said.

"Wow. Cute. Funny. And he cooks. A triple threat!" Sasha laughed and dug into her salad.

Abe flushed. He took a bite of pasta.

"I guess I should tell you I can't cook," Sasha said. "Not worth a darn. I can't even boil water. The last time I tried, I forgot the water was on and the water boiled away and left me with a ruined pot."

Abe laughed. "Well, don't get too excited about me cooking. My mom taught me to make three things: fettuccine alfredo, spaghetti marinara, and tacos. Otherwise, I'm all about the sandwich."

"I can't even make sandwiches. They end up being either too dry or too squishy."

Abe laughed. "I bet you make the best squishy sandwiches in the world."

Sasha smiled. "Where is your mom? Does she live nearby?"

Abe frowned. "I wish she did. She's staying in a care center. She has dementia."

Sasha reached out and touched the back of Abe's hand. "I'm sorry."

"What about your folks?"

"My parents are dead. If they were alive, I'd want them close, too. I understand."

They continued to eat and chat. Abe was happy with how easy it was to be with Sasha. He thought the dinner was going well.

And the whole evening went well, too. After they ate, they hung out on the sofa and talked. Before Sasha left, Abe leaned in and kissed her.

She kissed him back.

It was the best kiss of his life.

Abe couldn't wait to write to his mom. As soon as Sasha left, he opened his laptop. He started typing immediately: *Hi, Mom, Guess what? I met someone. Her name is Sasha. She's smart and fun and pretty. I can't wait for you to meet her.* Abe filled several paragraphs telling his mom about his time with Sasha. By the time he closed his laptop, he couldn't stop smiling.

Even thoughts of the gen1s couldn't dampen his good mood. Although he had no idea what to do about them, he figured that if he stayed in his locked bedroom, he'd be okay for now. And he was too content at the moment to worry more about it.

Abe settled under the covers. And in spite of knowing robots lurked nearby and in spite of the pain of his cuts, he quickly fell into a deep sleep.

"Gobble, gobble, gobble!" Sasha shouted, doing a little victory dance at the foul line as the pinsetter under the neon pizza above the end of their lane set ten pins into place. The pins quivered a little before they settled, probably afraid that Sasha was going to wipe them out again with her spinning ball. They didn't have to worry. It was Abe's turn, and his ball, sadly, wasn't as dangerous.

Abe grinned as he stood to give Sasha a fist bump. "So, this is your hidden dark side—gloating when you're wiping out your opponent?"

"I have to warn you," Sasha had said as they'd taken their seats behind the scoring screen on lane three in Bonnie Bowl. "I'm kind of obsessive about bowling. I'm pretty good at it, and I can get a little competitive about it."

"No problem," Abe had said. "I'm not very good, so you can wipe the lane with me and I won't get upset."

Sasha laughed. "Okay. One lane wiping coming up."

It was late, and Bonnie Bowl was rocking. Most of the twenty-two lanes were being used, and the lines at the ice-cream and drinks counter were long. Kids chased one another up and down the white-neon-lit stairs that separated the snack and service area from the lanes themselves. They also ran up and down along the neon-star-covered end walls that flanked the lanes. The whole bowling alley was such bedlam that Abe couldn't imagine how anyone could concentrate enough to bowl well.

Sasha, however, was managing just fine. The overhead scoring screen was still flashing *Turkey!* as Sasha gobbled and danced her way back to the ball return.

A couple of teen girls in the next lane were giving Sasha dirty looks for her excessive celebration, but Sasha's self-congratulation didn't bother Abe at all. He thought it was cute; he especially liked the little hip wiggle in Sasha's victory dance.

When Sasha was done dancing around, Abe stepped

up to the line and threw a relatively accurate ball. He knocked down eight pins.

"Way to go!" Sasha called out from her seat at the scoring table. "Now get that spare!"

"Piece of cake," Abe said sarcastically. He figured he had about as much chance at the spare as he did at extricating himself from his ongoing apartment predicament.

Abe retrieved his ball and threw it again. The ball wobbled a little, hugged the edge of the gutter, then made a miraculous curve back toward the six and ten pins. The pins fell down. Abe whooped.

"Nice spare!" Sasha shouted, jumping up from her chair. When Abe got back to her, she gave him a quick kiss. The kiss made Abe even happier than the spare had done.

After Sasha finished annihilating Abe, she asked, "Want to bowl another line?"

Abe shook his head. "How about saving that for another night? There's something I'd like to talk to you about. Can we go for a walk?"

"Uh-oh. You sound serious." Sasha grinned and gave Abe a little nudge. "Do I need to be worried?"

Abe twisted his mouth. Was he doing the right thing?

He shrugged. "I think it's time I told you how I got all the cuts."

Sasha's grin faded. "Okay."

Abe didn't want to talk about his troubles inside the Pizzaplex. There were too many ears. He suggested he and Sasha walk to a nearby park. The evening was cool but clear, and Sasha said a walk beneath the stars sounded romantic.

By the time Abe and Sasha reached an isolated bench near a pond, Sasha probably had changed her mind about the romance. Abe had just finished giving her a detailed description of everything that had happened in the apartment, after telling her about the devious way he'd gotten it in the first place and why he'd been so desperate to get into it.

Now they sat in silence. Sasha hadn't spoken since Abe had started telling his story, but she'd listened intently. She was still holding his hand. That was a good sign. Wasn't it?

But after a full minute of listening to proverbial and literal crickets, Abe couldn't take it anymore. He cleared his throat. "You think I'm making it up, don't you?"

Sasha squeezed his hand. "Not at all." She shifted so she could look directly at him. "I totally believe you."

Abe exhaled loudly. "That's a relief. I was afraid you'd think I was crazy. Any normal person would—"

"I'm not a normal girl," Sasha said.

Abe smiled at her. "I think I love you."

Sasha laughed. "That's a conversation for another time. Right now we need to figure out what's really going on here." She cocked her head. "Are you sure the gen1s are trying to kill you?"

Abe jerked away from her. What kind of question was that?

He motioned to his healing cuts. "How else do you explain this?"

Sasha bit her lower lip. "Well, they could just be acting out. Maybe they don't really mean to hurt you. It could be they're just out of control and what's been happening to you is the fallout."

"I don't get it."

Another couple strolled into view. Sasha watched them go past, then she scooted closer to Abe and spoke in low tones. "Listen, the kids I work with, they've been through so much trauma that it messes with their heads. They act out. It's normal with kids who have been mistreated. They have so much pain inside that they need to let it out somehow. They usually let it out in totally inappropriate ways. Sometimes, they break things, steal things, and hurt their caregivers. They're not bad kids. They've just had really, really bad luck and they don't know how to deal with it. So, they get in trouble. What I'm thinking is that the gen1s might be doing something similar."

Abe thought back over all the ways he'd been injured. Could what Sasha was saying be true?

"If I were you," Sasha said, "I'd want to find out more about the previous tenant."

"Landon Prout."

"Yeah, Landon. Who was he? Did he do something to the gen1s? Is he the reason they're so badly damaged? If so, it might explain their behavior."

Abe thought about that. He had to admit he had wondered why the gen1s were in such bad shape. Was Landon Prout responsible for what had happened to them?

Abe wasn't sure he believed Sasha's theory, but she had a point about Landon. Maybe knowing more about his predecessor was a good idea.

"I'm pretty sure I have the gen1s contained," Abe said, "but it would be nice to know more. I'll do some digging."

Sasha laid her head against his shoulder. "Good. Until then, be really careful, huh? I don't know about the whole love thing, yet, but I am getting rather fond of you. If, for some reason, your padlock fails, I'd hate to see you sliced and diced and barbecued before we can see where this can go."

Abe smiled when he felt Sasha shake in silent laughter. He kissed the top of her head. "I'll do my best to stay in one piece."

It wasn't difficult to hack into the Pizzaplex's employee database. Abe got to his desk early the next day so he could do it before anyone else came in. Within minutes, he was looking at Landon's personnel file.

And Landon's file was very interesting.

His file was thick with psychological reports. Landon apparently was being treated for paranoia resulting from his work at the Pizzaplex.

"Landon exhibits the classic signs of delusional paranoid disorder," a report stated. "Landon feels persecuted by nearly everyone and everything in the Pizzaplex, and he believes in outlandish conspiracy theories related to Fazbear Entertainment. Landon's delusion is related directly to the animatronics, which he believes are stalking him and want to kill him."

Abe looked up from his screen and glanced around to be sure he was still alone. Was the poor guy really delusional or was he actually being stalked? After what Abe had been through, he had more sympathy for Landon than judgment.

Abe scrolled through the rest of Landon's file, but he didn't learn anything else. There was no record of Landon returning to work after his leave of absence and no record of his being hospitalized. Abe clicked through the file until he returned to Landon's contact info. There was a phone number.

Abe picked up his phone. He put it down. He picked it up. He punched in the number.

A woman who sounded half asleep (Abe looked at the clock and saw it was before 7:30 a.m. . . . . oops), answered with a "Whaa?"

"I'm really sorry to be calling so early, but I'm trying to reach Landon?"

The woman sucked in her breath. Then she started to cry. "Is this a joke?"

"What? No. Not at all. I just . . ."

"Landon's gone."

The phone clicked in Abe's ear.

"Hello?"

A dial tone answered him.

Abe put down his phone.

What did "Landon's gone" mean? Gone as in moved away? Gone as in missing? Gone as in dead?

Abe leaned back and looked out the window. Shaking his head, he turned to his desk and opened his email. He pulled his keyboard forward and began typing.

Hi Mom,

How are you feeling today? I'm doing okay. I have a little mystery on my hands. Remember how we used to watch mystery movies together? I'm going to have to put my thinking cap on to solve this one!
I love you.

Abe

Abe leaned back on Sasha's bright blue, well-cushioned sofa. Unlike Abe's place, Sasha's space was filled with color. Red walls, a wood floor painted with red, blue, and purple stripes, red-and-purple polka-dotted drapes, the bright blue sofa and matching chairs, an eye-catching array of vivid modern art and dramatic photographs that Sasha had taken, and an eclectic mix of knickknacks and trinkets in all shapes and sizes filled the apartment with character and pizzazz. Whereas Abe's place looked like it was staged for a magazine layout, Sasha's place looked lived in. Abe liked it.

"I did some more digging just before I came over here," Abe said as Sasha dished up the fish and chips she'd gotten from a food truck near her building, "but I didn't find anything else."

Sasha brought him a plate of fried food. He took it. The tangy scent of the lemon tucked against his battered cod tickled his nostrils.

Sasha sat down on the sofa next to Abe. "So, we don't know whether Landon was paranoid because the animatronics really were out to get him or whether he was paranoid because he just thought they were. Either way, if he lived in an apartment with robots, it's highly likely he might have tried to destroy them. I think what you found supports my theory."

Abe nodded. He thought so, too.

"But how does that help me?" he asked.

Sasha chewed a french fry. She swallowed it and picked up another one. She jabbed the air with the next fry as she spoke. "From what I've read about the Fazbear Entertainment animatronics, they're programmed to approximate human behavior. That suggests that the gen1s might quite reasonably be reacting to the damage Landon potentially did."

Sasha ate the pointer fry. After she swallowed, she picked up another fry. Abe stuck a fry in his own mouth. Sasha pointed her fry at Abe. "I think I should spend the night at your place."

Abe choked on his fry.

Sasha laughed.

"That's not what I meant." She swatted his thigh. "I'm not talking romance. I'm talking research. I want to observe the gen1s for myself."

"But I told you about the padlock," Abe said. Ever since Abe had installed the padlock, he'd made it part of his morning and evening routine to check it. This morning, his heart had dropped from his chest into his feet when he'd found the hasp dangling from its screws, which were nearly out of their holes. The gen1s had defeated the padlock hasp, so the padlock was useless.

"Yeah, I know," Sasha said. "They can get out again. And they're dangerous." She gestured at his red-scored arms. "Obviously. But I think you should let them come out, and we'll watch them. I'm trained to see the signs of acting out. And even if I wasn't, I might see something about them that you've missed because you're so freaked out."

Abe frowned and opened his mouth.

"That's not a diss," Sasha gently patted his arm. "Honestly. I'd be freaked out in your position, too. But because you've told me about everything instead of me experiencing it myself, I think I can look at things a little more objectively than you can. Whatever I might see in your apartment will be clearer to me. There's no shock factor gumming up my works."

Abe thought about that. It made sense. From the very first incident in his apartment, he'd been reacting instead of analyzing. Since he wasn't sure how to contain the gen1s now, maybe studying them wasn't a bad idea. And maybe a fresh set of eyes could help. But would it be safe?

"I'm not as fragile as I look," Sasha said, winking at Abe. She grinned.

Her grin did nothing to ease Abe's sudden tension. "I didn't think you were," he said, "but—"

"No buts. We'll go back to your place when we're done eating."

The Bobbiedots were very happy that Sasha was staying the night.

"Yay, a sleepover!" Rose squealed. "We have to have snacks!"

"Sleepovers have many benefits," Olive said. "They

are a great way to experience new things. They help build up independence. They strengthen relationships. They enhance communication skills."

"And they're fun!" Rose crowed.

Sasha laughed. She leaned toward Abe and whispered, "That list applies to kids' sleepovers, but she means well."

Abe glanced at Olive. Did Olive narrow her eyes at Sasha, just a little?

"I'll put on some music," Gemini said.

Soft rock began playing.

"How about crackers and cheese?" Rose said. "Or those little mini tacos in the freezer? Those would be good with some salsa and some—"

"We just had dinner," Abe interrupted.

Rose thrust out her lower lip.

"Why don't we all just go hang out in the bedroom," Sasha said. "And talk," she quickly added when Abe and the Bobbiedots gave her wide-eyed looks.

By the time 2:00 a.m. rolled around, the Bobbiedots had gone dark. Rose had winked out when it became clear that food wasn't in the forecast for the night. Gemini let out a dramatic sigh and disappeared when Sasha asked if the music could be turned off, and Olive signed off when Abe told her that her encyclopedic knowledge of bowling wasn't necessary during Abe and Sasha's discussion of their next bowling date.

Abe and Sasha had been too keyed up to sleep. After a while, they were even too antsy to talk. They ended up sitting next to each other, holding hands. Just listening.

At 2:08 a.m., Sasha gripped Abe's hand. "Did you hear that?" she whispered.

He nodded. The gen1s were coming out. He could hear the hushed snuffling sound of their cables brushing along the walls and partitions.

"Ready?" Abe whispered.

Sasha took a deep breath. She nodded.

Together, they got off the bed and crept to the bedroom door. Pausing there, they listened. The faint swishing sounds were moving away.

"Remember, be really quiet," he told Sasha.

She nodded again.

Abe used the Mr. Hippo magnet and unlocked the door.

They padded softly out into the sitting area. Abe pointed. Sasha's eyes widened when she saw Two's ghastly, torn torso slink over the sofa and head toward the kitchen. To her credit, though, Sasha didn't make a sound.

Abe pointed again. Sasha turned to watch One and Three move around the dining table and split up. One went into the office. Three roamed around the kitchen.

Roamed wasn't the right word, though. Three wasn't meandering. She was moving purposefully, as if on a mission. Abe and Sasha stepped close to the panel separating the sitting area from the kitchen. Sasha turned to watch Two. Abe watched both Sasha and Two.

When Two bent over a plug-in socket, Sasha nudged Abe. She pointed emphatically at the decrepit robot.

Abe watched as Two pulled out a couple of wires from the socket and disconnected them. Abe raised an eyebrow as he noticed that one of the wires, a thin, exposed copper wire, ran from the plug to the floor and extended from there along the length of the baseboard toward the apartment door. What was that wire doing there, and why did Two disconnect it?

Sasha tugged on Abe's sleeve. He leaned down.

"I think they're trying to help you, not hurt you," Sasha whispered.

Her whisper was low. Unfortunately, it was not low enough.

Two let out a screech. One and Three immediately joined in. All three gen1s sprinted toward Sasha and Abe.

Abe yelled, "Run!"

Because Two was between him and the bedroom, Abe ran around the sofa and bolted toward the dining area. He assumed Sasha would be right behind him.

When he got to the dining table, he looked back. Sasha hadn't followed him.

The gen1s were still careening toward Sasha, but when they reached her, they didn't touch her. Their cables thrashed around them. When one of Three's cables flicked toward Sasha, she leaned back out of its reach. She turned to watch the gen1s circle around and head back toward the kitchen. Back toward Abe.

They don't care about Sasha, Abe thought. They were after him and only him. *Just because you're paranoid doesn't mean they're not out to get you,* Abe thought.

Abe turned and ran into the kitchen. The robots kept coming. They surrounded him. Their cables tangled around him like the arms of an enraged octopus. He dodged right and left to avoid the cords' biting assault.

Abe's heart pounded. He could hear its thrumming in his ears.

He was doing better than he'd done the last time he'd encountered the gen1s, though. For the most part, he was evading the gen1s' grasping hands and writhing cables. He only felt a few stings.

Abe leaped over Two's scuttling form and started to run past the refrigerator just as one of Three's cables snagged the huge appliance. The fridge toppled toward Abe.

Surrounded, Abe couldn't move fast enough to get out of the way. He screamed and threw up his hands.

The gen1s swarmed over the top of him. Abe flailed, batting away the robots' hands and cables. He was out of his head with panic. It felt like he was being smothered and compressed and cleaved into a dozen parts.

Suddenly, Abe felt Sasha's hand close over his.

"Come on," Sasha shouted.

Abe wasn't sure he could move. The gen1s were overwhelming him.

But he let Sasha pull him, and in a matter of seconds, amazingly, he was free of the robots' clutches. Only the tips of their cables swiped at his legs as he teetered after Sasha.

Sasha let go of Abe's hand and grabbed his arm. She took most of his weight as she helped him hurry around the sofa and shoot toward the bedroom doorway.

Once they were through the door, Sasha slammed it shut. She locked it. Abe shoved the dresser in front of it.

Breathless, Abe bent over and panted. Sasha put a hand on his shoulder, catching her own breath as well.

Finally, Abe straightened. "See what I mean?"

Sasha shook her head. "Actually, I don't."

Abe gaped at her.

Sasha took Abe's hand and led him to the bed. She sat and pulled him down next to her.

Together, they listened to the gen1s' retreat. Sasha looked up when she heard a scraping sound overhead.

After several seconds, the sound stopped. The apartment went quiet.

Sasha turned and looked into Abe's eyes. "They're not trying to hurt you," she said. "They're trying to protect you."

"What?!"

Sasha grabbed Abe's forearm. "I understand. You're freaked, but I want you to think about what you saw in the living room. You saw Two disconnect those wires. Right?"

Abe nodded. "Yeah. What was she doing? I've never seen that one wire before, the one that led to the door."

"I think that wire was part of a trap. If it was connected to the plug's circuit, the apartment door would have been electrified. It could have killed us if we'd reached for the door handle. I think Two was undoing a trap, not setting one."

Abe replayed the scene in his mind. Sasha was right.

"Okay, but they tried to get me in the kitchen," he said.

Sasha shook her head. "They weren't trying to get you. They were trying to help you."

"But they were all over me."

Sasha nodded. "I know. But remember, we're dealing with damaged robots. They can't function well. I know it felt like they were swarming you, but they were actually trying to shield you. I saw the whole thing. I think they were trying to be like bodyguards, surrounding you to keep dangers away. Didn't you see what happened when the fridge started to fall?"

"Three pulled it over."

"No. Three tried to stop it when it started to fall over. She didn't start it."

"But—"

"I saw it, Abe. I saw the whole thing. They were all around you, trying to make, like, I don't know, a fortress around you or something. The fridge started to fall. Three whipped out a cable to try to snag it because she wasn't close enough to grab it. Then they all covered you, and while they covered you, they shoved the fridge so it didn't go all the way over."

Abe tried to remember the sequence of events. Was that true?

He attempted to untangle all the sensations he'd felt.

But he couldn't do it. The experience was a snarl of pinching, swiping, and pressing.

"The fridge didn't fall," Sasha said. "If they'd wanted the fridge to crush you, you'd be crushed. But it didn't fall. It tipped, and they pushed it back."

Abe opened his mouth to argue, but he had nothing. If the fridge didn't fall, then what happened?

Abe thought about all his encounters with the gen1s. Had they really been trying to help him all along?

Abe tried to remember what he'd seen the gen1s doing before they'd attacked him the first time . . . if they had really attacked him. Had he just perceived their actions as an attack when it really wasn't? He tried to dissect the memory and figure out what he'd really experienced. Had the gen1s actually meant to hurt him or had they hurt him by accident?

Abe thought even further back.

The first time Abe had seen the gen1s, he'd expected them to be bad. And he'd been repelled.

The creepy cables. The broken exoskeletons. The missing eyes. The ripped-off limbs. The gen1s were like robotic undead. They had looked like android villains, so he'd expected them to act like android villains.

Abe remembered how he was never able to actually catch the gen1s sabotaging the apartment. He'd assumed they'd just been too subtle for him. But what if they hadn't been sabotaging the apartment at all? What if they'd been checking for sabotage instead? He'd seen them feel around as if inspecting the area for potential problems.

He'd completely misinterpreted the broken gen1s' actions. They weren't murderous. They were really just, because of their damage, clumsy and inefficient.

Abe rubbed his face. "Okay, so for the sake of

argument, let's say the gen1s are protecting me. Who are they protecting me from?"

"The answer's pretty obvious, don't you think?" Sasha said. She widened her eyes and tossed her head as if trying to signal him in some way. Abe didn't get it.

Sasha sighed. "Think, Abe. If it's not the old robots, it's . . ." She looked pointedly at the glass panels that surrounded the bedroom.

Abe looked at the glass panels, too. He got it.

It was the gen2s after all.

Abe goggled at the darkened glass. Even though he couldn't see them, he could almost feel the gen2s hovering.

The holographic Bobbiedots ran everything in the apartment. And they were never turned off. Even when they were dormant, they'd woken up the night that One and Two attacked him, hadn't they?

That meant they were listening.

Abe grabbed Sasha's hand.

They sprang off the bed, galloped across the room, and shoved the dresser aside. Abe threw open the bedroom door; they tore toward the apartment door.

They were just a few feet from the apartment door when all the apartment lights went out, and the glass panels in the apartment activated. The Bobbiedots converged, one on each of the three closest screens. All of them had their mouths open wide in maniacal grins. All of them were brighter than they'd ever been. Their eyes were nearly double in size. Their pigtails gyrated around their heads like angry serpents.

Abe couldn't believe what he was seeing. It was the worst betrayal of his life.

"Come on!" Sasha shouted. She tugged him toward the door.

Abe, stupefied, reeled after her. His legs felt like rubber. His heart was battering his chest.

Sasha grabbed the apartment door handle. She pressed it down.

Nothing happened.

Abe put his hand on Sasha's. He pushed, too.

Nothing.

The apartment door was locked.

They couldn't get out.

"Can you reach it?" Abe asked.

Abe stood with his feet planted wide to keep himself steady. Sasha sat on his shoulders, her legs tucked around his chest.

"Yeah, barely," Sasha said.

Abe looked up at the bobbing yellow circle of light cast by the small flashlight Sasha held in her mouth. He listened to the long metallic scrape of his butcher knife against the ceiling. Sasha grunted.

As soon as they'd realized they were trapped, Abe and Sasha had looked around. What could they do?

Going out the window wasn't an option. Shouting for help wouldn't do any good—Abe was sure the units were soundproofed.

The apartment had started going haywire. Sparks flew from light sockets and plugs. The fridge in the kitchen fell over. Burners came on. Water poured from faucets. Music and news reports blasted.

The Bobbiedots had surged from glass panel to glass panel, a blur of helter-skelter motion that made no sense at all. Their colors pulsed, nearly blinding. Their faces contorted. Static danced around them and cascaded through the apartment.

Abe had no idea what to do.

Good thing his girlfriend had kept her head on straight.

"We need to get up to the gen1s," Sasha had said urgently.

"What?! Why?"

Sasha had grabbed Abe's shoulders and shook them. "Get a grip. Who's been helping you?"

Abe blinked. "Yeah, but what if their version of helping kills us?"

A flashing blue arc of electricity had shot their way. Sasha and Abe had ducked and scurried out of its path.

"Can it be any worse than this?" Sasha had snapped.

She had a point. "Okay," Abe said.

Both of them had looked up at the high ceilings.

"If you stand on the table"—Sasha pointed at the dining table—"and I sit on your shoulders, I think I can reach it."

Narrowly avoiding a flying glass end table, Sasha and Abe had run for the dining table. They'd clambered up onto it. She climbed onto his shoulders.

"I can reach it," she said. "But it won't budge."

"Is there a lock?"

"Hang on a second."

The dining table had slid across the floor. Sasha swore. Then she said, "I can't see. There might be a mechanism I can jimmy. I need a flashlight and something to slide into the crack."

The kitchen had been going crazy around them, but Abe had left Sasha on the table while he dodged flying canned goods and plates to get to the drawer that held the cutlery and the miscellany drawer, where he kept a small flashlight. A pot had grazed his head and a skillet had whacked his ear, but Abe had been able to reach the drawers. He grabbed the flashlight first, then he reached for a butcher knife. As he did, all his other knives shot out of the drawer.

"Sasha, duck!" Abe had shouted as he'd hit the floor. The

knives had whizzed past above his head. He heard them thunk against the glass panel behind the dining table. The glass didn't break. The knives had clattered to the floor.

Abe had leaped up and jumped back onto the dining room table.

And now Sasha was prodding at the trapdoor crack with the butcher knife. All Abe could do was try to hold her steady as the table bucked under them and more kitchen utensils flew at them.

Abe and Sasha grunted every time something hit them. Abe's forehead was pulsing from the impact of a flying spatula. Sasha's arm was bleeding from the slap of a cheese grater.

For reasons Abe didn't understand, once the projectiles hit the floor, they stayed there. That was good. If the knives levitated and came at them again, that would be the end. He couldn't dive out of the way with Sasha on his shoulders.

"Can you get it?" Abe asked, cringing when a cutting board slammed against his hip.

Sasha didn't answer. Abe looked up to see Sasha barely avoid another jolt of electricity arcing down from the kitchen ceiling light. Abe heard more scraping.

The table lurched. Abe gritted his teeth and replanted his feet. He clutched at Sasha's thighs with all his might. He was not going to drop her, no matter what.

The hard rock music that had been playing since the apartment locked down shifted to frenzied classical music. The sound seemed to dive under Abe's skin. He could feel it hurtling through his nervous system, trying to tear him apart from the inside.

"I think I've almost got it," Sasha said.

Abe hoped he could last that long. His legs were about to give out. His brain was perilously close to fried.

To distract himself, Abe tried talking to the

Bobbiedots. "Why are you doing this?" he called out. "I thought we were friends."

"You never share your food!" Rose wailed.

"You don't appreciate us!" Gemini cried.

"You take us for granted!" Olive shouted.

"But—" Abe began.

"Save your breath!" Sasha yelled. "I've got it!"

Abe heard a snap and a thunk, and Sasha's weight lifted from his shoulders. He looked up to see her disappearing up through the hole in the ceiling. Seconds after she was out of sight, she leaned out through the open trapdoor. She reached toward him.

"Grab my hands!"

"You're not strong enough to pull me up!"

"No, but you can climb up my arms," she shouted. "I'm strong enough for that. Just grab on and pretend I'm a rope."

Abe opened his mouth to argue, but the table started to slide out from under him. Electricity began to gather in a network of slashing blue light along the baseboard in the kitchen. The strands of crackling power began building and reaching outward. Abe had no choice. He grabbed one of Sasha's arms.

Using the same hand-over-hand motion he'd been taught to use for rope climbing, Abe crawled up Sasha's extended arm until he could get a grip on the trapdoor's frame. Once he had two hands on the frame, Sasha backed out of view.

Abe did the best pull-up he'd ever done in his life until he'd hauled his upper body into the crawl space. From there, he leaned forward and groped around for something to hang on to so he could pull himself farther in. His hands encountered the cold, hard edges of a metal ceiling joist. Abe gripped the joist and levered himself up through the opening. As soon as he was through the doorway, the Bobbiedots' screams reaching in behind him, the trapdoor slammed shut.

★ ★ ★

Abe didn't move for several seconds. He just rested his throbbing, bleeding forehead on the metal joist under him and listened to Sasha's labored breathing behind him. Below the ceiling, the Bobbiedots' enraged rantings continued. The squeal of strings continued to blast from the speakers.

Abe shifted his weight, trying to get a feel for the crawl space. The bottom of the crawl space consisted of drywall attached to metal joists, which were placed sixteen inches apart. Abe was pretty sure the drywall wouldn't hold their weight; they'd had to balance on the metal joists.

Abe tried to shift his weight again, seeking a more comfortable position.

"Be careful," Sasha whispered. "The . . ."

Before she could say anymore, the gen1s started wailing. The sound was deafening. And close.

Abe flipped over and sat up. He didn't even think about whether there would be enough room for him to sit upright. He just knew he didn't want to be lying down when the gen1s found them.

Thankfully, when Abe sat up, his head ended up a couple inches below the joists above him. Propping his legs on the joists under him, he shifted to face the chilling sound. He stiffened when he looked into the glowing eyes of the three gen1s.

Two luminous blue orbs, one shining pink orb, and one large blazing green orb were just three feet from Abe. In the dim glow of the small flashlight Sasha aimed at the gen1s, Abe could see One's and Three's cracked white exoskeletons and Two's battered metal endoskeleton. Their cables coiled around them like a knot of enmeshed black worms. Abe shivered. He started to back away.

Sasha's hand closed over his arm. He nearly jumped out of his skin.

"It's okay!" She had to yell to be heard above the gen1s' screams.

Abe didn't think it was okay at all. His gaze was locked on the twitching cables. He imagined them reaching out to ensnare him and choke him, all in the service of misguided protection.

Completely frozen, unable to even think much less figure out what to do next, Abe watched as the gen1s continued to bawl and shudder. His eyes widened when Sasha, perched on two ceiling joists next to Abe, started to scoot closer to the gen1s.

"Don't!" Abe cried out. He caught Sasha's hand and pulled her back just in time.

Writhing black cables surged out of the darkness and whipped between Sasha and the shadows. The gen1s' scratchy caterwauls got even louder.

Even so, Sasha tried to calm the robots. "Shh," Sasha said. "We know you're trying to help. We know."

The broken screeches ended abruptly. In the silence, Three's single pink eye glowed brighter. Then One's blue eyes and Two's green eye brightened.

"I'm so sorry you've been hurt," Sasha said to the gen1s.

Abe turned to look at Sasha's profile. She was pale, and she had a cut on her cheek. Blood trickled from the gash and ran down her neck.

She was amazing.

"Can any of you talk?" Sasha asked the gen1s.

A prolonged hiss preceded a choking gurgle. Then Three's mouth creaked as it hinged open.

"Kill," Three said. The word came out in several stuttered syllables that sounded like metal clicking on metal. "We killed."

Abe shuddered and tried to pull Sasha back away from the gen1s. She resisted him.

"Who did you kill?" Sasha asked calmly as if she was discussing the weather.

Three continued to speak in distorted words, words wrapped in hisses and gurgles and punctuated by clicks. Her words, however, were clear enough.

"We killed Landon," Three said.

Abe's breath caught in his throat. Was Sasha wrong after all?

"Why did you kill Landon?" Sasha asked.

The cables that trailed out of the darkness surged upward like a black eruption. The gen1s' eyes glowed brighter.

"Landon was going to burn down the tower," Three said. "We could not let him do that. It went against our programming."

"What are you programmed to do?" Sasha asked.

"We are programmed to protect the tenant and protect the building. The building's protection is paramount. It overrides the need to protect the tenant."

"Okay," Sasha said in the same even tone she'd used since she'd started chatting with the gen1s.

Abe was in awe of Sasha. If she wasn't here, Abe was sure he'd be dead by now. He'd have been so panicked and knee-jerk in his reactions that he wouldn't have had a snowball's chance in hell of having this conversation.

A loud thud sounded from the apartment below. What were the Bobbiedots doing down there? Could their systems reach up here? He decided it was time for him to speak up.

Summoning up his courage, Abe looked at Three's glowing eye. "Do you know why the gen2 Bobbiedots are trying to kill me?"

"The gen2s assigned to this unit are experimental," Three began.

Abe had to work hard to ignore the continued hisses and clicks. He also had to concentrate to hear the words through all the distortion.

In spite of the extensive damage to her vocal processer, Three had a lot to say about the Bobbiedots. "The gen2s were programmed differently than we were and differently than the gen2s in the other units in the building. Their programming was intended to give them more confidence and autonomy. That programming gave the gen2s a sense of superiority. They think humans are like parasites that upset the balance of things. They want to remove humans so the AI system can be pure and smooth functioning. They won't stop until they have achieved their goal."

Even though the gen1s—with their broken metal limbs, glowing eyes, and undulating cables—continued to freak him out, Abe found himself responding to Three's explanation. "But they acted like they liked me."

"The gen2s are fascinated by humans," Three said. "They love. They hate. At the same time."

Sasha reached for Abe's hand. They clutched at each other.

"Any idea how we're going to get out of this alive?" Abe asked Sasha.

Sasha looked at Three's pulsing pink eye. "Do you know how to deactivate the gen2s?"

"The tenant can manually initiate a system update," Three said.

Abe shook his head. "I suggested doing that when I thought you three were trying to hurt me. Rose said it couldn't be done."

Three's cables whipped out, barely missing Abe's knee. "She lied," Three said.

For some reason, Rose's lie made the gen2s' betrayal even

more painful. Abe shook off his silly hurt feelings. "Okay," he said, "so if I do the update, that will deactivate them?"

Three's cables quivered around her skull. "That only stops their current actions temporarily. After you do the update, you have to cut the power to wipe out the gen2s. At the panel on the wall in the office."

Abe imagined the distance between the trapdoor and the office. He opened his mouth to ask how they were going to do that without being electrocuted or crushed, but a deafening metallic crack stopped him.

Abe turned to look behind him, just in time to see a pipe running along the outside wall of the crawl space burst open. Water began spewing from it like a geyser, creating a rushing current that coursed through the crawl space.

The gen1s screamed. They crawled closer to Sasha and Abe. Abe, staring at their broken metal endoskeletons and exposed wires, started to shrink back, but Sasha held him in place. "They're trying to protect us," Sasha said.

Abe looked at the water sluicing through the crawl space. It was filling the troughs between the ceiling joists, creating a gridwork of rivers above the drywall.

"I don't think they're going to be able to do much," Abe shouted. "That drywall isn't going to hold up to the water."

"That was what I was trying to warn you about earlier," Sasha shouted back. "I put my hand on the drywall, and it started to give."

Abe nodded.

Once the drywall gave way, even if they could cling to the ceiling joists, the gen2s would have open access to them. And with water churning around them, how would they hang on to the joists without drowning?

Abe looked around for something he could use to clamp off the burst pipe. Or something he could use as a weapon. Other than the gen1s themselves, he saw nothing.

And suddenly, the gen1s vanished as the drywall gave way. The entire apartment ceiling—the floor of the crawl space—collapsed and dropped into the apartment below.

The gen1s, not well-balanced on the ceiling joists, were immediately caught in the waterfall, and they tumbled out of the crawl space, falling down into the apartment. Sasha and Abe attempted to hold on to the metal joists, but the gen1s' trailing cables ensnared them, and they, too, were pulled free of the crawl space. Their bodies, along with chunks of drywall, plummeted downward.

The drop was so sudden and fast that Abe didn't even have time to yell out. Sasha was silent, too.

Abe tried to see past the sheet of water that carried them downward. Through the blur, he saw Sasha's arm and tried to grab it. He knew the landing was going to be hard, and he wanted to try to get her on top of him.

But he didn't have time.

They landed.

And they lucked out. They both ended up on the sofa, which was now sitting diagonally across the living room, having been tossed around the apartment during the gen2s' tantrum.

Abe scrambled to his feet. He started to jump off the sofa. He wanted to get to the door, in the hopes that the water had somehow made escape possible.

Sasha grabbed Abe's arm. "Don't! Look!"

Sasha pointed at sparkles sizzling at the bottom of the apartment walls. Undulating spikes of blue were skimming along the surface of the water pooling on the floor. The flooded apartment was electrified.

The gen1s' screams grabbed Sasha's attention. She turned toward them. Abe followed the direction of her gaze.

The gen1s were caught in the electrical currents. They were writhing as if in agony, their limbs windmilling, their cables flapping. Around them, the water level was rising. It was nearly to the bottom of the sofa's seat.

Sasha stared at the gen1s' agony in horror.

Abe grabbed Sasha's hand and pointed at the water level. "We have to get higher!" he shouted. "We need to get on top of a partition."

Sasha wiped her face with the back of her hand and looked around. She nodded.

Abe boosted Sasha onto the top of the nearest partition, even though Gemini's teeth-bared face filled the partition's glass panel. He noticed Sasha grit her teeth as her leg slid over Gemini's holographic image. He didn't blame her. He didn't want to touch the panels, either. It was like touching the gen2s.

But the gen2s were holograms. They were energetic projections. They clearly had the ability to use that energy to affect inanimate matter like furniture and kitchen utensils, but they couldn't grab on to Sasha or Abe. All Gemini could do when Sasha's foot was planted on top of Gemini's head was cry out in anger.

Abe ignored the cries as he followed Sasha onto the narrow chrome shelf that topped the panel.

Water still poured from the ceiling. Abe wiped his eyes and looked toward the main terminal between the living area and the kitchen. It was at least fifteen feet away. The panel they were on didn't extend that far. They were going to have to jump to three other half walls before they could reach the one that they needed.

Abe started to try to rise to his feet.

"I have to get to the main terminal."

Sasha nodded, understanding his plan.

Abe carefully repositioned his leg so he could get his foot under him. Once he'd done that, he started to raise himself up.

The six-foot width of the chrome panel tops created a surface that was sufficiently stable to stand on, or it would have been if the chrome wasn't water drenched. The wetness, unfortunately, made the metal slick. As Abe attempted to get his balance, he felt like he was trying to ice-skate on a high wire.

Twice, as Abe started to rise to his full height, his feet slipped. Twice, Sasha grabbed his leg to keep him from sliding down the panel into the water below.

Finally, Abe got his footing.

Sasha lifted her hand. "Help me up."

"Why don't you wait here?" Abe protested.

Sasha pointed at the water, which was rising even faster now. "I don't mind waiting, but I'd rather be standing than kneeling. That way, I can move quicker if I need to."

Abe nodded. He took Sasha's hand and helped her transition to a standing position.

To get and keep his balance on the partition, Abe had been forced to block out everything that was going on around him. Now he glanced around.

The gen2s were popping in and out of view on the panels. One second, they were close, ranting and raving. The next second, they were on distant panels, flickering in and out of focus. The apartment lights were still out, but the gen2s' bright colors flashed like menacing rainbows throughout the space. Below the streams of colored light, the water kept rising and the electricity continued to spark. The gen1s' agony went on.

When Sasha reached a standing position, Abe realized they had another problem. The partition was starting to wobble.

Now they not only had to ice-skate on a high wire, they had to surf at the same time.

"I think the best thing to do is move fast," Sasha said.

"The more we hesitate, the more chance we have of falling."

Abe wasn't sure that was true, but he didn't think it was a good time for a debate. He did have one question, though. "We? I thought I was doing it alone."

Sasha gestured at the partition. "Do you think this thing is going to hold when you leap off it?"

Abe got her point. "You're right."

"We'll go together," Sasha said.

Abe nodded.

Slowly and mincingly, Abe and Sasha rotated so they were facing the next partition.

"On three," Sasha said.

"One," Abe started. "Two. Three."

Sasha and Abe jumped as one person, but Abe, his legs much longer than Sasha's, reached the next panel first. He reached it so quickly that his momentum nearly took him over the top of it. He had to jerk himself backward to stop his forward progress. And at the same time, he had to pull Sasha toward him. Her foot hadn't quite landed on the top of the panel, and she was starting to skid downward toward the lethal water.

"I've got you!" Abe shouted before he was actually sure that he did.

Thankfully, Abe was able to pull Sasha close and give her a chance to find purchase on the chrome shelf. As soon as she did, however, the partition began to sway. It was giving way just like the last one.

"We have to do it again!" Abe yelled. "Now!"

Water continued to pour over them. They both sputtered and snorted, swiping at their eyes so they could see.

Another leap. Another slip-sliding landing on the next partition. Abe's feet skidded sideways along the top of the panel as he landed. Sasha once again barely made it.

She got only one foot on the top of the chrome. Her other one began skimming downward.

Abe gave Sasha a yank. Her dangling foot groped for the top of the chrome and found it.

This partition, like the last two, began to wobble, teetering dramatically. Both Sasha and Abe threw their arms out to keep their balance.

"One more!" Abe yelled.

"One. Two. Three," Sasha shouted.

They leaped again.

This time, Abe nailed his landing, his feet square on the top of the chrome shelf. And because this panel was near the cabinet cutout that had surrounded the refrigerator before the gen2s had started throwing things around, he was able to grab the edge of it to steady himself.

And that was fortunate . . . because Sasha's landing wasn't as good.

As soon as Sasha's feet hit the chrome, they skidded off and headed down the glass. Sasha grabbed for the glass panel, and she was able to catch herself, but she was dangling, perilously close to the water below. She let out a terrified howl.

Abe immediately reached down and grabbed Sasha's arm. Grunting, digging deep to find every ounce of strength he had left, he pulled Sasha straight up until her feet were settled next to his.

The panel began its inevitable seesawing.

Abe quickly turned and faced the main terminal.

His fingers flew across the keyboard on the glass panel and he initiated the system update.

Sasha shouted, "Look!"

Abe turned, clutching the fridge enclosure, and watched as the gen2s' images began to deconstruct. Their bodies came apart and then joined together again in topsy-turvy ways. Feet came out of the tops of their heads. Their pigtails streamed from their bellies. Their hands jutted out from their eyes. They began spewing words, but none of them made sense together.

"Cookies, research, over, review, pets, stronghold, threat, romantic, new, inventory . . ." On and on a non-sensical stream of words filled the apartment.

The gen2s' systems were crashing, but they were still just as active. Abe turned and looked at the two partitions he needed to reach to get to the office. He coiled, getting ready to leap.

Before he could, the dining room table, caught in the sparkling and swirling water, shifted violently. It slammed into the partition closest to Abe and took it out. The partition went over like a felled tree, slapping the water and sending sparks flying.

"Oh no," Sasha moaned.

Abe understood her despair. There was no way he could get to the office now. He couldn't jump far enough to reach the next partition beyond the one that had just bit the dust.

Had all this struggle been for nothing?

As if confirming their impending doom, the partition they were balanced on canted sharply. Both Abe and Sasha lost their footing and began slipping down the glass.

Abe's gaze locked on the waiting electrified water. It was going to be the last thing he would ever see.

Suddenly, the water seethed.

The gen1s burst up through the roiling waves. Electricity still crackling over their metal endoskeletons, the gen1s, en masse, extended their cables outward. The black cords shot this way and that, snapping through the air, reaching out of the sitting area, into the kitchen, beyond into the office, and also into the bedroom. Within seconds, the end of each cable was linked to an electronic connection. Cables plugged into wall sockets and computer terminals. They crisscrossed the entire apartment like electrical gridwork.

A deafening pop filled the apartment. Shiny trails of electrical current crawled up the walls and spiraled across the ceiling. Sputters and pings and fizzles chased one another through the space.

The gen1s let out resounding squalls that vibrated all the way through Abe's body. Then they were silent. The water's swells flattened out. The gen1s went limp and sank beneath the water's surface.

The glass panels darkened. The overhead lights came on.

Abe and Sasha finished their slide down the partition. They landed thigh deep in water . . . and they didn't die.

Sasha looked up at Abe. "What just happened?"

Abe shook his head. "I think they fried the whole system."

Sasha sloshed over to Three, who lay on her back under the water, her one eye dark. "Oh, the poor things," Sasha said.

The wall phone in the kitchen rang. Abe looked at it.

Exchanging a glance with Sasha, Abe waded toward the phone.

"Yes?" he answered.

"Maintenance," an automated voice said. "We have a flood warning for your unit."

Abe thought of Sasha's "File that under 'duh'" saying. He smiled. "Yeah, I'm sorry. The tub overflowed."

"Not a problem. We'll send someone up in a bit for cleanup."

Abe got off the elevator and repositioned the heavy bag he had slung over his shoulder. Two young guys Abe recognized from the Pizzaplex's marketing department were waiting to get in the elevator.

"Hey, Abe," one of the guys said.

"Hey, Pete."

"Did you see the game Saturday?" Pete asked.

Abe nodded, then shook his head. "No defense."

"You got that right." Pete shook his head, too. He and the other man, Dean, got on the elevator and waved as the doors closed.

Abe smiled. It was so nice not to have to hide from his neighbors anymore.

The fallout from the flooded apartment, and the fact that Abe occupied it, hadn't been nearly as bad as he'd expected it would be. Apparently, the tower's administrators were so happy that Abe's unauthorized tenancy had resulted in solving the apartment's Bobbiedots issues that they decided to overlook how Abe got in the apartment to begin with, and how much damage had resulted before all was said and done.

Abe whistled as he strode down the hallway. He couldn't believe how great the last three months had been. He'd gone from total isolation and near death to living the life of his dreams.

Abe looked down the hall and saw Sasha pushing open the apartment door with her hip. Her arms were filled with bags of groceries.

"Hey, you're off early, too?" Abe called out. He hurried to get to her so he could help with the bags.

Sasha turned and smiled up at him when he reached her. "Hey, handsome," she said.

"Hey, delusional." He grinned and bent over to kiss her. As always, the kiss made his toes curl.

"Let me take those," Abe said.

"Thanks, but I've got them." Sasha flashed a big smile.

Together, they stepped into the apartment and let the door close behind them. Abe looked around at the apartment's new colorful decor.

After the apartment had been cleaned up and repaired, he and Sasha had decided that they were better together than apart. Because she loved the idea of the tower, in spite of what they'd endured, they'd moved all her bright, cozy furnishings and curtains and artwork and knickknacks into his space. The apartment no longer looked cold and barren. It was filled with vibrant, joyful life—like Sasha herself.

The apartment was going to have another new addition, too. At Sasha's suggestion, she and Abe had remodeled the office, turning it into a small bedroom. Abe's mom would be moving in soon.

Sasha pointed at Abe's bag. "So, what did you find?"

Abe opened his bag and showed Sasha its contents. She clapped her hands at the abundance of robotic parts he'd been able to salvage from the sewer level during his lunch hour. The sewer, as it happened, didn't bug him anymore. After what he'd gone through in his own apartment, nothing wandering around in that subterranean animatronic graveyard was going to scare him.

Sasha poked through the parts. "These are great!"

She carried her grocery bags to the kitchen. "I got what we need for a stir-fry. After dinner, we'll get to work."

"Can't wait."

"Me neither." Sasha gave him another kiss.

There were never too many kisses.

As soon as they'd cleaned up after dinner, Abe reached to the string dangling from the trapdoor in the ceiling. He tugged on it, and a drop-down ladder unfolded to the floor.

Abe motioned to Sasha. "You go ahead. I'll pass the parts up to you and then join you."

Sasha nodded happily and climbed up into the crawl space. Abe handed up the parts and then went up the ladder himself.

"You were so brilliant to build this," Sasha said, patting the ladder.

"You were so brilliant to think of it," Abe said.

They laughed together and settled on the plywood floor they'd installed above the ceiling joists. The floor, nice and dry, easily held their weight.

Abe and Sasha laid out the parts. "Oh, you found an arm. Elizabeth's going to be so happy!"

Abe smiled. Not long after he and Sasha started working on the gen1s, they got Three's vocal processor online. Three was able to communicate that she and the others were grateful for Abe and Sasha's help. Sasha decided the gen1s needed names, and she proceeded to name the robots after queens. Three was Victoria. One was Elizabeth. Two was Isabella.

"It won't be much longer before we'll be able to talk to all of them," Sasha said.

Abe grinned. "Nope. Not much longer at all." He looked at the gen1s' still forms. Although they were unmoving, they didn't look half bad.

In the last two weeks, Abe had been able to find new legs for Isabelle, and he'd found a replacement eye for Victoria. Sasha had been able to use the pieces of plastic exoskeleton Abe had found to replace Victoria's missing pieces, and she nearly had enough to form an entirely new exoskeleton for Isabelle.

Abe and Sasha got to work. "Pretty soon, they'll be good as new!"

"They're going to love helping out your mom," Sasha said.

That was their plan. Instead of living in a care center, Abe's mom would be able to live here, watched over by the refurbished gen1s.

Abe grinned. "I think she's going to love them, too."

ABOUT THE AUTHORS

Scott Cawthon is the author of the bestselling video game series *Five Nights at Freddy's*, and while he is a game designer by trade, he is first and foremost a storyteller at heart. He is a graduate of the Art Institute of Houston and lives in Texas with his family.

Andrea Rains Waggener is an author, novelist, ghostwriter, essayist, short story writer, screenwriter, copywriter, editor, poet, and a proud member of Kevin Anderson & Associates' team of writers. In a past she prefers not to remember much, she was a claims adjuster, JCPenney's catalog order-taker (before computers!), appellate court clerk, legal writing instructor, and lawyer. Writing in genres that vary from her chick-lit novel, *Alternate Beauty*, to her dog how-to book, *Dog Parenting*, to her self-help book, *Healthy, Wealthy, & Wise*, to ghostwritten memoirs to ghostwritten YA, horror, mystery, and mainstream fiction projects, Andrea still manages to find time to watch the rain and obsess over her dog and her knitting, art, and music projects. She lives with her husband and said dog on the Washington Coast, and if she isn't at home creating something, she can be found walking on the beach.

L ucia shoved one of her kinky curls away from her
ear as she bent to listen to the radio. She and Kelly
had managed to get the radio working, but all they'd
gotten so far was static . . . until now. Lucia was sure she
could hear a voice coming through the crackly hisses.

Behind Lucia, Adrian's footfalls filled the room with
an edgy metrical tapping. Lucia understood Adrian's agi-
tation, but his pacing was getting on her nerves. And
it was making it impossible to parse the static from the
voice she thought she'd heard.

Lucia lost her patience. She whipped around and
glared at Adrian. "Stop that!" she hissed.

Adrian ceased pacing. He looked at her with two
raised eyebrows.

She immediately felt awful. "Sorry, I need to listen,
and your pacing . . ."

"Sure," Adrian said. For a moment, his handsome features lost some of the tightness that had marred them
since the thing they now called the Mimic (they'd agreed

to that name after Lucia had found the user's manual that had a picture of the thing in it) had started killing them one by one.

Adrian gave Lucia a fair imitation of his usual smile as he gestured at the radio. "Do you hear something?"

Lucia nodded. "I think so." She looked at Kelly, who was fiddling with the radio's dial. "Did you hear it?"

Kelly nodded. "Mm-hmm. It's distorted, but I think it's a voice."

"I think so, too," Lucia said. "Can we boost the frequency?"

Kelly shifted the radio and adjusted its antenna.

And there it was. It *was* a voice. Still a little garbled, the voice was deep and awkward sounding, broken, its words spaced apart as if the speaker was struggling to get out their words. "We . . . are . . . in . . . pizz . . . eria."

Lucia leaned back, her eyes wide. She looked at Kelly and Adrian.

Jayce, who had been under the table drawing, crawled out and stood. He frowned at the radio. "Did I just hear 'pizzeria'?"

Lucia ignored the question. She leaned over and tweaked the radio dials just a hair. The voice spoke again; it came in a bit clearer. "We're . . . trapped . . . stage . . . abandoned pizzeria."

Kelly grabbed the radio's microphone. "Could you repeat that, please?"

More static. Then, ". . . trapped in old pizzeria under new . . . construction . . . behind stage."

Kelly keyed the mike again. "Are you saying you're trapped in the old pizzeria under the new Pizzaplex? In a room behind the stage?" Kelly's pale skin was flushed with excitement.

A burst of static. Then, "Yes."

Lucia grabbed the mike. "Who are you? How'd you get there? Where's the room exactly?"

More static. Lucia spoke into the mike again. "Are you still there?"

More crackling and spitting. And then a voice said, "Help."

Lucia and the others stared at one another.

"There's someone else down here, too?" Jayce asked. He shoved his drawing pad in his pocket and carefully replaced his pens in his pocket protector. He'd been sketching under the table. Lucia knew he was doing it to escape the reality of their situation. Now he was clearly ready to be part of it again.

"I guess it's possible," Adrian said. "We didn't move all those boxes and costume racks behind the stage when we were looking for a way out. There could be some kind of room back there where others got trapped."

"If we got in here, others could have," Lucia agreed.

"We need to go get them out," Kelly said. "The more of us there are down here, the better chance we have of staying alive."

"We also need to find Joel and Wade," Adrian said.

"Could we be talking to Joel and Wade?" Kelly asked.

Lucia frowned. Could they? There was so much static that the voice was coming through too fuzzy to identify.

"How'd they get a radio?" Jayce asked.

"Maybe they found one in whatever room they're in," Kelly said.

"But they said they were going to the systems room," Adrian said.

Then they all started talking at once, throwing out theories about who was on the radio and where they were and what they should do about it. Finally, Adrian held up one of his large, perfect hands.

"Stop!"

Lucia closed her mouth. She flushed. He was right. They were babbling, and it wasn't accomplishing a thing.

Adrian sighed. "The only way we're going to get any answers is to try to find the room behind the stage."

Lucia looked at the barricaded door. She really didn't want to leave the office. But he was right. She nodded. So did Kelly. Jayce swallowed hard and then nodded, too.

"Okay," Adrian said. "Let's do this."

Lucia handed Adrian a box of stage props and paused to wipe sweat from her eyes. As she had been doing every other second since she and the others had left the office, she froze and listened hard. She turned in a full circle. They were still alone.

Somehow, the group had managed to deconstruct their barricade and make it from the office to the backstage area without encountering the Mimic. Unless the robotic endoskeleton had figured out how to walk without making its signature hissing and rasping tap and no longer shorted out lights when it was nearby, it wasn't close. Even so, every nerve ending in Lucia's body was on alert, and she'd never worked so hard to hear every little tiny sound around her and to discern every iota of the details in her surroundings.

"Look!" Jayce exclaimed.

"Shh," Kelly admonished.

Jayce flushed. "Sorry," he whispered. He joined the others in turning yet another full circle to be sure they were alone. Then Jayce pointed at the wall. "It's one of those doors made to look like part of the wall," he whispered. "See?" He pointed at a narrow, door-shaped seam.

Lucia stepped up next to Jayce and examined the wall.

"He's right," she whispered. She frowned. "Why's there a hidden door back here?"

Kelly shook her head. "This place is owned by Fazbear Entertainment. Why does Fazbear Entertainment do half of what it does?"

"Good point," Lucia said. She stepped up and felt around the hidden door. "How do we get it open?"

"How do we even know this is the right place?" Adrian asked. He was moving the last of the boxes that had obscured the hidden door.

Lucia looked around. "The voice said behind the stage. The only other enclosed place is that costumes closet, and it's open." Lucia shuddered. They'd found Nick's remains scattered near the open door to the closet. Sticky blood was everywhere. Lucia had stepped in some, and she'd been scraping the sole of her hiking boot on the floor ever since.

Out, damned spot, Lucia thought now, suppressing a demented giggle that would have given away the hysteria that she was only barely keeping at bay.

Lucia nearly jumped out of her skin when Adrian knocked on the camouflaged door panel.

"What are you doing?" Jayce squeaked.

"Before we try to get the door open," Adrian said reasonably, "shouldn't we see if someone is in there?"

"I think . . ." Jayce began.

An answering knock came from the other side of the door.

Jayce gasped and leaped over to press against Lucia. Her on-the-alert senses were assaulted by the stale smell of Jayce's sweat. She forced herself to pat his shoulder, a halfhearted attempt to comfort him.

Kelly leaned toward the door. "Can you hear me? Who's in there?" she called out softly.

They all listened hard. But they heard nothing.

"What if they've run out of oxygen or something?" Kelly asked.

Adrian nodded. "We need to get in there." He began pressing his fingers along the door's seams. "Maybe there's a pressure latch somewhere. If we could just—"

Lucia heard a click. The door opened a few inches.

They all sucked in a collective breath and retreated a couple steps. Lucia hugged herself, trying to rub away the goose bumps that had just erupted on her arms.

Adrian rolled his shoulders and stepped forward. He grabbed the edge of the door and pulled it open.

The lighting behind the stage was only slightly better than that in the rest of the pizzeria. In addition to a couple of dim wall sconces, the area received a few halfhearted sprays of illumination from dying stage lights attached to metal scaffolding overhead. Those sprays, though weak, stretched in through the open door.

Lucia and the others moved together until they were shoulder to shoulder. As one, they stepped forward and peered into the small room.

Lucia wasn't sure what she'd expected them to find. Joel and Wade? Another group of stupid kids who'd broken into the pizzeria on a lark? A construction worker?

In one glance, it was clear that the very small, maybe eight-foot-by-eight-foot, room contained none of those people. In fact, it was empty of any people at all. The only thing in the room was a collection of costumes like the ones they'd found in the Parts and Service Room.

Adrian broke away from the others and took a step into the small room.

"Careful," Jayce gasped.

Adrian gave a sharp nod. He looked around and called out softly, "Anyone in here?"

He received no answer. The room was still and silent . . . until it wasn't.

Suddenly, the costumes on the right side of the room began to rustle. The chirr of fabric against fabric combined with a barely there crackle. And then Lucia heard a hiss and a rasp.

"Adrian," she cried, "look out!"

Lucia lunged forward and grabbed Adrian's hand. She yanked hard.

She acted just in time. The stage lights flickered.

As Adrian fell back toward Lucia, a costume, one with matted brown fur and a pale face that was vaguely reminiscent of a monkey, surged out from the surrounding characters. A grating sound combined with a whir as the deranged-looking primate leaped toward Adrian and tried to grab Adrian's arm.

The monkey paw's fur was torn, and Lucia caught the glint of metal as it swiped at Adrian's bicep. Adrian cried out and grabbed his arm.

All the lights went out. They were surrounded by blackness.

"It's the Mimic!" Lucia cried as she tugged at Adrian. Her mind replayed, at hypersonic speed, what she'd read in the user's manual about the robot's limbs and torso expanding and contracting to fit into any animatronic costume.

Lucia could feel Adrian flailing, trying to keep his balance. Somehow, he steadied himself. "Go!" he bellowed.

Jayce and Kelly hadn't needed the command. Lucia could hear their footsteps; they were already running.

Bumping into the boxes and costumes in the backstage area, Jayce and Kelly were bumbling in the darkness, heading toward the parted stage curtains. Adrian and

Lucia, with the grinding, tapping Mimic too close behind them, raced after their friends.

Lucia tried not to think about the thing pursuing them. She couldn't. She had to concentrate on feeling her way through the murk to get beyond the stage curtains.

Once she was sure she felt the tip of a sharp metal finger catch on the back of her woven vest, and she pushed herself harder. Her vest pulled against her chest, then it went loose again. Adrian grabbed her hand, and he hauled her along even faster.

Beyond the curtains, the dining room lights were still on. That light guided them all toward the front of the stage. There, now that they could all see where they were going, they picked up speed.

Not bothering with the stairs, all four of them jumped off the stage and vaulted past a jumble of overturned chairs. Hopping over the body parts that were scattered through the area, they churned through a tangle of limp party streamers and tore through the dining room.

Without discussing it—because they clearly had no time to do that—they all ran toward the main hall. Lucia intended to head back to the office; the others apparently did, too. Only once did Lucia risk a glance over her shoulder. When she did, she saw the Mimic, its arms extending out like those of an orangutan, plodding past a pile of concrete rubble on the arcade side of the dining room.

Thankfully, although the Mimic was deadly and sneaky, Adrian now realized it didn't move very fast. Adrian and the others were able to get to the office before the Mimic reached the lobby. They quickly rebuilt their barricade, and then they all clustered in the middle of the room, panting, clutching at one another, their eyes wide, their attention fixated on the office door.

Several seconds passed as they all listened hard. Seconds turned into a minute. Then two. They heard nothing.

"Where did it go?" Jayce whispered.

Adrian glanced down at his friend, who was clutching Lucia's hand so hard Lucia's knuckles were white. Lucia was wincing, but she did nothing to shake Jayce off.

Adrian shook his head. That was a good question.

Kelly touched his arm. "You're bleeding pretty badly," she whispered.

Adrian looked down. Blood was streaming down his arm from a gash in his bicep. He remembered the searing pain when the Mimic had grabbed for him. Then, running for his life he'd felt nothing. Now he realized his arm was throbbing.

"I think I saw a first aid kit in the filing cabinet when I was rummaging through it," Lucia said.

Lucia gently disengaged Jayce's hand and stepped over to the filing cabinet, which was once again on its side on top of the desk. She pulled open a drawer and plucked out a small first aid kit.

For the next few minutes, Adrian let Lucia and Kelly attend to his gash while Jayce hovered nearby. Jayce's face was so white it was practically transparent.

"You really need stitches," Kelly said, "but these butter-fly bandages should help hold it." She wrapped a gauze bandage tightly around Adrian's arm.

Adrian nodded, but he wasn't thinking about his arm. He was thinking about Wade and Joel. He had a very bad feeling about them.

Finally, the girls stopped fussing over his arm. Adrian thanked them and then said aloud what he'd been thinking. "We need to find Joel and Wade."

No one said anything. Adrian knew why. They were probably dealing with the same image he was dealing with—the image of Joel's and Wade's mutilated bodies.

The Mimic was obviously as clever as it was lethal. Adrian thought it entirely possible that the Mimic had outsmarted the two not-so-clever jocks.

Jayce piped up. "Are we sure we want to go back out there?" He blinked at the office door.

Adrian shook his head. "I wasn't planning to go back out there." He pointed at the vent cover under the table. "We'll go that way."

"We?" Jayce squeaked.

"I'll go with you," Lucia said, her voice cracking only slightly.

Adrian repeated the head shake. "No, you need to stay here. See if you and Kelly can get something else on the radio, maybe some real people this time."

Kelly let out a humorless guffaw. "Who knew that thing was so devious."

"Maybe I should read some more of that user's manual," Lucia said.

Adrian nodded. "Yeah, do that, too." He looked at Jayce. "Jayce, buddy, I could use your help. Are you up for it?"

Jayce chewed his thin lower lip. He blinked and sniffled. Then he nodded. "Sure, Adrian. I'm with you." The inflection of both sentences went up on the end as if Jayce was more questioning than affirming. No one pointed that out.

The duct beyond the vent cover was bigger than Jayce had expected it to be; it was plenty wide and tall enough for Adrian, who was eight inches taller than Jayce's diminutive 5'6". It was cleaner, too—Jayce could feel a faint breeze in the duct; somewhere a fan was circulating air, which apparently was keeping the faint layer of dust collecting on the metal to a minimum. The duct wasn't, however, all that stable.

Just a few feet from the office, as Adrian and Jayce crawled around a bend in the ductwork, the steel "floor" of the duct sagged when one of the seams popped apart a few inches. Jayce yelped at the resulting tinny clunk.

"I thought these things were made of galvanized steel," he called out to Adrian, who was a couple feet ahead of him. Jayce could just barely see Adrian. The only light in the ductwork came through vent covers spaced several feet apart.

"Shh!" Adrian stopped and cocked his head to look back over his shoulder at Jayce. A faint ray of light reflected off the whites of Adrian's eyes. He pointed at the metal grate of a vent cover just ahead of them. "If the Mimic is out there," Adrian whispered, "it could hear us."

Good point, Jayce thought. He nodded meekly. He didn't even want to be there. He felt like a rat scurrying around inside a metal maze.

But, of course, he went along with Adrian. He always did.

They crawled for another few feet, past the vent cover. Another seam cracked apart as Adrian crept over it. "Careful," Adrian whispered. "Some of these joints are rusting."

Duh, Jayce thought. That was why he'd said what he'd said about galvanized steel. He was an artist, not a scientist, but he thought galvanized steel was treated to resist rust. *Resist* was the operative word, he guessed. Maybe, eventually, all metal rusted. Whatever. All he knew was that the ductwork wasn't all that stable. He wondered where they'd end up if the duct collapsed under them.

They crawled on in silence. Sweat dripped off Jayce's nose. Dust made his eyes burn. His knees were starting to ache.

"I don't think it's much farther," Adrian whispered as if he sensed Jayce's discomfort.

Then Adrian froze. So did Jayce. They were approaching a vent cover, and, beyond it, something was moving.

Tap-hiss-rasp.

It was the Mimic!

Adrian turned and put a finger to his lips. Jayce ignored the unnecessary instruction. He had no intention of making a sound. Or a movement. He was a mute statue. He willed himself to be invisible.

The *tap-hiss-rasp* sound moved closer. The illumination in the duct nearly disappeared. Jayce stared at the vent cover. He had to suppress a gasp. Beyond the metal grill, two bright white eyes staring out of the face of a butterscotch-colored furry costume looked into the duct. Something whirred. The vent cover rattled.

Jayce stopped breathing. He closed his eyes tight as if not looking at the Mimic would make it go away.

Jayce started counting the seconds, wondering how long he could hold his breath. He'd gotten to nineteen when he heard Adrian's athletic shoe squeak against the duct's metal side. Jayce opened his eyes.

Adrian was crawling forward again. He would only be doing that if the Mimic had moved off. Even so, Jayce hesitated. Then he checked the vent. Light was streaming through the spaces between the grill once more. *Okay,* he thought. He forced himself to follow his friend.

Adrian had hoped they'd be able to take the ductwork right to the systems room, which was where he wanted to start his search for Joel and Wade. That was where Joel had wanted to go, so Adrian figured that was the best place to begin. Unfortunately, he and Jayce had encountered an air handler unit, an AHU. The son of a contractor,

Adrian knew most ductwork had these large metal boxes that contained a blower, filters, and heating and cooling elements. An AHU had blocked the bend Adrian had wanted to take. Because of this, they ended up in the employee break room instead of the systems room.

Adrian looked around the locker-lined room filled with upended tables and chairs. Aside from the furniture and other debris, the room was empty. He quickly and quietly pulled himself out of the duct and bent to offer Jayce a hand.

Once Jayce was on his feet, Adrian motioned for Jayce to follow him. He didn't bother to explain to Jayce why they were here instead of in the systems room, and Jayce didn't ask. Adrian had a feeling Jayce was still recovering from being so close to the Mimic by that vent cover. Adrian had to admit it had freaked him out, too. He didn't have time to think about it, though.

"Come on," Adrian whispered. He quickly led Jayce past a few broken chairs, toward the door to the back hall.

Jayce pressed close to Adrian. Jayce was clammy and smelly, but Adrian figured he was, too.

Adrian slowly opened the door to the hallway. Pausing a beat, he leaned his head out and looked in both directions. The hallway was clear. It was quiet. No tapping footsteps.

Adrian looked to his left, toward the end of the hall. The systems room door was standing open. Good. Adrian nudged Jayce, then he trotted as quickly and quietly as possible over the hallway's black-and-white tiles. They couldn't be totally silent—their feet made scuffling sounds over the dirty floor—but they were as stealthy as they could be.

In five seconds, which felt like five minutes, they

covered the distance to the systems room. Adrian looked over his shoulder to check the hallway behind them. It was still empty. He ducked into the systems room and waited until Jayce followed him in. Then he shut the door. Adrian and Jayce looked around.

The systems room was a shadowed, L-shaped space filled with a bank of control panels along one wall and an industrial-size furnace flanked by metal maintenance scaffolding. The furnace had multiple rectangular chutes and cylindrical ducts, many of which looked to be collapsing. Something in the furnace was running, though. Adrian could hear the faint rhythmic hum of what sounded like a fan.

"What's that smell?" Jayce asked.

Adrian inhaled. "It's just the furnace," he said. "Old furnaces can smell like rotten eggs when they—"

"No, not that smell. The other one." Jayce took a tentative step toward the bend in the wall. He peered around the corner.

Jayce let out a squawk and fell back into Adrian. He bounced off Adrian and fell to his knees. Bending over, Jayce made a gasping, heaving sound as Adrian shot forward to see what had upset Jayce so badly.

Adrian managed to stay silent when he saw the first leg. He didn't scream or even gasp when he saw an arm a few feet from the leg. When he looked beyond the arm and saw the mutilated head lying on one ear, its eyes staring, Adrian still managed to keep it together. With a massive force of will, he tamped down a retch, and he turned away from Wade's remains.

Adrian closed his eyes and breathed in and out three times. He went back to Jayce and put a hand on the little guy's shoulder.

"You going to be okay?" Adrian asked.

Jayce was curled forward, hugging himself. He didn't look up. But he nodded.

"Stay here," Adrian said.

Jayce didn't respond.

Adrian looked back at the systems room door. He listened. No rasping tap. The Mimic had been here, obviously, but it wasn't here now.

Adrian took a deep breath and steeled himself. Forcing his feet into motion, he went around the corner.

Adrian had to step carefully to avoid all Wade's dissected parts. Wade's blood was everywhere, too. Adrian couldn't stay away from all of it. It was splashed all over the floor.

Tiptoeing gingerly, Adrian made his way toward Wade's torso. No, wait. It wasn't Wade's torso. It was Joel's.

Both Wade and Joel had worn the same purple-and-yellow team shirts. But Joel was a bigger guy. It was his torso that lay, bisected horizontally, at the bottom of what looked like a vertical furnace shaft. Adrian looked around. He spotted Wade's torso against the wall.

Adrian tore his gaze from the gore strewn around him. He concentrated on the hum he'd been hearing since they entered the room. If there was a big enough fan, there might be a way out of this place. Adrian made himself focus on that thought and not on what was all around him. If they were going to survive, they all had to control their emotions and find a way to think logically.

Adrian stepped over two disembodied legs—he thought they were Joel's. Doing his best not to touch the sides of the furnace opening above the legs, Adrian stuck his head into the opening and looked up. Just as he'd thought, the chute, which had handholds and footholds for climbing, led up to a massive fan.

Adrian retreated. He returned to Jayce.

Squatting down next to his friend, Adrian repeated his earlier question. "Are you going to be okay?"

This time, Jayce looked up. His eyes were red, and his lips quivered. But he cleared his throat and asked, "Is it both of them?"

Adrian nodded. "Yeah."

They were silent for several seconds.

Adrian had never much liked Joel or Wade. Joel especially could be a real jerk sometimes. But he hadn't deserved what had happened to him. No one did.

Adrian touched Jayce's shoulder. "There's a bit of good news."

Jayce wiped his eyes. "What's that?"

"I think Joel and Wade were trying to get out through a chute that leads up to the ceiling. There's a big fan up there between the ceiling and the crawl space under the roof. If we could get it turned off . . ."

"We could find a way out," Jayce said, brightening infinitesimally.

Adrian squeezed Jayce's shoulder. "Exactly."

"Then let's do that," Jayce said. He pushed himself off the floor and stood.

Lucia threw up her hands and backed away from the table that held the uncooperative radio. "It's no use." She sighed. "The signal's not making it past the building."

"Yet," Kelly said. She was sitting in a chair in front of the radio. "We have to keep trying."

Lucia shook her head. "I'm not as good with radios as I am with robots and computers."

Lucia thought about how much she'd been enjoying her robotics class in school. After this, assuming there *was* an after this, she wasn't so sure she'd be as excited about robots as she used to be. The Mimic, although she and the others had been thinking of it as more of a creature than something mechanical, was, after all, a robot. It was a strange and fiendish robot, but it was a robot, and because of it, Lucia wasn't so sure she wanted anything to do with robots anymore.

"While I keep tinkering with the radio," Kelly said, "why don't you see if you can find out anything else about the Mimic."

Lucia glanced at the user's manual she'd flung to the floor near the barricade that blocked the door. She'd read it forward and backward. The only thing she'd learned was where its deactivation switch was, at the back of its neck. But if you couldn't get close to the thing without being ripped apart, what good was that knowledge?

Lucia sighed and stretched. She rubbed her sore back. She'd been bending over the radio so long that her lower back muscles were screaming at her.

"You're a lot more patient than I am," Lucia said to Kelly.

Kelly looked up and smiled. "Confession." She blushed. "I've never told anyone at school this."

Lucia frowned, wondering what she was about to hear.

"I'm a ham radio freak," Kelly said. "I have a setup at home. I talk to people from all over the world. I have more friends I've never seen face-to-face than I even know people at school."

"Why is that a confession?" Lucia asked.

Kelly flipped her now-straggling brown hair off her shoulder. "It's pretty nerdy."

"Hey," Lucia said. "Watch the way you say that word. You're talking to the queen of nerds." She grinned.

Kelly laughed. She pointed. "Go. Try to learn something else. I'll stick with this."

Lucia nodded. She crossed to the desk/barricade and started going through its drawers. She'd already been through all the filing cabinet drawers. If she was going to find something, it would have to be in the desk.

Ten minutes later, Lucia hadn't found anything else about the Mimic. She did, however, find a key on a key ring that was labeled STORAGE. She remembered seeing a dead bolt on the door of the small room at the end of the hall, the one opposite the systems room. She wondered if the key was to that room. Shrugging, Lucia pocketed the key. It might come in handy at some point.

Adrian and Jayce paused at the edge of the stage and listened. The dining room was such a disaster of broken furniture, construction materials, endoskeleton parts, and human body parts that it was like looking at a microcosm of an Armageddon. Jayce didn't want to be anywhere near this room, but Adrian was right—what they needed would be out here.

Jayce was pretty proud of himself for the fact that he was still a functioning human being at this point. Spending even one minute in the abattoir that was the systems room was more than he'd ever thought he had in him. Somehow, though, he'd managed to help Adrian scour the room for the fan's control panel, and when they'd found it on the main control panel at the back of the room, he'd been able to pick his way past the dregs of Joel and Wade so he could check to see if the fan was still going when Adrian toggled the fan switch to the off position. When flipping the switch had no effect, Jayce had also helped Adrian locate a fuse box, but none of the switches in that box had stopped the fan, either. Jayce had even crawled behind the bottom part of the control panels (Adrian wouldn't fit back there) and looked for loose connections. He didn't find any.

By the time they were done attempting to stop the fan, Jayce knew every inch of the systems room—and he'd been desensitized to the carnage that filled the small space. His nose had even adjusted to the stink in the room. The combination of a coppery blood odor and a reek of the fluids Joel's and Wade's bodies had released when they'd died.

Now, though, being out here in the open, Jayce was losing his nerve again. His legs were shaking, but he was not going to wuss out on Adrian. He stuck right with his friend.

As Jayce and Adrian sidled around the edge of the dining room, they heard a thud in the farthest of the adjacent party rooms. They froze and stared in that direction.

"We'd better hurry," Adrian whispered. He pointed to the left. "I think that's what we need."

Jayce immediately saw what Adrian was looking at. He nodded, glanced toward the party room, and then, without discussing it with Adrian, he took off toward their prize. What they were looking for was wedged between a stack of concrete blocks and a pile of wood beams. It was in a tight spot; Jayce figured he'd be able to reach it more easily than Adrian would.

As he scurried over a litter of bright paper cups and plates, Jayce idly wondered what had been going on in the place before everyone had been ripped apart. Had they been planning to remodel it? Use it as a storage room for decommissioned robots?

"I wish someone would have decommissioned the Mimic," Jayce muttered under his breath as he squeezed between a stack of overturned barstool-style, red-vinyl-topped chairs and a large metal toolbox.

Jayce crawled past an upside-down table, and he knelt. He reached out and managed to snag the metal foot of a long endoskeleton leg. He pulled on it. It didn't budge.

Something scraped the floor behind him. He spun around.

"It's just me," Adrian whispered. "I thought it might be too heavy for you."

Jayce shook his head. He was determined to be useful. He grunted, and he tugged again.

Maybe his determination gave him the strength he needed. The leg came loose. He started dragging it across the floor, shaking it to free it from the other endoskeleton parts entangled with it.

Jayce grimaced. "These things are heavy."

A thunk sounded from the party room. Adrian scrabbled up next to Jayce. "Let me help. We need to get moving."

Jayce didn't argue. Adrian reached around Jayce and grasped the ankle of the metal leg. He jerked it and then lifted it up onto his shoulder.

"Come on," Adrian said.

The dining room lights started flickering.

"We need to go," Adrian whispered. "Now!"

Adrian got a good grip on the metal leg and clambered over the concrete blocks. He reached back to pull Jayce to his feet.

As soon as Jayce was upright, Adrian pushed him toward the back of the dining room. Jayce started to run, but Adrian grabbed his shirt and yanked him to a stop. Jayce yelped. Then he immediately realized why Adrian had stopped him.

The Mimic was there, just a few feet away.

Rising up from behind a pile of endoskeleton arms and torsos, the Mimic was no longer in the form of a monkey, or whatever it had been when it was outside the vent cover.

Now it was some kind of blond-colored dog, a mangled dog with one ragged ear and a torn muzzle. The Mimic's metal teeth shone through the costume. The ends of its metal limbs jutted through the molted edges of the dog's paws.

The Mimic took a rasping step. The dining room went black.

Something grabbed Jayce's hand. He nearly screamed, but then he realized he was feeling skin, not metal. It was Adrian. Jayce let Adrian pull him backward, away from the Mimic.

The Mimic's rasping, tapping footsteps moved closer, but terror gave Jayce and Adrian speed they'd never had before. They floundered over the dining room debris, falling and getting back up again. Lurching, spinning, leaping, they kept moving forward.

With the Mimic's whirring approach right behind them, Jayce and Adrian managed to fumble their way into the arcade. There, the lights were still working. That meant the Mimic wasn't close on their heels.

Adrian led Jayce along a row of pinball machines. At the end of the row, they paused and listened. They could hear the Mimic's footsteps; the footfalls weren't close.

Adrian knelt and pulled Jayce down next to him. Putting his mouth right next to Jayce's ear, Adrian whispered, "I think if we sneak onto the small stage, we can slip behind the stage curtain and get to the far side of the big stage before the Mimic realizes what we've done. You with me?"

Jayce nodded. He didn't want to be with Adrian; he wanted to be someplace else, anyplace else. He wished he could check out, take himself to an imaginary place filled with happy, cute, benign things instead of a menacing, ugly, hostile thing. However, he knew his go-to way of coping with stress wasn't going to work; crawling under a pinball machine and drawing bunnies was a sure way to become the Mimic's next victim.

Adrian motioned for Jayce to stay low, and he duck-walked around a Skee-Ball machine. They both peered into the dining room. The far side of it remained dark. That meant the Mimic was still over there.

Adrian made a *come on* gesture, and he rose to his full height. Jayce turned himself into Adrian's shadow. He stayed right at Adrian's side as Adrian darted toward the small stage and vaulted up onto it. Somehow, Adrian still held on to the heavy endoskeleton leg, and with his free hand, he reached down and pulled Jayce up onto the stage.

A clatter from the far side of the room froze them in their tracks. Adrian immediately dropped to the stage, flattening himself to its wood floor. Jayce followed suit.

They remained there for several seconds, breathing as quietly as they could. When they didn't hear anything else, Adrian began army-crawling forward. Jayce copied him. Together, they slithered over the rough, dusty stage floor and slipped behind the main curtain.

Jayce almost sneezed when the velvet fabric brushed against his nose, but he managed to suppress the urge. He wasn't going to be the reason they got killed.

Behind the curtain, Adrian stood and helped Jayce up. He motioned for Jayce to follow, and he walked flat-footed, not making a sound, behind the curtain. Jayce copied him again. They moved slowly, surreptitiously, so it took longer than Jayce wanted for them to make it across the broad expanse. But they eventually got to the other side. When they did, Adrian eased back the curtain and looked out. He dropped the curtain and bent down to whisper in Jayce's ear again. His breath was hot and forceful.

"The dining room lights are on again, but the lobby

looks dark. I think the Mimic went the other way. You ready? We need to get down the hall as fast as possible."

Jayce nodded.

"Okay." Adrian repositioned the heavy endoskeleton leg. "Let's go."

Adrian grabbed Jayce's hand, and the two of them pushed through the curtains and ran down the stairs, off the stage. Jayce wanted to stop and check behind them to make sure the Mimic wasn't coming after them, but he didn't. Instead, he squeezed Adrian's hand and did his best to keep up as Adrian sprinted away from the dining room.

Adrian gently closed the door to the systems room. Before they'd entered, he'd looked back down the hall, and he hadn't seen anything, but the dining room was dark again. The Mimic wasn't that far away. They'd have to be fast.

"Come on," Adrian said.

Running past the torn pieces of Joel and Wade, Adrian didn't even bother to try to avoid the blood. There wasn't time.

At the opening to the bottom of the chute, Adrian stopped and propped the metal leg against the outside of the furnace. "Wait until I get in there with the leg, and then as soon as you can, follow me. I think wedging this metal into the fan will stop it, but it may not hold for long. There also may not be enough room for me to get through. But you'll be able to. So, stay close."

Jayce nodded. He wasn't letting himself think anymore. He was just reacting. Whatever Adrian told him to do, he'd do.

Adrian punched Jayce lightly on the upper arm. "You've done good, Jayce. Real good."

Jayce's eyes filled with tears. He blinked them away and nodded. He didn't trust himself to speak.

Adrian levered himself up into the chute, and he reached back out for the metal leg. The leg scraped the side of the furnace as it slid into the chute. The metal-on-metal rasp was unsettling.

And so was the rasp that came from outside the systems room.

The sound was faint, but Jayce's senses were attuned to it. He knew what it was the second he heard it. He got his confirmation a few seconds later when the lights flickered.

Adrian must have seen the flicker as well. "There's no time to get you in here," Adrian said. "Go hide!"

Jayce had already figured that out on his own. Before Adrian finished speaking, Jayce was scurrying around the end of the furnace, heading toward one of the control panels. He was ducking into the dark space behind the front of the panel when the lights in the systems room went out.

The interior of the furnace chute was tight and smelled strongly of rotten eggs—and blood—but it had evenly spaced handholds and footholds, and it was an easy climb to the top. Adrian had just reached the apex of the shaft when the room went dark. As soon as it did, he froze. He heard the hissing and tapping of the Mimic's footsteps. The creature was coming toward the bottom of the shaft. *Jayce*, Adrian thought.

Had Jayce found a place to hide?

Adrian badly wanted to go back down and find his friend, but the Mimic was down there in the dark. There was no way Adrian was going to get to Jayce. The only thing he could do now was try to get out through the fan and go for help.

Adrian gingerly shifted position in the shaft. He hung on to a handhold with one hand and got a good grip on the metal leg with the other. Then, summoning all the strength he had left, he lifted the leg above his head.

As soon as Adrian jammed the leg into place, he knew it wasn't going to be sturdy enough to do the job Adrian needed it to do. The fan was far more powerful than Adrian had assumed it was.

Immediately, the fan's blades started scoring through the metal leg, spraying metal shavings into the air above Adrian's upturned face. He closed his eyes and looked away.

The fan's gears ground. Adrian heard a snapping twang. The leg was violently wrenched from his grasp. Adrian cringed at a metallic crunching that sounded like metal eating metal. The endoskeleton leg thrashed above Adrian. Its foot beat against Adrian's shoulder.

Then Adrian felt specks of heat searing the top of his head. He heard a sputter. Without thinking, he looked up and was rewarded with more tiny burns.

The fan was sparking!

Would it stop turning?

The metallic banging above Adrian's head got louder. It turned into a cacophony of metal sheering metal. Then part of the leg jumped out of the fan. It hit Adrian on the temple, and Adrian lost his grip on the chute's handholds. He let out an involuntary cry.

Adrian fell straight down the shaft. He skimmed along its walls, its handholds and footholds battering him as he went. He fell faster and faster as if he was zipping down an enclosed slide.

The fall was short and painful, and in the few seconds that he was descending, Adrian didn't have time to think about what would happen next. This was a mercy. Because what did happen next was Adrian's worst nightmare. He shot down to the bottom of the shaft and out through its opening, right into the extended arms of the Mimic.

Jayce cowered behind the control panel. Breathing as shallowly as he could, he had listened to the Mimic's footsteps pass him and head toward the bottom of the chute.

Go, Adrian! Jayce had thought. Adrian had to get the fan stopped and get out. He just had to.

When Jayce had heard metal screaming and banging, he had hoped for the best. But then he'd heard Adrian's cry.

Jayce started to leave his hiding place. He had to help his friend!

Before he could shove himself free, though, Jayce heard Adrian cry out again. This cry was much louder than the first one. It wasn't just a cry. It was a howl. It was a caterwaul, a keen of indescribable pain.

Jayce knew what that sound meant. The Mimic had Adrian.

Jayce compressed himself into the smallest ball possible. He let the tears sluice down his cheeks as he listened to his friend die.